If I Say Yes

Brandy Jellum

Booktrope Editions
Seattle WA 2014

Copyright 2014 Brandy Griffin

This work is licensed under a Creative Commons Attribution-Noncommercial-No Derivative Works 3.0 Unported License.

Attribution — You must attribute the work in the manner specified by the author or licensor (but not in any way that suggests that they endorse you or your use of the work).

Noncommercial — You may not use this work for commercial purposes.

No Derivative Works — You may not alter, transform, or build upon this work.

Inquiries about additional permissions should be directed to: info@booktrope.com

Cover Design by Shari Ryan
Edited by Jacy Mackin

This is a work of fiction. Names, characters, places, brands, media, and incidents are either the product of the author's imagination or are used fictitiously. Any resemblance to similarly named places or to persons living or deceased is unintentional.

Print ISBN 978-1-62015-367-3

EPUB ISBN 978-1-62015-392-5

DISCOUNTS OR CUSTOMIZED EDITIONS MAY BE AVAILABLE FOR EDUCATIONAL AND OTHER GROUPS BASED ON BULK PURCHASE.

For further information please contact info@booktrope.com

Library of Congress Control Number: 2014907244

*To my husband,
for allowing me to follow my dreams.*

Acknowledgments

To the Booktrope family; thank you for making my dreams become a reality. I am blessed to be part of an amazing company, full of hard workers helping make each book the best they can, and being a part of a large group of talented people.

To my husband, for not allowing me to quit and walk away when I wanted to the most. You encouraged me and pushed me to follow my dreams. For taking care of the children, meals, and housework while I typed away on my computer. For listening to me talk for hours on end about my characters, plot twists, and my usual book talk. Thank you for the laughs you have given me while trying to convince me that my book needs a scene with women wrestling in chocolate pudding and not getting mad when I didn't put it in the story. (Sorry hun, maybe next time!) More importantly, thank you for being the best supporter I have and for loving me.

To my mother, for always being there to support me in everything I do.

To my grandparents, for loving and nurturing me. For believing in me and encouraging me to always be the best person I can be and driving it into me that I should never give up.

To Jessica, Sara, and Amanda, my trusted beta readers, none of this would have been possible if it weren't for you. Your honesty, your love for the story and characters, are what drove me to complete this story. You ladies have been there since the very beginning, and have helped me mold this story into the best possible one it can be. Thank you for the time you have put into this book, and thank you for loving it just as much as I do. And thank you for helping me realize that there is much more to the series than I ever planned. All the books I write, I owe to you. (Sara; if it wasn't for you… a certain character would've never gotten his own book!)

To Lisa, my best friend, for always being there during the good times and the bad. You are the epitome of what a best friend should be and have always believed in me. Thank you for listening to my endless rants, my frustrations, and for telling me that I can't quit chasing after my dreams.

To Cindy, for being one of the best chicks hands down. I love our late night texts. Being able to rant to one another. No one makes me laugh as much as you do. In the short time we have known each other, I feel like we have become best friends. Soul sisters. Thank you for encouraging me to do what I think is best when it comes to my writing. I look forward to many more years of friendship. Here's to being wild, crazy, and as vulgar as we want to be.

To Rachel, for our late night writing chats, and exchanging ideas with one another. For always being there when I have needed it. For always telling me that everything will work out. And for always believing in me. I still have to come up and have you make me one of your delicious dinners.

To Tess, for allowing me to take your writing workshop and helping me perfect my craft. For being genuinely honest and sweet. You always give me encouragement when I am feeling low and always reach out to me when I need it the most. I can't wait to have that celebratory glass of wine with you.

To Amanda, you have been a huge support in getting the word out about this book. You understand that I'm not in fact crazy because of the voices in my head and just have an overactive imagination. I love talking to you, talking characters, and stories. Your never-ending support these past few months have been amazing, and I look forward to many years of friendship.

To my ladies of Our Writing Nook, I am glad to have found a group of such talented authors, and thank you for all your support, advice, and love you have shown me.

To my street team, you ladies rock. I love how you guys get excited when I share pieces of a story and how involved you are with everything I do. Thank you for taking time out of your personal lives to help spread the word about this story/series. You are what makes this story get out there and I don't know what I would do without you. xoxo.

And finally, to my readers, thank you for taking the time to read this story. These characters mean a lot to me and I am so happy to share them with you. I hope you fall in love with them as much as I did and that their story takes you on a ride. Thank you for the support. Because of you, this is all possible.

Prologue

Six years ago

BLOOD COVERS EVERY SURFACE. On the pristine, white marble flooring, the grand staircase and handrail, and what used to be a tall, square wooden end table by the large double doors I just walked through. The table now lays scattered across the foyer, broken into jagged pieces. The large, antique ceramic bowl that served as a key holder had set on the table, but now it too is scattered amongst the broken wood and the blood bath. I follow the trail of dark crimson fluid up the stairs, my hands shaking and my breath catching. Upstairs is worse, far worse. The plush white carpet is saturated a deep shade of red; splatters and droplets are everywhere.

My heart is pounding, urging me to go, to leave, to run and call for help. My head tells me otherwise, to follow the trail of blood down the hall. The blood is smeared on the walls, as if someone was trying to grab ahold of something to prevent being dragged this way. The trail leads to my parents' bedroom. My heartbeat quickens, and a bead of sweat forms along my hairline. The door to my parents' room is slightly ajar, and I nudge it open a little farther, just enough that I can slip past the door.

A piercing scream escapes, and I quickly clamp a hand over my mouth. My eyes are glued to the sight before me. I can't mistake the familiar blonde hair attached to the crumpled body on the floor, discarded as though she is a piece of garbage that nobody wants. Just lying on the floor, with a pool of blood surrounding her body. The blonde hair, the only thing I share with my mother, is drenched in the dark fluid. Another cry escapes my lips as I rush across the room and collapse next to her, brushing the hair out of her face. My heart drops to the pit of my stomach, and I feel bile rising to the back of my throat. I can hardly recognize my mother's soft, delicate face; she was a natural beauty, one that everyone wanted to star in their next movie at the height of her career. Her face is mangled with large, jagged cuts that run across it. The blood is already starting to dry. Examining the rest of her body, I see she is covered from head to toe with multiple stab wounds. Under the cross-hatch of wounds, faint bruises form from the multiple contusions she has suffered as well.

"Mom," I whisper. I scoop her body into my arms and pull her close to my body. Her head rests against my chest as I begin to rock back and forth. "Don't be dead... please, don't be dead." I know my plea is useless; she is already gone. The amount of blood throughout the house and pooling around her and the blank expression in her blue eyes is proof enough. Tears form in my eyes. "You can't be dead."

I cry out loud, and my body begins to shake involuntarily. "I didn't mean what I said... I forgive you." My voice breaks and barely comes out. I think back to the last conversation we had. Which, honestly, wasn't anything outside the norm, since we fought constantly the little time we were around each other. We had a toxic mother-daughter relationship. If there's an award for worst parents ever, mine would win, hands down. But today, today's argument was different. It had been the final straw in her attempt to break me down. I had yelled at her, uttering all the same obscenities and same 'I hate you'. I had told her that she was the worst mother in the world, and that I would be better off if she would just die. I never really meant that last part. No matter how unloving, cruel, and horrible they were, neither of my parents deserved to die, at least not like this.

I shake my mother slightly, but she doesn't stir. Of course she doesn't; she is long gone. "Please... please... just come back." I choke out the last three words. It doesn't matter that I have spent a lifetime hating her, nor does it matter that she took the one thing that made me happiest in the world right out from under my nose. At the moment, I could care less about all the horrible things she has said and done. Nothing, I repeat: *nothing*, she has done warranted her death. I begin to cry, sobbing uncontrollably. I cry because however rotten she was,

she is gone, and I never got to say goodbye or to take back any of the things I have ever said to her.
"It's a shame things had to end like this." I snap my head up and find my father leaning against the door frame. His dark brown hair is a tousled mess. He is still wearing the charcoal suit I last saw him in, minus the jacket and tie. His forehead is creased, and his dark brown eyes, the exact same shade as mine, narrow. In one hand, he is holding a large, white, terry cloth towel stained with blood. In the other is a large butcher knife, dripping blood. His lips quirk up into a sinister grin that sends a chill down my spine. "You can't really be sad, can you? Not after what she did to you... to me... to us."

His words linger in the air.

"Y-Y-You did this?" I ask weakly.

He struts across the room toward me, and I pull my mother closer, as if I can protect her from any further harm. I glance up at him hovering over me, and my eyes flicker to the knife in his hands. My father follows my gaze and smiles. He tosses the knife onto their oversized poster bed and wipes his hands off with the towel before tossing it onto the bed as well.

"Of course I did," he sneers. My father smiles, not showing one ounce of remorse for what he did.

"Why? Why would you do this?"

"The bitch had it coming." He smiles again and sends another wave of chills down my spine. "I did it for us. But more importantly, I did it for you, Elizabeth." Then he lunges for me...

Chapter One

Present Day

DULL. BORING. PATHETIC.
 I exit out of the email screen on my computer and push away from my wooden desk. A frustrated groan escapes my lips. It's the same thing, over and over again. An author wishing and hoping to land an agent, to be published, to become the next big thing. Me, and about a million other people in this world. If one thing is lacking from being involved in the world of books, it's imagination. No one has it anymore. Most books are all the same. The only books that can both thrill and excite me are the books that belong in the Horror/Thriller genre. That is where the real art form of writing lays, the books that truly hang on the verge of being genius. Everything else is wretched, worthless. Simply put, everything besides horror is mundane.
 And the reason why being forced to work on the Romance floor of Harder's Literary Agent House is the worst job I can possibly have.
 I shouldn't complain. I'm lucky to even have such a prestigious job fresh out of college, especially since I only spent the last year interning here for experience. When I interned here, I worked alongside one of the biggest agents representing authors in the Horror/Thriller genre. Nothing like a good thriller keeps me on the edge of my seat, turning page after page, trying to figure out what is going to happen next, and who is behind it all. Trust me; it's a much better alternative than sitting in the dark, wiping away tears, rooting for the guy you want to win the girl's heart, and waiting for that happy ending. Nonetheless, when Lawrence Harder hired me full time, it came with one condition: "I had to spread my wings and fly." His exact words. Either work in Romance,

or try my hardest to land a delivery job at another literary agency and work my way to the top. Which could take years, if I succeeded at all. I couldn't risk that, since it doesn't fall in line with my list. So I took the job, regardless of how much I despise it.

Three months ago, I took the coveted agent position here, and I haven't signed a single author yet. Mr. Harder assures me that it takes time to shift into a new genre, and that I will eventually adjust and find the perfect author. Let's be real for a second; not many authors are flooding the email of a twenty-four-year-old agent just starting out in the world. Then we have Viola Harder, my boss' most recent wife. She is problematic in the most ridiculous ways. The only things she has going for her is that she is strikingly beautiful and in the best shape any woman of twenty-five can be. Other than that? Nothing, absolutely nothing fills that stupid, bottle blonde head of hers. She walks around the floors, strutting around like she is God's gift to earth, and she is large and in charge. All because she is married to the man who owns the company. Viola's had it out for me since my first day at orientation over a year ago, for who knows whatever reason, and she has been trying her best to get me fired ever since.

Viola's newest arguments are that I bring absolutely nothing to the table and that my place in the company is a waste of space, time, and money. I'm easily replaceable. As if she can hear my thoughts from six floors above, my email screen pops up on the computer, flashing with a new message from the devil herself.

> From: hotblonde69
> To: LWinter@hlah.com
> Ms. Winter,
> Tick-tock. Tick-tock. Tick-tock.
> Do you know what that is the sound of? That is the sound of the clock ticking, a reminder that your time here is quickly running out. You still have yet to sign anyone, and it's only a matter of time before LJ takes notice and rids the company of you, once and for all. I, unfortunately, cannot say that it would be with the utmost sadness to see you leave HLAH. I will be absolutely thrilled when that day comes. Believe me, that day will come. Sooner than you think.
> Signed,
> Viola Harder
> Vice President of HLAH

I shake my head and laugh at the sheer lack of professionalism in her email. First of all, who has an email account with the screen name hotblonde69? Seriously, how old is she again? Sixteen? Her threat, however immature as it may seem, is quite valid, though. I hate to agree with the woman, but it's only a matter of time before Mr. Harder decides to get rid of me. Am I going to sign an author anytime soon? Especially if I can't even get through a single sentence of a query letter? I have to do something to fix this. I have to get out of here and back to where I belong—in Horror/Thriller. I quickly grab the phone resting on top of my desk.

"Heidi," I say into the receiver. Heidi is my assistant, a year younger than me, and an intern with the same aspirations I have. She has been a godsend. "I need to talk with Mr. Harder. Can you see if he is available?"

"Right away, Ms. Winter." Her voice still holds a trace of a southern accent. I look up from my desk, out the panel of windows in front of me, to see her sitting at her small oak desk and shake my head.

"How many times do I have to remind you to call me Liza?" I hate being called Ms. Winter. It sounds too formal and makes me feel older than I am.

Heidi runs a hand through her long, strawberry blonde hair and releases a sigh into the phone. "Yes, Ms. Win— I mean, Liza." I smile and see her return the smile through the window. "I'll call up to his office now."

"Thank you." I hear the receiver click, indicating that she hung up, and watch her dial Mr. Harder's secretary. A few seconds later, a smile spreads across her face, she nods, and hangs up the receiver. I pick up my phone on the first ring.

"Mr. Harder can meet with you for a few minutes. But you must hurry," Heidi says quickly. I nod my head, acknowledging her through the window, and hang up the phone.

* * *

The elevator opens up to a small desk just outside a set of large wooden double doors. Jennifer smiles at me as I step out of the elevator. Her sleek blonde hair is pulled back into a tight bun, and she wears a black skirt suit. Mr. Harder has a thing for blondes. Luckily, I have a head of unruly black, wavy hair. It's reassuring knowing that I was most likely not hired on for some sick, perverted idea of his. The man could be a pig, but he is the best businessman out there. Jennifer nods at me as I walk past her desk and push open one of the doors. The door swings inward into a large office, with nothing but windows overlooking the bustling city below. Near the furthest wall is a large modern desk with steel legs curved into arches and a glass tabletop. The oversized, overstuffed leather chair behind the desk is facing towards the window, blocking my view of the man.

"Mr. Harder?" He doesn't turn around. I clear my throat and take a deep breath. "Mr. Harder, I really appreciate the opportunity you have given me to work for your company, but my particular skills would best serve you and the company outside of the Romance department. Each query letter I read leaves me wanting more, and I fear that we've lost a number of potential authors due to my misplaced skills. I believe a transfer to Horror and Thriller would serve the company best, as my talents lay in that area."

The words spill out of my mouth in a frantic rant. When I finish, I stand glued to the floor, waiting for what is about to come. Nothing. The room is quiet. My body is shaking, and I am still trying to wrap my head around the fact that I really just said all of that to Mr. Harder. I probably just secured my name at the top of the next-to-go list. I am finally able to move and turn to leave. I might as well start packing up my office now, what little I do have in there. "What is it about romance that you don't like?" The voice doesn't belong to Mr. Harder. The leather chair turns around and reveals that it is definitely not him, but a much younger, more handsome man.

"I-I-I'm sorry," I stutter. "I thought you were Mr. Harder."

"Of course you did." The man stands up, walks around the desk, and leans back on it with his arms supporting him. He crosses his legs out in front of him, and he smiles. His is the kind of smile that is utterly alluring, one that melts a girl's heart and sweeps her off her feet. He's gorgeous, with his dark brown hair and nearly black eyes, and he knows it. His white button up dress shirt tightens around his chest with his arms extending behind him, showing off the curves of his muscles. His black dress pants aren't tight in the way that he should be humiliated, but rather in a way that conforms to his legs. I'm sure the view from behind is just as nice as the view from the front. "So… what about romance novels is it that you don't like?"

My heart flutters. His voice is smooth and deep, one I could sit and listen to for hours. *What is going on with me?* No man has this kind of effect on me. Not anymore. "I just don't," I say sharply.

"I see." His smile falters for a moment before returning to full-wattage once more. "Care to elaborate?"

For some reason, I feel compelled to do just that. "The plot is the same in every book." I glance away. My heart is beating rapidly just looking at him, and I can't let him get under my skin. I'm a girl with a list that has to be followed down to the very last bullet point, and I can't be bothered by the likes of a man like him. "Boy-meets-girl, girl-meets-boy, one has a dark past that makes them feel they are unworthy of love. The two endure a long challenging road, facing inner demons. Eventually, everything turns out alright, and they find the love that they didn't even know they were searching for."

The words sound cold and bitter.

"That's the beauty of it, though, isn't it? That's what keeps the readers coming back for more, time and time again." He sounds so sure of himself.

"What?" I snap my head back towards him. "For what? A happy ending? One that doesn't truly exist. One that everyone in this world secretly hopes happens for them. It's a bunch of crap. It's just fiction, not the real world." I stare into his eyes as if to prove to him I mean every word I say. "Life isn't like any of the romance books. There are no happy endings. Nothing ever turns out the way anyone plans. At least, not in my world."

"Ah, I get it," he murmurs, causing me to pause. To my dismay, he pushes off the desk and crosses the distance between us in four long strides. Stopping just in front of me, he brushes back a strand of my wild, black hair. His touch causes me to jump, but I refuse to pull away. The man is standing too close, close enough to smell the rich scent of his cologne and to notice the stubble on his chin. He leans forward, close to my ear. A chill runs down my spine as his breath caresses my face. "Tell me, who was it that broke your heart?"

I turn away, walking as fast as I can without glancing back over my shoulder. He's struck a nerve. I don't know how he did it. I don't know how he figured it out so quickly, but he did. I need to get out of here as quickly as I can. With my head hanging low, I can't see where I am walking and walk right into someone. I look up and find Mr. Harder standing in front of me. "Oh my, I didn't see you there," I say quickly. "I'm sorry."

"That's quite alright, my dear," he says in his deep voice. "I see you met my nephew, Reid, my brother's son. He's just come back from overseeing our branch across the Atlantic for the last four years."

Of course, it has to be his nephew. Though my boss has salt and pepper hair and green eyes, I can see a bit of resemblance between the two of them. My face heats up, and I am sure that it is beet red by now. "I'm a lucky man to have met such a bold and beautiful woman," Reid chimes in.

I glance over at him, only to find he is now standing right beside me, grinning wider than before, if that's even possible. Irritation courses through my body at the sight of his smile. I do my best to grin at Mr. Harder. "Your nephew was quite enchanting." *Irritating is more like it.* I still want to know how he figured out so quickly something that I have been working hard to keep hidden. I am not an open book or anything. I don't mope around, acting like a woman who has had her heart stomped on, even if it was six years ago. Something about the man standing beside me sets my veins on fire.

"So what can we do for you, Lisa?" Harder Senior asks.

I groan inwardly. "It's Liza," I say softly.

"What was that, dear?" Mr. Harder raises an eyebrow and stares at me curiously. I can feel the heat of Reid's eyes on me. My chest tightens, and I struggle to breathe. He is standing so close that when he makes the slightest movement his arm brushes against mine and sends electricity dancing through my veins. *I. Need. To. Get. Out. Of. Here. Now.*

"It's Liza," I say louder. I clear my throat and take a breath.

I feel Reid wrap his arm around my shoulder, the touch startling me, and I hear him laugh softly. He drops his arm and I don't dare look at him. "Liza here came to talk to you about working in Romance," he says.

"Oh, really?" My boss raises his eyebrow again. "Now remember, Liza, it's going to take some time, but I think that you will find it a very good fit for you there."

"Yeah, who doesn't like a good story about love and overcoming your demons?"

I glare at Reid. Did he really just use my own words against me? I feel the heat rushing to my face again, only this time it's anger I'm feeling rather than embarrassment.

"Besides, I'm sure Reid here will be able to make the transition smoother from here on out." I glance at Mr. Harder. I must have seemed scared, because he laughs loudly. "Don't fret, darling; you are in capable hands." Still confused, my eyes dart back and forth between the two men. What is he talking about? "Silly me! I forgot to mention that Reid is filling the open Senior Agent position on your floor."

Oh boy, Harder's nephew is my new boss, which means I will be seeing him every day. This is not good, not good at all. I need to get out of here quickly, by any means necessary.

"So what do you say, Liza? You up for giving Romance another chance?" Reid flashes his million dollar smile as my heart flutters and my knees feel like jelly.

"What choice do I have?" I barely manage to say.

"That's the spirit." Mr. Harder says as he claps a hand down on my shoulder. I smile softly, tell them I have to get back to work, and walk as quickly as I can out of his office.

Chapter Two

MY LIFE OFFICIALLY SUCKS. Not only did I not achieve getting out of Romance, but I am now stuck with Harder Junior for who knows how long. Something about him drives me insane, something that irritates the hell out of me. Yet I can't get him out of my mind.

I stare at my computer screen, attempting to read another query letter, but I'm too distracted. I cannot stop thinking about Reid's smile, the kind I always swore I would never fall for on a guy. When he smiles, his face lights up, softening his deep, dark eyes. I can't forget the way I felt when he stood close to me, brushing the strand of hair out of my face, or his breath against my ear. I can still smell his cologne and hear the sound of his sultry voice bouncing around in my head.

I grab my phone, pushing the button to call Heidi's desk, and wait for her to answer. She picks up on the first ring. "What can I do for you, Ms. Win— I mean Liza." I laugh quietly as she catches herself yet again.

"Let's grab lunch," I reply quickly. "My treat."

Through the window, I see her smile. She nods her head, and that's all I need for an answer. I hang up the phone, open the drawer in my desk, and pull my cell phone out. One of the very few things in the office that is mine. My office is plain, barren of any personality, and shows no sign that it belongs to me. In every office, each agent has pictures of their families and clients. Some even have their college degrees plastered on the wall. Others have wall art personalized by their children. Even Heidi has decorated her desk with mementos of her family and her boyfriend. My walls and desk are empty. I don't have any pictures to hang, at least none that I wanted the world to see. All my photos hold horrible memories of a broken past. Of being hurt, disappointed. That life is behind me now. This life is a new day and age, a new Liza Winter.

I grab my purse and jacket off the coat rack in the corner of my office before I step out the door and close it softly behind me. Heidi has her coat on and is ready to go. I nod at her. She smiles, and falls into step next to me. We don't say a word as we weave through the cluster of desks out in the bull pen, where all the assistants' desks are, and head towards the elevator. In the short time we have spent together, Heidi has become the closest thing to a friend I will allow someone to be. She's already learned how to tell when I'm in a foul mood, frustrated, or don't want to talk. Clearly, now is one of those times.

The air is brisk and cold as we step out of the towering glass building. We turn to the right, walking down the sidewalk to the same little bistro we eat lunch at every day. The walk is short, and we arrive in just a few minutes. The bistro is emptier than usual, probably because there's still at least another hour until everyone in the business district is fighting to get in here to grab some lunch. Out of the eleven restaurants on the block, everyone wants to eat here. Some days, I send Heidi out a bit earlier to make sure we can get some food and bring it back to the office.

Today, I am glad we came earlier. I need the peace and quiet, plus the time and space to calm and collect myself. We order the same thing we always do: chicken and raisin salad for Heidi and a cheeseburger with fries for me. Heidi seems to think she can't indulge in fat, greasy foods for fear of gaining too much weight. From what I have learned of her, she grew up in the south, feasting on large home cooked meals, and isn't any bigger than a twig. I have insisted that she is absurd for feeling the need to watch her weight, so now she finally joins me in our traditional strawberry milkshakes. Although she orders hers with soy milk.

The waitress brings our food in a timely fashion, faster than we have ever been served before. I make note to grab lunch early every day from now on. Getting away from the four blank walls that stare at me only a daily basis is nice. I'm halfway through stuffing my face when the bell chimes as the door opens. My back is towards the door; however, I notice the sudden change in Heidi's demeanor.

"Oh… my…" she says slowly. I turn to see what has drawn her attention. My heart stops beating and drops to the pit of my stomach. Here, in my very own private sanctuary for the moment, is *him*. Reid Harder. I groan loudly and turn back to my food, hoping he doesn't see me sitting here.

"What is *he* doing here?" I mutter to myself. Heidi glances up at me and raises an eyebrow.

"Wait... you know him?" *Know him?* Hardly. Had the unfortunate mishap of meeting him and making a fool of myself less than an hour ago? I wish the answer isn't yes. I catch Heidi staring at him as he stands at the register, her mouth gaping, eyes wide open and filled with infatuation.

"That's Mr. Harder's nephew."

"You're telling me that that is Harder's nephew? That irresistible, mouthwatering, I-wanna-take-him-to-my-room-and-have-my-way-with him, God-like man is the boss's nephew? No way!" Heidi stares at me in disbelief. I say nothing and nod my head, aware that her attention is turning back to him. Jealousy sparks in me at the way she is gawking towards him. Who am I kidding? It's not like he belongs to me. I just met the guy. He's annoying, like the getting under your skin kind of type, fully aware he's attractive and uses it to his advantage. But man, I can't get him out of my head. Great, now I can't even stop peeking at him.

Oh crap, he's turning around, and then he sees me. Reid heads towards our table as I turn my attention back to my plate, and I suddenly lose my appetite. I can feel him watching me, but I can't see to gaze at him. I'm fully aware of his presence and smell his lingering cologne. "Liza..." he says my name, which sounds like music to my ears. Now that he has approached us, I can't ignore him. I can't pretend that he isn't hovering right above me. I turn my head and glance up at him. "Reid," I say plainly. "Please don't tell me you followed me here?"

What the hell? Why did I say that?

"You're only wishing I did." He laughs, which is sweet and light. It's one of the most beautiful things I have ever heard. I can feel the blood rushing to my face, which I'm sure is beet red by now. "That cute little blonde down in reception suggested I come here for lunch."

Like uncle, like nephew? Now I'm officially annoyed. "Who is this little beauty you got here?" Reid asks.

I hear Heidi giggle and see her flushing face. I roll my eyes and shake my head. "Reid, meet my assistant, Heidi. Heidi meet Mr. Harder's nephew, Reid," I say rather sharply. What is it about this man that gets my blood boiling so quickly? One minute I'm swooning over him, and the next he opens his mouth and I instantly become irritable.

"Heidi, such a beautiful name for a beautiful girl." He's flirting with her. *He is totally flirting with her right in front of me.* I know it shouldn't bother me, but it does. "How did you get the pleasure of becoming the assistant for the lovely Liza?"

Lovely Liza? Who the hell does this guy think he is?

"She's an intern from LPU," I answer quickly for her.

"Ahh, Long Port University, huh?" Reid looks at me and smiles. "Isn't that where you graduated?"

How does he know this? "Yes," is all I can manage to say.

"Well, good for you," he says, turning his attention back to Heidi. "I'm sure you'll do great."

"Thank you," Heidi says softly.

His charm is working. Her face flushes a deep red again, and she turns her head to the side in attempt to avoid him seeing it. It's too late. He knows he has her hooked, like a helpless fish drawn to the worm dangling from a fishing line. Reid says something to her, but my heart is pounding in my chest so hard that my ears are ringing, and I don't catch what he says. The same waitress that brought our food appears with his order in a bag. Thankfully, he is taking it to go. It's obvious the waitress is totally enraptured by him as well, since she lingers, explaining practically every ingredient in his meal, which is totally unnecessary. The girl finally leaves, blushing, giggling, and stealing glances over her shoulder as she walks away. I watch Reid checking her out from behind. He doesn't even have the decency to be polite about it. *What a pig.*

"See you ladies back at the office." Reid finally turns his attention back to Heidi and I. "Liza, when you get back, I'd like to meet with you in my office to talk about the direction we need to guide you in."

I can hardly breathe, let alone think. Being alone in his office isn't the smartest idea, but I nod my head regardless. He flashes that million dollar smile of his, and I swear Heidi is going to lose it right here in the bistro. As soon as the door closes behind him, I let out a long deep sigh. I can finally breathe again.

"Why does he want to meet with you?" Heidi asks. Her face is placid, showing no emotions, but I can feel the jealousy radiating off of her.

"That," I pause momentarily and sigh again, "is my new boss." Unfortunately. This is my worst nightmare come alive. Well... almost.

Chapter Three

I HAVE HAD A LIST made ever since the summer after my second year of college, detailing almost every aspect of the next ten years of my life. Nowhere on the list does it say to be irrevocably attracted to my new, arrogant, annoying, beautiful boss. In fact, at the bottom of the list, I wrote in big bold letters '**NO MEN!**' with the exception of my best friend, Elias.

I cannot deviate from the list. I carry the slip of paper around with me in my purse everywhere I go, scratching off and adding things as I go along. The list was created to keep me on track, to keep my eyes set on one singular goal— being the best damn literary agent this world has ever seen. Though I haven't made much progress on that just yet.

I don't have the time to date or to make many friends. It's just Elias and I. In school, I was always work and no play. That's carried over into my career as well. My life is perfect that way. I like having control over my life, and Reid is making me consider losing my self-control.

I sit in my office staring at my cell phone, contemplating whether I should call Elias or not. He's been the only constant throughout my life, and the only man who hasn't let me down. Elias, or Eli for short, is the polar opposite of me. He's wild, carefree, and has a different woman on his arm every chance he gets. I'm slightly jealous that he has no problem with letting loose and seeing where life leads him. I can't do that. I would probably have a heart attack and land myself in a mental ward. Everything has to be perfect, everything has to be my way, and everything has to be under my control. No control equals one psychotic wench, and nobody wants a psychotic wench on their hands.

I finally decide against calling Eli. He's probably wrapped up in bed with his newest fling of the week, and I do not want to interrupt that. When he's free, he will call, as he always does to check up on me, and when he does, he can talk some sense into me. He can bring me back to my happy place.

I glance up from my phone and see Reid walking across the lobby of our floor, immediately realizing he's heading straight towards my office. Damn the wall of windows that look out into the lobby. They make me feel exposed. Vulnerable. I quickly open the drawer to my desk, drop my phone in, and slam it shut. I turn to my computer and pull up my email program. Only five new query letters since I left the office. I open the first email and pretend to be working just as Reid walks into my office like he owns the place. Technically, he does— or his uncle does, at least.

"Excuse me," I say without taking my gaze off the computer. "The door is shut for a reason. Try knocking next time." I hear him laugh, the door close, and the sound of knocking. I glance up, unable to hide the smile that creeps up on my face. Reid stands outside the office door, arms folded, and his left foot tapping against the floor, waiting impatiently for me to let him in. I nod my head. He opens the door quickly and closes it behind him.

"There," he says. "Is that better?"

"Much." I turn back to the computer screen, ignoring his presence and doing my best to seem busy. Out of the corner of my eye, I see Reid cross the distance between the door and my desk. He pulls out one of the chairs closest to him and takes a seat, leaning back comfortably with his legs stretched out in front of him and his arms resting on the arms of the chair. I do my best to ignore him, but my eyes keep drifting over to him, absorbing his beautiful features. If looking like he did was a crime, he would spend life in prison without the possibility of parole. A few minutes later, Reid begins whistling some tune I have heard, and I sigh. "What do you want?" I finally ask, still not shifting my gaze towards him.

"Oh, I'm sorry." He straightens up in the chair. "Are you busy or something?"

"I'm trying to work," I say casually. It's a lie. I have been staring at the same damn query letter since I noticed him walking towards my office. I haven't read one single line. I close the email and move to the next one. It's the same thing.

"You and I both know that you aren't doing anything more than staring at the computer screen, pretending to be busy." He chuckles. My body stiffens, and I catch my breath. "You can stop pretending now and look at me."

I release a slow, low breath before closing the email and turning my attention to him. His dark eyes stare into mine, and the world is still for one brief moment. I shake my head and clear my throat. "What do you want?" I ask again.

"I believe I asked you to come to my office when you got back from lunch." His eyes darken for a moment before lightening back up to his normal shade of dark brown.

"I forgot," I say nonchalantly. He stares at me, and the way he stares at me is making my heart race. I take slow, deep breaths to calm my beating heart and fail. The sight of him is enough to make my pulse go crazy.

"Well..." Reid gets up out of the chair. "Let's go."

"You're here now," I say. Reid stops and settles back down in his seat. "So what do you want to talk about?" I cross my arms and rest them on top of the desk, doing my best to not show how he is affecting me by just sitting there. Reid is quiet for a long time. He starts to laugh, breaking the silence. I tilt my head to the side and study him. "What is so funny?"

"Are you always so serious?" His laughter bothers me, and I feel the irritation starting to bubble under my skin.

"I thought we were going to talk about work? About how you can supposedly help my transition to Romance an easier one?" I stare at him, unmoving. Reid releases a hearty laugh again, the sound like a beautiful one-of-a-kind song.

"I'd much rather continue our conversation from earlier." His voice is soft. He leans forward, resting his elbows on his knees and gazes up towards me. *Our conversation from earlier?* Is he talking about in his uncle's office? If so, that's territory I do not want to venture in, much less alone with him.

He has figured me out quickly, from the moment we met, and it scares me. I have never been one to wear my emotions on my sleeve or to give any inclination to my past. I've worked too hard to keep it behind me. That old life is dead and gone. His question earlier, the one about who broke my heart, caught me by surprise. Those few words he said were almost enough for the memories to come back. And that's something I can't have. "I am here to work," I say sharply. "If you do not want to discuss anything relating to our job here, then you might as well leave now."

"Okay." He raises an eyebrow. "On one condition." Reid stands up and runs his hand through his hair. "Say you will have drinks with me, tonight after work, at Gravity."

"Not a chance." The words come out automatically. Hell would have to freeze over before I ever return to that place. Reid frowns, and without saying another word, he walks towards the door. I watch him open it, pause, and look back at me.

"I want you to have three potential authors you are willing to sign and an explanation as to why in my office by three o'clock or I *will* be having a talk with my uncle." His voice is cold. He walks out of my office and slams the door behind him.

I sink back in my chair. *What the hell just happened?* Reid goes from asking me out for drinks to potentially firing me because I said no. Ah hell, I should have just agreed. Now my job is on the line. This is such bull. How am I ever going to get three authors chosen when I can't even make it past the first sentence of their letters? I could always just choose three random authors, but Reid seems smart. He'll know that's what I have done. Especially since I have to give legit reasons as to why I chose them.

Just great, Liza, just great. See what you have gotten yourself into.

Why did I let him get under my skin? Why did he have to be the boss's nephew? Me and my big fat mouth, I should have just kept it closed and given him what he wanted. I should have agreed to meet him for drinks. But I couldn't. I know having drinks with a guy is nothing. It's no big deal. People do it all the time. That wasn't even the problem. The problem is that he wanted to grab drinks at Gravity, only the biggest, most exclusive night club in town. That place is no good for a girl like me. It is the last place on Earth that I want to find myself in with the likes of a guy like Reid Harder. It's also a place filled with bad memories, ones I fight to keep hidden away.

What do I do?

Not hesitating, I open my drawer, grab my phone, and dial Eli's number.

Chapter Four

THE PHONE RINGS several times as I tap a pen on top of my desk and wait impatiently for him to answer, but it goes to voicemail. I sigh and hang up the phone. I lean back in my chair and stare up at the white ceiling. The shrill of my phone ringing startles me, and I jump in my chair. I reach for the phone immediately, press talk, and bring it up to my ear. "Liza, what's wrong?" Eli asks right away. His voice is eager and shaky.

I say nothing. I hear shuffling on the other end of the line and realize that he is probably still in bed. The joys of being carefree. "Talk to me... what is it?" he says softly.

"I just wanted to hear your voice." I sigh and lean back in my chair again. It's only a half lie. I really did want to his voice. He brings me a sense of calm and grounding.

"I know you better than that, *little rabbit*." I smile when he says the nickname he gave me when we first met in kindergarten. I could never stay still, I was always bouncing in my seat and moving around. Eli said I reminded him of a little rabbit, and the nickname has stuck ever since.

"It's just..." I sigh. "It's just work." How can I explain to him about Reid? I only just met the guy this morning. Eli says nothing and patiently waits for me to continue. "I got a new boss today, and he's..." He's what? Annoying? Irritating? Infuriating? Dangerously gorgeous? "He's something else," I finally say.

"Define something else?" I can sense the hesitation in his voice.

"He's an ass."

Eli laughs loudly into the phone, and I smile again. "According to you, all men are asses."

"That's because they are," I say lightly. In my experience, every guy is an ass. They are good for nothing other than breaking your heart. But talking to Eli is already easing the tension built up inside of me.

"Well…" Eli says. "Except for me."

"You are a rare treat." I laugh. "For the most part."

"I'll take that." Eli chuckles softly and then goes quiet for a few seconds. "Seriously, Liza, what is it?"

"I-I-I really don't know what to do? My boss, Reid, he isn't just some random guy they hired. He is Mr. Harder's nephew, as in the owner of my company, and he irritates the hell out of me."

"Why?"

No way can I tell him about the way Reid drives me crazy and not just in the literal sense. "He's arrogant, nosy, and… and, well, he had the audacity to ask me to grab drinks with him after work," I say. "To talk about some work related things," I add quickly.

I can hear the humor in Eli's voice. "And that's reason enough to irritate you?"

"He asked me to go to Gravity," I say coldly. Just saying the name out loud threatens to bring back the memories I stored away years ago.

"I see." Eli is quiet again. He knows why I can't go back there, the real reason. I can't go back to Gravity. Ever. That life is in the past, which is where all the memories are. Of everything that has to do with a person who longer exists. I can't… I won't ever go back there.

"You know you can't avoid all those places forever, Liza. Long Port is only so big." Eli's voice is soft again, but I can hear the seriousness in his tone. We have had the same talk time and time again. Sometimes I feel sorry for him. I feel like I hold him back from doing the things that he wants to do. That any twenty-four-year-old male wants to do, like have fun and go crazy. Most of the time, we spend our time locked up in the safety of my small apartment. We never go anywhere, except for dinner or an occasional movie. Every time we do, however, Eli wears a disguise, something to keep attention being drawn to us. Being the son of one of the most popular actresses of her time and a big time attorney, he's sort of a celebrity, and recognized everywhere he goes. I can't have that kind of attention, or everything will fall apart. My life as I know it would cease to exist. "You may not live that life anymore, but it's still a part of you. You can't undo your past."

"I'm not that person anymore." The words barely come out a whisper.

"That part may be true, but you can't escape being Jared Lewis's daughter forever. No matter how much you want to."

I sigh. Eli's right, as he always is. I may be able to change my appearance, who I associate with, the places I go, the things I wear, the car I drive, and the house I live in. Hell, I can even change my name. But I can never change who my father is, or what he has done. Even if he is twenty minutes away, spending life without parole at Long Port's Correctional Facility.

But I can try.

Sometimes I question why I stay so close by, but then I remember that no one expects to find me here. I'm right under their nose and they have no idea. They don't have the slightest clue that I haven't really gone anywhere. I'm right here where I've always been, a place I have always known, and that is my greatest advantage I have with the changes I've made. I know the places not to go and I am familiar with my surroundings. My risk at running into someone I may know is high, but it's a bigger risk going out into the unknown. At least here, I'm in control.

Damn it, talking to Eli was supposed to make me feel better. It usually does. Somehow he's managed to turn the conversation around on me and mention my father. Someone else I do not think about if I have the choice. "Is that all?" Eli's voice is still the same soft tone.

"No." I take a deep breath. "After I told him no, he didn't take it very well, and well.... well, he—"

"Liza." His voice is filled with concern and seriousness. "What did he do?"

"Relax; he didn't do anything you have running through that overzealous, overprotective mind of yours." I laugh, knowing all too well what it is he is thinking. "He told me that I had to choose three potential authors I want to sign with a reason why and be in his office by three or he's talking to his uncle"

"I don't know why you are on the phone with me then. You've got work to do!" Eli laughs.

Once again, Eli is right. It's useless keeping score as to how many times he has been right; all I know is my count is zero. The enthusiasm in his voice brings a tiny smile to my face. However, this phone call hasn't really done what I was hoping it would do. "I guess," I say softly. "I'll talk to you later."

"Yeah," he says. "I'm sure you will." With that, he hangs up the phone.

I'm alone again in my office. I let out a deep breath and mentally prep myself for the task at hand. I open the email up again on my computer. No new messages; only about forty that I have pretended to read. I scroll down to the bottom of the messages, figuring I should start with the oldest ones first. One more mental pep talk and I give the computer screen my full attention.

* * *

I take a deep breath before knocking on Reid's office door. I know he saw me coming, because his office has a wall of windows facing towards the lobby, just like all the others. I can see through the glass door that he is on the phone, so I knock softly. Reid motions for me to come in, so I open the door and close it quietly behind me. I stand near the entrance and wait for him to get off the phone. He motions for me to sit down in the plush leather chair in front of his desk, and I oblige.

"It'll be my pleasure to represent you and your book, Ms. Collins," he says into the phone. I try to ignore his conversation, not wanting to eavesdrop, but sitting in front of him makes it a little hard. "You, too, Ms. Collins. I'll see you next week." Reid hangs the phone back on the receiver and shifts his focus to me. "So what do we have?"

I hand him the piece of paper I have spent the better part of my day working on, struggling to get the right words out. It might be one of the hardest things I have had to do lately.

"What's this?" Reid raises an eyebrow and eyes me curiously. He reaches over the desk and takes the sheet of paper. I watch him as he reads it, and his eyebrows furrow every few seconds. "A resignation letter?" He narrows his eyes at me, his jaw clenches, and his face turns red. "Are you serious?"

"As serious as I can be," I say bluntly. "I can't do it. I just simply cannot work in the Romance department, representing authors who write a genre I despise." This is the last thing I want to do, but I feel like I have no other option. I would prefer to quit before being fired; that way, during interviews when asked why I no longer work at HLAH, I can honestly say that the job and I didn't mesh. Which is a lot better than being fired for not succeeding in my line of work.

"I don't get you, Liza," he says softly. His face starts to relax, and he looks at me. "I know you must know what you're doing, and that you're good at it. My uncle wouldn't just hire some girl fresh out of college otherwise." I wince when he refers to me as just some girl, the way he says it makes it feel degrading. Often I have wondered why Mr. Harder hired me. It was probably out of sympathy— because besides Elias, his parents, and my therapist, he is the only other person who knows my true identity. He only knows the truth because I arrive late to the office every Monday morning due to my weekly therapy sessions, and I felt obligated to tell him since he offered me a job right out the gate. "My uncle sees something in you. What is the problem? Why can't you sign anyone?"

"What's there to get?" I say, avoiding his gaze. "It's being here, on this level, with this genre. Romance and I, we don't go hand in hand." Reid says nothing but continues to stare at me with his dark eyes. "I can't force myself to work if I can't even make it past a single sentence in a query letter."

Reid's lips curl up into a smile. "I'll tell you what... you take this back." He slides my resignation letter across the desk. "And I'll make a deal with you."

"I'm listening." I cross my arms and lean back in the chair.

"Give me a month..." The hesitation in his voice strikes me, and I feel almost compelled to take it easy on him. Almost. I keep my arms crossed and stare at him, waiting for him to continue. "Just one month, with the two of us working side by side, trying to make this work." He pauses and shakes his head. "I mean make this *job* work. At the end of the month, if I haven't helped you sign anyone, I'll talk my uncle into letting you transfer to whatever genre you want."

I answer all too quickly, "Deal."

He smiles, a smile both beautiful yet menacing all at once. He's up to something. "Hold on. One more thing..." I really don't like where this is heading. "You have to have drinks with me at Gravity tonight. Nine o'clock."

I gulp. My throat is dry, and I can't breathe. What the hell am I supposed to do now? He is offering me the best alternative in the world, one that is a million times better than resigning. I can handle working side by side with him for a month just so I can transfer out of here. Well, at least I hope I can manage a month of working with him without caving in and ripping his clothes off in the process. But drinks at Gravity? That's asking too much, even if he doesn't know why.

"If I say yes..." Reid's full attention is on me. "It comes with one tiny exception… we sit at a table of my choosing." He nods his head in agreement, and I let out a deep breath. *Okay, this may work.* I know the perfect table at the club where no one will see us. I take a deep breath and let it out slowly. "Fine." The word barely comes out as a whisper.

Reid smiles as I stand up. This time his smile speaks volumes of triumph, that he has finally won. I turn, walking toward the door, and make no effort to close the door softly behind me. The sound of it slamming captures the attention of everyone in the lobby. As I walk through, I keep my head high and pretend to ignore the fact that they are all whispering about me. Heidi races over to me and brushes her bright red hair out of her face. "Everything okay, Liza?" She stares at me with her large, soft green eyes.

"Just peachy," I say harshly. I storm into my office and slam the door behind me.

Chapter Five

THE LAST TIME I had been in this alley, I was running in high heels and a wearing a tight black dress with tears streaming down my checks. I shudder at the memory and keep walking in my skinny jeans, flats, and plain, white baby doll T-shirt, an outfit that totally sticks out like a sore thumb at this club. I'm starting to second guess my outfit choice but realize that it's not a big deal. I have no plans on going far enough into the club for anyone to really take notice. I plan on snagging one of the tables in the farthest, darkest corner, out of view of everyone.

The alley is poorly lit as I walk down between the two brick buildings. I cross my arms over my chest and rub my arms in effort to keep them warm. I finally reach the back door and knock three times. The door is opened by a big, burly man with short black hair and arms the size of tanks. The sound of music blaring inside the club comes through the door, and I can see strobe lights flashing in the distance behind him.

"Excuse me, miss, but this is not an entrance." He steps out of the door frame and takes a possessive stance in front of it. "You'll have to go around front if you want to try and get in."

"Not even for an old friend?" I mentally slap myself. *What am I doing?* I cannot tell Preston who I am, but the sight of him makes me miss him. The way he stands there reminds me of all the times he stood like that to protect me from awaiting paparazzi. It also reminds me that he is a man I can trust, a man I once considered my friend, and I want to tell him. Preston cocks his head to the side, raises an eyebrow, and eyes me curiously. "Elizabeth? Elizabeth Lewis?"

"In the flesh." I smile, and we both begin to laugh. Preston drops his big man façade and wraps me up into one his big ol' teddy bear hugs. The man is ridiculously bulky, so much so that it is intimidating, but really he has the kindest of hearts.

"I didn't recognize you with the black hair." He shakes his head and brushes a strand out of my face.

I smile. "That's kind of the point."

"I'm afraid your usual table is no longer available," he says.

"That's quite alright. I have no intentions of sitting there." And I don't. My old table, the one directly in front of the dance floor, is in plain view for everyone to see. Literally. It doesn't matter where you sit or stand in the club or which direction you are staring from, you have a direct line of sight to the people sitting in the fancy VIP booth. "Any of the tables in the back will do. Preferably one in the darkest corner."

Preston nods his head and moves to the side to let me pass. I walk down the dimly lit hallway with him close on my heels. The hall opens up to the familiar club that once was a constant part of my life. The scene remains unchanged. This club attracts a variety of people, but appeals more towards the upper social class and quite popular. The most gorgeous men and women come here. Women wearing skimpy dresses grind their bodies up against any man who's willing on the dance floor in the middle of the club. Other women run their fingers up and down the arms of men having drinks at the bar on the left side of the club, regardless of the fact that they are wearing wedding rings. The rest of the women have arranged themselves on the laps of the men sitting in the private booths that circle the dance floor. The men are just as sleazy, if not worse. They take pleasure in the attention they are receiving and have no regard for their wives at home. It's disgusting, and the men are nothing but pigs.

It's amazing how little a place can change in six years.

"Will this work?" Preston says as he points to a table on the right. He clearly understands what I meant when I said I wanted the darkest, most out of sight table in the club.

"This is perfect. Thank you." I smile. "And if you could, please tell no one of my presence here."

"Your secret is safe with me, darling." I slide into the booth and stare up at him. I never realized until now how much I have missed him. "It's good to see you, Elizabeth. It's been six years too long."

My heart pulls at his words. Maybe there are some people I should have never cut out of my life, him included. I don't have the heart to tell him that this is the last and only time he will see me step foot in this club. After tonight, I plan on never ever coming in here again. Well, as long as I am not blackmailed into it again. Preston begins to walk away, and I call out to him. "Oh, and Preston..." He stops and glances towards me. "I'm supposed to be meeting someone here. He'll be searching for me under the name of Liza Winter, so if you can, bring him to my table when he arrives. His name is Reid Harder."

The look on Preston's face says he knows who I am talking about. How? That I didn't know nor did I care to know. I just want to get this dumb drink and meeting thing over with and get the hell out of here. "Anything for you, Ms. Elizabeth."

At twenty minutes past nine, Reid still hasn't shown up. If he isn't here in the next ten minutes, I'm leaving. It's as simple as that. I have already been here longer than I want to be. It's only a matter of time before someone comes trekking through this area, seeking for a hiding place to do who knows what. I glance around to see if I can spot him. In a club this large, though, it's nearly impossible. I notice a couple of people I knew from the past and shrink back in my chair. I'm sure if I can see them from where I am sitting, they can probably see me. Though they probably aren't looking at me like I am at all of them.

My heart aches momentarily as I realize none of my old friends are searching for me. That they are here, having the time of their lives on a Friday night, without a care in the world. I am long out of their minds. I know this is what I wanted, what I set out to do in the beginning, but even after six years, it still hurts that they all gave up so easily on our friendship when I shut them out. So much for being friends for life. The only one who didn't give up on me and made it perfectly clear he wasn't going anywhere was Elias. For which I am eternally grateful. If it wasn't for him, I would truly be alone in this world.

I peek at my phone again. Its twenty-five minutes past nine, and still no sign of Reid. *I'm not going to wait any longer.* I start to stand up and leave my table when Preston reappears. "Excuse me, Elizabeth, but it seems your Reid Harder guy has already arrived and is waiting for you at his table."

"Can you let him know that I will only meet him here?"

"Already did..." Preston is still efficient as ever. "But he is insistent that you come to him. He also asked me to remind you that Horror is on the line, whatever that means."

"That bastard…" I mutter under my breath. He isn't oblivious to my reluctance about coming here. He may not know the story as to why, but he can't be that stupid. "Where is he?"

"Platinum booth."

"Of course he is." My old table, which is the most open, most visible booth in the club. He is putting me on display when I least want it. My head screams at me to leave now and to turn in my resignation letter to Harder Senior on Monday and leave it at that. Nothing is worth what I am about to endure. "Is there a less visible path to get to it?" I know the answer to my question, but I still ask it regardless."

"'Fraid not, Elizabeth; you know that."

Yes, I do.

All eyes are on me as I walk towards the platinum booth. The booth is in front of the dance floor, up on a high stage, on display for everyone to see and eye with jealousy whoever is sitting there. There's only two ways to get to it. The first is to walk along the narrow walkway between the dance floor and the ring of booths that surround it. The second is to go right through the middle of the dance floor. I choose the first option. No one seems to notice who I am, but they still stare at me, no doubt because of my clothes. My outfit is the polar opposite of the women in the club with their too short dresses, their butt cheeks hanging out, and strapless tops that leave their cleavage in danger of falling out.

I recognize more people now that I am down on their level. Some stare at me with disgust as I weave past them. Some shake their heads, while others just stare at me with disbelief. I really should have rethought my outfit tonight. I keep my head held high and my eyes straight forward. This walk is the longest five minute walk of my life.

Reid is alone in the booth as I reach the top of the stairs. He is wearing a pair of dark wash jeans, a plain dark green shirt, and a pair of Converse. He looks even hotter than he does in a suit. A smile spreads across his face as he stands in front of the long, white sectional couch. The booth has not changed, much like the rest of the club. "You captured a lot of attention on your way up here," he says, and another smile spreads across his face.

I stop in front of the low glass table in front of him, cross my arms, and glare at him. Reid frowns and sits down on the couch. I walk around the table and sit on the far opposite end, as far away as I possibly can, making it perfectly clear that I am not happy to be here. "Oh, come on," he says over the music. "At least act like you're going to enjoy yourself."

"Why did you ask me here?" I ask brusquely. Reid moves closer to me on the couch, close enough so we no longer have to shout over the music.

"To get to know you better outside of the work place. That way I can figure out how to help you."

"But why here? Why not a restaurant or someplace..." I catch myself before I say someplace intimate in the nick of time. I never want to find myself in an intimate setting with him. "Someplace else."

"I like the atmosphere."

"Right." I laugh. "If you really want to get to know me better, you should know this isn't my kind of scene. I don't really fit in here." I make a gesture to my clothes, and he moves closer. Our bodies are nearly touching now. I can smell the same rich cologne he was wearing earlier. My body vibrates with a hum of energy I have never felt before. His smell is intoxicating, so much so that I just want to reach out and touch the curve of muscles that defines his arms.

"You could fit in anywhere you go," he leans in and whispers in my ear. Another hum of energy dances through my body, and I move away. He's too close. "You didn't see everyone staring at you the way I did."

"It's because I stand out with my clothes." I try to move further away from him again and realize I am out of room on the couch. "What do you really want, Reid?"

What all men want, I think to myself. I shake my head, trying to get the thought out of my mind. What I wouldn't give to see him standing in front of me naked, to be tracing the lines of his body. *Stop it.* I mentally slap myself in the head. I cannot think about him like this. I cannot ever go *there* with him, or anyone. Reid is staring at me with a wide grin on his face, and I glare at him. "I want to get to know you better. To see what makes you tick, to know why you don't like romance… and to see what makes you smile."

The last part comes out barely a whisper, and I'm almost sure I made it up. "Why do you need to know these things?" I ask breathlessly.

"I can't figure you out. But I want to…" His voice is eager. His eyes shift, dropping his mask, and revealing something much deeper to him. A need to feel loved. Something I can never give him. "I need to."

I say nothing and stare straight ahead. I can't look at him, I better not even think about glancing at him, because if I do, all my hard work will blow right out of the window. I set these rules I have so I never risk falling in love again, so I never get my heart broken again, but Reid makes me want to throw caution to the wind and say to the hell with it. Something about him ignites my veins, and that feeling isn't something I can trust. It's a feeling I don't know what to do with.

"Dance with me?" he asks as he stands up and holds a hand out to me. I snap my attention back at him, and I swear my jaw hits the floor.

"E-E-Excuse me?" His question came out of left field, and I never saw it coming. "No," I say defiantly.

"Dance with me… just one dance. What harm can it do?"

Chapter Six

"**OKAY.**" The word is out of my mouth before I can even register what I have said. My body betrays me by standing up and placing my hand in his. The touch of his hand in mine sends a wave of excitement coursing through my body. Reid is smiling like a kid in a candy store, and before I can change my mind, he is dragging me down to the dance floor.

A few heads turn to watch at us as we brush past them on the dance floor, but that's all. A momentarily flicker of fear flashes in my mind. *What if someone recognizes me?* I don't have another second to get my thoughts together and get off the dance floor before Reid pulls me against him. Our bodies began to sway to the music, my legs fitting perfectly between his, my body grinding against his. I wrap my arms around the back of his neck as he rests his hands on my waist and nuzzles his face near the nape of my neck. We lose ourselves in the music, and I don't know how long we dance. I didn't realize until now how much I missed this.

I turn around, pressing my backside against his growing length, and his hands wander up and down my body. My body is on fire, yearning for his roaming hands to touch me in all of my sensitive places. I cast my eyes around the room, but no one is paying attention to us, and it's just Reid and I against the music. That's when I see *his* eyes on us, the dark blue eyes that belong to the guy who broke my heart all those years ago.

All the air leaves my body, and I can't breathe. I stop dancing and return his stare with horror. He smiles at me and winks; that's when it hits me that he knows who I really am. "What's wrong, beautiful?" Reid's seductive voice whispers in my ear.

I spin on my toes and stare at him. His dark eyes have filled of lust and hunger. "This was a mistake. I have to go." I shove my way through the crowd as fast as I can. I don't glance back out of fear that if I do, I may never leave. I pass the table where I sat when I first arrived and hustle down the hallway just as the tears begin to stream down my face.

How could I lose control like that? *Why did I have to dance with him?* I shake my head and continue down the dim hall. "Elizabeth, everything okay?"

I stop to see Preston walking towards me, worry filling his eyes. "Thank you. I'm fine." I brush past him and shove the door open. The cold air hits me in the face, and I start to run. Just like I did six years ago. It's funny how time really doesn't change anything.

* * *

"It's all your fault, Elizabeth." I hear the sound of my mother's voice. I sit up in my bed and glance around the dark room. It can't be my mother; my mother is dead.

"Mom?" I say softly, allowing my eyes to adjust to the darkness. Like a flash of lightning, she appears at the foot of my bed. My mother looks just like she did the last time I saw her, with her blonde hair and clothes saturated in blood and puncture wounds everywhere. I cringe and cast my eyes away, unable to face her.

"Elizabeth Rose!" she shouts. "Don't you dare turn away! Look at me... see what you have done to me." Reluctant, I slowly turn my head back towards her. Tears sting my eyes, and I barely breathe. "Are you happy now? Did you get everything you wanted from my demise?"

"Mom..." I choke out. "I didn't... I never wan—"

"Enough!" she shouts again. "You should be rotting in jail alongside your father, you stupid bitch." My mother lunges across the bed, arms extending out in front of her, revealing several jagged cuts along them. A scream escapes my throat.

I'm awake now. Alone in my dark room. The sound of my cell phone ringing snaps me out of the nightmare. It's been a long time since I have had one. I glance at the digital clock on my night stand; it's a quarter after two in the morning. I snatch my phone from the nightstand to see a picture of Elias and me illuminating the screen. A calming wave washes over me. *It was just a dream.* A really vivid, horrid dream. I sink back against my pillow with my phone in my hand and answer. "Hel—" My voice cracks, and I clear my throat. "Hello."

"Did I wake you?" Eli's smooth voice comes over the phone. "I figured you might still be out."

"Nope, I'm home in bed and trying to sleep."

Eli takes a deep breath and sighs loudly. "So, tell me… how was your date?"

I groan. "It wasn't a date." The thought of being on an actual date with Reid Harder is enough to make me want to laugh out loud. He is exactly the kind of man I would date, which is exactly why I have to stay away from him. I've already broken enough rules. "And it was worse than I ever expected." That's a lie.

"What did he do, Elizabeth?" Eli's voice is cold and hard. I take a sharp deep breath; it's been years since he has called me by that name.

"Nothing," I answer quickly. "What is it with you and assuming he has done something?"

"I don't like him."

I laugh loudly. "You don't even know him."

"Exactly." His voice is serious. The doorbell rings and I jump.

"There's someone at my door," I whisper.

I hear Eli's voice catch before he finally speaks. "It's after two in the morning. Who would be at your door?"

"Hold on…"

"Liza, don't you ev—"

I lower the phone from my ear, missing the rest of whatever Eli is saying. I climb out of my bed and tiptoe down the hall towards the front door. My body is trembling, my heart is pounding hard against my chest, and my mind is racing. No one knows where I live, except for Eli and his parents. I can hear Eli shouting on the other end of the phone, but I hold the phone away from my ear. The doorbell stops ringing and is followed by loud, aggressive knocks against the door. I stop just in front of it, flicking on the light and unsure if I want to open the door. The one thing I never got around to doing is getting a peephole installed so I can see whoever is on the other side. This is a moment I really wish I hadn't put it off. Another knock comes across the door, and I start to tremble. My hand is shaking as I crack the door open, leaving the chain in place, and glance through the tiny opening.

"Reid?" I quickly close the door, remove the chain, and find a disheveled mess of a man. Reid's beautiful dark brown hair is sticking up every which way, his eyes are dark with circles around them, and he seems like he is going to be sick. I bring the phone back to my ear where Eli is still shouting, but I block out everything he is saying. "I-I-I'll call you back," I say quickly and hang up the phone. I stare at Reid, who is running a hand through his hair and won't meet my eyes. "What are you doing here?" *And how do you know where I live?*

Instead of answering my question, he pushes past me into my apartment. I gaze at him in astonishment for a moment before I close the door and stare at his back. Reid's body is tense, and I can hear his ragged breathing loud and clear. Quickly, he turns to face me. Without saying a word, he crosses the few feet between us in three short strides. He pushes me up against the wall and presses his lips against mine.

I am surprised by the sudden connection, but it only takes a split second before I succumb and return it. The kiss is raw, full of hunger and desire. His tongue brushes against my lips, and I open my mouth to let him in. He tastes like bitter, aged barley from the alcohol he has consumed, but delicious nonetheless. I run my hand through his hair and feverishly press my lips against his as if my life depends on it. He tugs on my lower lip with his teeth and bites down gently, causing a wave of desire to radiate through my body. His hands wrap around my waist, pulling me close as he starts to move with me towards the living room. Not once do his lips leave mine. Reid gently lays me down on the couch and leans on top of me. I run my hand up his shirt, tracing the lines of his muscles, just like I have imagined doing a thousand times since meeting him less than twenty-four hours ago. I moan as our tongues collide again, doing the familiar dart and dance, and press my body against his growing erection.

Reid pulls away and looks bewildered. I watch him shake his head, stand up, and say nothing. He gazes at me once more storming out of my apartment, leaving me there to figure out what the hell just happened. The kiss is over as quickly as it started.

Chapter Seven

I'M A CATASTROPHIC MESS over the weekend. Elias comes to check on me the morning after the kiss, and I don't tell him anything other than someone had the wrong door. He knows I'm lying, but doesn't press me any further. One of the many things I love about him. In reality, what could I tell him? That Reid showed up to my house, kissed me like I have never been kissed before, and then left me there. No, lying was the better way to go. How did Reid know where I lived anyway?

The thought takes over anything else for the rest of the weekend.

To say I am a bundle of nerves as I head to work this morning is an understatement. I decided to skip my appointment with my therapist this morning because I really didn't want to talk about anything. I didn't want Reid popping up in our conversation somehow. Not until I try and make sense of it myself. Now I'm wishing I didn't miss out, because I am a train wreck, car wreck, and plane wreck all bundled into one as I enter the elevator. I nervously tap my foot against the floor as I wait for the doors to close. My breath catches as Reid steps in at the last minute. No trace of the man who showed up at my apartment at two o'clock in the morning and kissed me. No, instead, he is looks amazing in his smoky gray suit that clings to his body in all the right places. Our eyes meet briefly, staring at one another before he breaks away and presses the button that takes us to our department. The ride is quiet, unnerving, and tension ripples through the air.

A couple of people join us as we stop on different floors on the way up. Reid exchanges quick hellos with them and never once glances my way again. I can't help but wonder what the hell his problem is. We finally reach our floor, and Reid motions for me to step out first.

I nod my head slightly and exit the elevator. I start to head towards my office when he stops me by touching my elbow, sending energy humming through my body. I turn to look at him and he pulls me off to side. He seems different, almost angry, and I don't know why. I'm the one who should be angry.

"My office. Ten o'clock. Don't be late," he says in a cold, sharp voice.

Before I have a chance to respond, he lets go of my elbow and walks away. I'm left there alone, watching him walk away. Again. My pulse begins to quicken, and my blood boils. *That's all you have to say to me?!?*

I shake my head and storm toward my office. Heidi greets me and I brush her off, slamming the door in her face. I sink down in the chair behind my desk, open the drawer to place my cell phone inside, and slam it closed. "What the hell, Liza?" I say out loud to myself. *Why am I letting him get on my nerves?* I can't put the blame on him, not all of it at least. I did nothing to stop the kiss, so I have to take some of the blame, I suppose. I let out a deep sigh and turn on the computer.

Five new messages. The first four are from authors who are seeking representation, of course. I spend a few minutes on each of them, trying to read them before I give up and move on to the next one. The final email comes from an unknown sender. Curiosity gets the better of me, and I open the email. My heart stops, and my hands shake as I reread the message over and over again. It's simple and straight to the point.

From: Unknown Sender
To: LWinter@hlah.com
Dear Ms. Winter,
It is my greatest pleasure to indulge you with a bit of information I have acquired. You see, you are not who you say you are. You are merely playing the charade of being someone else. How long do you expect this to last? You cannot hide from being Elizabeth Rose Lewis forever. The truth will come out. And when it does, I will be there to relish in the delight of your failure. You can run, but you can't hide. Watch your back.

Someone knows. Someone, other than the few people who should, knows the truth. I forward the email to my personal account and delete it off my work email as quickly as I possibly can. Everything is starting to slip out from beneath me. *What is going on?* I want to call Eli, but I decide against it. It will only worry him more than he already does. I lean back in my chair, rub my eyes, and sigh loudly. I glance at the clock, and it's nearly ten. Almost time to make my way to Reid's office.

I'm not going to go. If he is going to be an ass and ignore me like he did in the elevator, then I'm going to ignore him and pretend I didn't hear his demand. With one last deep sigh, I sit up and open my inbox again. There aren't any new messages, just the forty old ones that are sitting in my inbox. I click on a random message and attempt to read it.

I find myself in the same predicament always. I simply cannot get through a query letter. I attempt five more before giving up and just staring around my office. I catch a glimpse of gray out the corner of my eye, and I look to see a livid Reid storming my way. I quickly turn my attention back to the computer screen. Maybe if I act busy, he'll buy my story of merely being so caught up in my work that I forgot to go to his office. *Fat chance.*

My door flies open, and Reid storms in, slamming it behind him. I am tempted to remind him to knock, but the deathly glare he is sending me makes me think otherwise. "Liza." He says my name like a growl. "Look at me, goddamn it." I turn my head and face him. His face is flushed, and his hair is slightly messier than the pristine style from this morning, as if he has ran his hand through it multiple times. And he's panting like he just finished running a marathon. "I told you to be in my office an hour ago."

"Oh, I'm sorry." I smile, which is the wrong thing to do because his nostrils flare and his eyes darken. I shrink back in my chair ever so lightly and glance at him. "I must have forgot. Just as you forgot to knock once again." I clamp my big, fat, stupid mouth shut. What am I thinking? I'm only going to piss him off further. *Like I really care.*

"Liza." My name rolls off his tongue like its dripping with acid. "I am your boss. If I tell you to meet me in my office at a certain time, you damn well better show up." He's right. He is my boss, but that doesn't mean he has to be such an ass.

Reid circles around my desk, stopping behind my chair, and places a hand on either side of my arms. His chin nearly rests on my shoulder, and I can smell the invigorating scent that sends my blood pumping through my veins. I try not to stare at his lips. The soft, sweet lips that were pressed against mine just two days ago. He's staring at the screen, reading the email I have pulled up. I watch his eyes furtively scan the message, his eyebrows raising slightly whenever he reads something that intrigues him. He is totally in his element right now. "Sign her." I swivel my chair around and gaze up at him.

"E-E-Excuse me?"

"I said sign her." I shake my head. "See, her letter is impeccable. The book she is proposing is just what we are looking to represent. This could be your big break."

My big break? I don't want a big break in Romance. What I really want to do right now is rewind back to Saturday morning and finish what we started. Reid stares at me, oblivious to the fact that licking his lips is really turning me on. My breathing slows, and we don't break eye contact for several long seconds.

In a blink of an eye, his lips are on mine again. The kiss is nothing like the first one we shared. This one is soft, sweet, and gentle. "I've been wanting to see you again all weekend just so I can do that again," he whispers against my lips. He pulls away and walks back around my desk. I turn in my chair, and my eyes never leave him. "Right…" he says, running a hand through his dark hair. "So… um… since you apparently can't seem to follow directions and be somewhere when told to be, you can accompany me to lunch, and we'll discuss what I wanted to talk about there."

There he goes with the demands again, like he can just boss me around. Technically, he can. But I have a right to decide where and who I eat lunch with. I should just say no, not give into his demand, but I can't.

Chapter Eight

REID SHOVELS FRIES into his mouth acting like it isn't a big deal, and I can't help but to think how long he's going to work out to burn off all those calories. I can picture him shirtless, running on a treadmill, with sweat dripping down his body. I shake my head, trying to get the image out of my mind. *What is wrong with me?* I hear Reid laugh and turn so I can get a good look at him. "What's so amusing?" I ask him.

He leans back in his chair and glances around the café we are sitting in, the same one I ran into him last week. "Are you even going to eat that?" He reaches over and plucks a few French fries off my plate. "You know…" He chews the fries quickly before speaking again. "I still can't figure you out."

"I think you've said that before."

"It's true." He takes a sip of his water, places the glass alongside his plate, and rests his hands on top of the table. "Back there… in your office… you have the perfect opportunity. Something to make a lot of money off of."

"I don't need the money." It's true. I really didn't. When my father was arrested, he transferred all the money to me, stating that he would have no need for it any longer. I have never touched it. I don't feel right taking money from the man who murdered my mother in cold blood. So instead, I let millions of dollars just sit in the bank, untouched.

"Yes, you do," he says plainly. Rage begins to boil under my skin. *Who is he to tell me what I need?* "I have seen that death trap of a car you drive around in."

"Hey! That car gets me where I need to go. That's all that matters."

He smiles. "And I've seen that small, crammed apartment of yours."

"Speaking of which, how did you even know where I live?"

"I went to the office and checked your file." He acts if it isn't a big deal. My heart starts to race. If he peeked into my file, does that mean he knows the truth about who I really am? "Why don't you have a boyfriend?"

His question takes me by surprise. "Who says I don't?" Reid shrugs his shoulders and he eyes me curiously, like he isn't stupid. "Not that it is any of your business, but I don't date guys."

"So you're a lesbian then?"

I laugh loudly, and the water I just began to sip sprays everywhere. I feel the heat of embarrassment creep up my face. The few people in the café turn their heads and glance at me. *Me, a lesbian? He can't really believe that after our kiss Saturday.* "No, I'm not a lesbian," I whisper. "I just don't have time to date, that's all."

"What? With your busy work schedule?" He laughs. "With all those authors you have signed, you must be quite the busy lady." He's mocking me, full on mocking me. I don't know whether to laugh along with him or to be mad.

"All jokes aside, why did you want to meet with me?"

Reid's face falters for a moment before he regains that aura of being in control of himself. Neither of us say anything, and we just stare at each other. The silence gives me time to absorb more of his good looks and the memory of the kiss.

The same waitress that flirted with him on Friday is back, throwing herself all over him. She stands facing him, with her back toward me. She keeps touching his arm every time he says something she finds funny. I watch the two of them, who appear to be completely ignorant to the fact that I am sitting here. Reid indulges the waitress and flirts back with her. I want to tell her to back off, that he is mine, but I have no claim to him. Yeah, we have shared two kisses now. One that makes me hot every time I think of it, and one that was soft and sweet. But he isn't my boyfriend, and I don't want him to be.

"Ahem." I clear my throat. Both of them ignore me, so I clear my throat louder. The waitress turns around and glares at me. Reid drops his hand from where it sat on her waist and stares out the window. I hold up my glass towards the waitress. She glares again, and then snatches the cup out of my hand. I hear Reid laugh lightly, and I watch the girl's face turn red. She turns on her heel and heads to get another drink for me.

"So…" Reid says after the waitress is gone. "The company's charity dinner is this next weekend. What would it take for you to accompany me?"

My heart stops. How could I forget about the dinner? It's less than two weeks away. Last year, I managed to escape due to something with school, but I was only an intern. This year, however, I am agent, and there's no getting out of it. Every agent is required to be there, along with any authors who have available time in their schedule. I completely forgot about it until now. It's a black tie event which means I have to dress up. Everyone who is anyone in this town will be there, including the very people I cut out of my life years ago. I start to hyperventilate.

"Liza?" I hear Reid say my name softly. "Liza… are you okay?" He is kneeling next to me now and gently shaking my arm.

"I… I'm sorry. I'm fine," I barely answer, snapping out of my trance-like state.

"What's wrong?"

"It's nothing."

Reid returns to his seat. His eyes soften, revealing a small glimpse of a gentler side of him. "So what do you say? Care to be my date next Saturday night?"

"Why did you kiss me?" I ignore his question and ask the one that has been burning in the back of my mind. I wait, and I wait, and he hasn't answered me. He stares out the window for a long period of time before finally glancing at me.

"I don't know why." It barely comes out a whisper, and I almost didn't catch it.

I shake my head and gaze into his eyes. "Yes." He lowers his head. "Yes, I will be your date."

Reid's eyes light up, a stark contrast to his dark brooding ones, but only for a moment before the darkness seeps back in. "I'll pick you up at seven o'clock sharp." He stands up and places a fifty dollar bill on the table. "Now, if you'll excuse me, I have to go."

And he leaves, just like that. What is it with this man and leaving me hanging every single time? I sit there, unable to eat the rest of my food. The waitress brings back my glass and stares at the empty chair across from me with disappointment. She isn't the only one. I know how she feels. I allow myself to stare out the window at the bustling street outside for a while before I grab my purse and make my way back to the office. My head is spinning with my thoughts going a mile a minute.

My email is blinking with one new message for me when I get back to the office from another unknown sender. I am hesitant to open it. I pace around my office, contemplating whether not I want to read it. After about twenty minutes of pacing I finally sit down behind my desk and open it.

> From: Unknown Sender
> To: LWinter@hlah.com
> Trouble in paradise? It seems to me that you are sprung on a certain boss of yours. I wonder what his uncle would think of this. Doesn't this go against all your rules? Ah, yes, I know all about your silly rules. You haven't been as careful as you think. Leaving your purse behind or talking about it adamantly over lunch with your assistant or best friend. Not very wise for someone who is trying to hide her past. Don't worry. Your secret is safe for now. But stop and think for a moment, what would that man you are drooling over think once he learns the truth about who you are and what your father has done? Tread lightly, Elizabeth, for you never know when your world will come crashing down.

Tears stream down my face. Who is this person? How do they know so much about me? Only one thing is for sure. They are stalking me, watching my every move. The thought alone sends chills down my spine. I send the email to my personal account again before deleting it. I really need to tell Elias, but I can't. Not yet. Whoever it is wouldn't be toying with me if they didn't want something. I just have to figure out what that something is.

Chapter Nine

REID NEVER SHOWS UP to the office the next day, or the rest of the week. I try to distract myself with work, but that only reminds me of the deal we had made in his office a week ago. A deal where he isn't keeping up his end of the bargain. I should be happy, honestly, because then at the end of the next three weeks, I'll be back in Horror. Yeah, it may be by default, but that's on him, not me.

It's been nearly a week since the hot steamy kiss, and three days since the gentle one that sent my heart spiraling out of control. I can try to deny it all I want, but as frustrated as he makes me, he also has me wanting more. I haven't told Eli about this. Seeing the dark office that is Reid's tears at my heart. I can't wait for the end of the day to come. At least I'll have the weekend away from staring at his empty office. That doesn't mean I won't stop thinking about him, however.

Eli texted me earlier today to let me know that he was going to head back home after spending the past few days at my house. So that means I'm on my own for the evening, with nothing to do. I decide that today is the perfect day to go for a walk in the park. After work, I park my car in my assigned parking space and head towards the park without glancing back at my apartment.

The neighborhood I live in is nothing short of horrible. Break-ins happen all the time. Cops are being called for domestic disputes constantly, and apartments are being raided in search of drugs. It's bad enough that Eli considered staying and opted to go to LPU with me to make sure I would be safe. He even insisted that he would move in with me and sleep on the couch in my one bedroom apartment. Eventually, I convinced him to go off to college a few hours away, with the help of his parents.

With the neighborhood I live in, no one would guess such a beautiful park would be only a three minute walk away. A cement pathway winds throughout the park with thick, luscious, dark green grass on both sides. Trees are planted at regular intervals from each other, lining the sidewalk. In the distance, I can hear and see children scream in delight as they either run around the playground or are pushed on the swings by their parents. It's a sight that makes my heart ache just for a moment, yearning for something I never had.

My parents were never home. Not ever. Sure, I had a nanny who would take me to the park when I was younger, but it was never the same. I always sat on the edge of the playground, kicking the sand with my feet, while my nanny stood in a group with other nannies, puffing away on a cigarette like a chain smoker. However, you can't see that here. No, here the parents engage with their children.

I follow the pathway to the small bridge that crosses the pond in the middle of the park. I stop in the middle of the bridge and stare out over the water. This place always brings me a sense of peace and calm. A light breeze picks up my hair, causing it to dance across my face. I brush it out the way just in time to see a flock of geese swimming underneath the bridge. I turn around to walk to the other side and watch them come out when I see Reid standing there, staring at me.

I take one look into his eyes and keep walking as if I can't see him. I brush past him and ignore the call of my name. I grip the railing on top of the bridge, close my eyes, and take a deep breath. Now that I know he is here, I can't stop feeling his presence behind me, or the flames coursing through my body. Just the mere sight of him brings back the memories of his delectable lips on mine.

I hear his footsteps behind me. I open my eyes and groan quietly when I realize I missed the geese coming out from under the bridge. I can't explain why, but it's my favorite part of being here. Just watching as they carelessly swim across the water, with no destination in mind, and the only thing that matters is that they stick together in the end. The kind of loyalty only one person has ever shown me: Eli.

"Liza." Reid says my name softly as he approaches the railing. I turn away from him and begin crossing the bridge the rest of the way. "Liza... please wait!" he calls after me, but I continue to ignore him. I turn right on the path, along a secluded pathway with vines and flowers entwining amongst one another above my head.

A firm hand stops me a few steps underneath the trusses. I turn and see Reid fully for the first time. He looks like he did that Saturday morning when he appeared at my apartment: dark circles under his eyes, hair disheveled, and his clothes unkempt and wrinkled all over. The only thing missing is the scent of alcohol. "What do you want, Reid?" I ask harshly.

"I… I… uh…" Reid stumbles over his words. He brings his hand up and runs it through his hair, causing it to be messier than before. He holds up a loaf of bread I hadn't noticed in his hand and flashes a boyish grin. "I… uh… well… I thought we could feed the geese."

I glance at the loaf of bread and back at him. A laugh escapes my lips before I can stop it. I clap my hands over my mouth in an attempt to stifle it. Reid stares at me, tilts his head to the side, and furrows his eyebrows. "I'm sorry. That isn't funny." Reid only nods with his head. I cast my eyes away for a moment before I snap my head back to him and glare. "Wait a minute… how did you even know I was here?"

"I followed you." His voice doesn't waver. He says it so simply, like it isn't a big deal.

"You followed me?" I raise my voice. I hear the sound of wings fluttering as birds fly off the vines above us. "How long have you been following me?" I lower my voice.

"From the office to your apartment to here." Once again, his response is so simple.

"Isn't that stalking?" I stare at him and shake my head. "You disappear for the rest of the week and now you're stalking me? Do I even want to know where the bread came from?" He starts to laugh hysterically, his laugh sounding like sweet music to my ears. "What is so funny?"

"I wish I had a mirror so you can see the face you are making," he says. "It's priceless."

"This isn't funny." I'm angry now. "You left me hanging… we have a deal." *Not to mention that you've kissed me twice and asked me to be your date to the biggest event of the year.* But I don't say that out loud. "You just up and disappeared."

Reid brushes past me, and I turn to follow him. "I had something important to tend to." As I follow him, I can't help but think about how nice his butt is in his dark blue dress pants. I eye the outline of his rumpled button-up white shirt, accentuating the shape of his muscular arms, with one end of his shirt tucked in and the other dangling out. "Are we just going to keep walking, or are you going to tell me where the hell you have been?"

"I'll tell you if you will sit down with me." We clear the pathway with the vine roofing, stopping where it opens up to a very concealed and intimate area. A single wooden bench sits close to the pond with flowers blooming on both sides. It's set back far enough in the corner of the park so that others walking on the other side of the pond can't see us. Reid motions to the bench and waits for me. "Sit down, help me feed the geese, and I'll tell you anything you want to know."

I glance around, my nerves on the edge. Sitting here, alone with him, I can't deny the urge to reach out and touch him. To press my lips against his. But damn it, I can fight off the urge. I have to. I can't deal with another rejection from him when my body craves his. I nod once, pass him, and sit down on the bench. Reid takes a seat next to me, and our arms brush against one another. This is the closest we have been since Monday. My body is humming with pure energy and the desire to take him, right here and right now.

I fight the feelings down as best as I can, tucking them away just barely beneath the surface. I stare straight ahead, listening to Reid breathing in and out. Out the corner of my eye, I see him open the bag of bread and pull out a slice. He hands the piece over to me, and our fingers touch and linger against one another's. A bolt of electricity swamps my body, and I hear Reid take a sharp breath and then tense beside me. I pull my hand away, taking the piece of bread with me. I rip off a portion and throw it in the water, where geese appear out of nowhere and swarm it. Reid and I say nothing as we go through the loaf of bread, each of us ripping off pieces and tossing them to the geese. I squeal when a goose tries to nab a piece of bread that fell close to my foot and mistakes one of my toes for food.

I pull up my feet out of reach of the goose, lose my balance, and fall onto Reid. He laughs gently and brushes my hair out of my face. He traces his fingers over my lips and gently presses his mouth against mine. My breathing hitches momentarily before returning the kiss. The kiss is soft and sweet and over all too soon. "Where were you?" I whisper.

"I had to tend to something," he replies rather sharply. "Something important."

"So you've said."

Reid adjusts in his seat, pulling my legs into his lap, and resting his hands on top of them. I turn away, not wanting to meet his gaze. "Liza…" I cross my arms and make a 'hmmph' noise, like a little child. "I'm sorry… I didn't mean to come off rude." I glance at him out the corner of my eyes and catch a glimpse of sadness in his eyes. The sight almost breaks me, and I stare at him now. "I-I-I just have a really hard time talking about it. In fact, I've never shared it with anyone." With that, I give in and place a hand on top of his. "I was with my mother."

"Your mother?"

"Yes…" His voice cracks. "My mother. She's sick… she has cancer. The doctor says it doesn't look hopeful."

I feel like a bitch, a total bitch. Here I am being angry at him this entire time, being rude and a complete snob, when his mother is sick and dying. What the hell is wrong with me? I know it isn't my fault. I didn't know, but I can't help to feel guilty. "I'm sorry," I say softly. "Is she going to be okay?"

A tear forms in the corner of Reid's eye, I want to reach out and wipe it away, but I can't seem to move. "She says she is, but the doctors say otherwise. That's where I have been all week. I was with her… in the hospital."

"I'm sorry," I whisper. It's the only thing I can manage to say.

"Don't be." He shakes his head. "She wouldn't want that." Reid stands up and offers his hand to me. I respectfully decline by shaking my head and stand up next to him. He lets out a deep sigh and starts to walk back under the vines. I follow him, taking a few quick steps until we are walking side by side. We walk silently through the narrow pathway. I replay all my actions lately in my head. How could I be so rude? Well, it's not like he's exactly been a chip off the ol' block. He's had his fair share of rude qualities. The bridge comes into view. Out in the more public area, I can relax a bit more. Reid continues to say nothing, and I glance at him. He's just staring straight ahead.

"Tell me about her," I say. Reid stares at me, a slight smile tugs at the corner of his lips. "Tell me about your mother."

"She's amazing," he says affectionately. "The epitome of what every mother should be: sweet, caring, loving, and funny. She is stern when it is necessary, but never cruel or hateful. I have never come across anyone who isn't affected by her infectious smile or her humor. Everyone adores her. She goes out of her way to help others..." I listen to his clear as day admiration for his mother and feel a twinge of jealousy. My mother was nothing like that. She was the complete opposite. "I remember one year, my father was out of town—"

"Why was he out of town?" I interrupt.

"Most likely a business trip. I can't remember." He squeezes his eyes shut for a moment like he is trying to remember.

"I'm sorry," I reply automatically. "As you were saying..."

"Anyways, the year after my parents split, I became obsessed with Batman. Like so obsessed that I wore my Batman cape everywhere, even to bed. My mother had to sneak in every night to remove it just so it could be washed." He laughs gently as he recalls the memory. "That year for Halloween, I, of course, wanted to be Batman. But what is Batman without his trusty sidekick Robin?" He gazes down at me, and I smile. "So my mother said she would be Robin, and she was. Not the girly costume version of him but the actual Robin. Mask and all." Reid pauses for a moment. "I know that sounds silly..."

"No, it really doesn't." And I'm not lying. It really doesn't. "She sounds like a magnificent person."

"She is..." He pauses, as if remembering more memories. "That she is." His smile is big when he says it. Reid glances at me and raises his eyebrows. "What about your mother?"

My breath stops for a split second. He doesn't know. He really doesn't know about my mother. I sigh a breath of relief. If he doesn't know about my mother, it means he doesn't know about my father, and he certainly doesn't know the truth about who I am. "She's dead," I answer plainly and stare straight ahead.

"I'm sorry."

"Don't be. I'm not." It's only half of a lie. Some days, I really do miss her, and whatever dysfunctional relationship we had, it worked for us. And most days, I'm really glad she's gone. Out of my life and never able to hurt me again. Call me cruel. Call me a heartless bitch. Call me whatever, but the woman was just as cruel and heartless.

"And your father?"

"I stopped talking to him as soon as I could get away from him." Tears threaten to form in my eyes.

Reid stops me by the arm. He turns me so I am facing him, tucks another wild strand of my hair behind my ear, and rests his hand on my cheek. The world seems to fade away, disappearing behind us, leaving only the two of us standing there. We stare into each other's eyes, and I try to ignore the pull between the two of us, but still find myself tilting my head up and leaning in. Our lips are about to meet for the fourth time when our moment is interrupted by the sound of screaming, and a young, sandy blonde haired girl pushes between us. A tall, slightly built man comes running towards us and stops just in front of us.

"Sorry 'bout that." He smiles. "It's time for dinner, and she doesn't want to go home."

"Not a problem." Reid snaps back in a cold, strident tone. *What is Reid's problem?*

The man, with the same shade of hair as the girl, nods his head, circles around me and continues to chase after the girl. "Amyra! It's time to go... get over here!" he shouts after her.

I laugh lightly. Reid shifts on his feet and starts walking again. I jog a few steps to catch up and fall in step with him as we continue down the path. The path curves, circling back in the direction I came from, towards my apartment. The rest of the walk is silent.

We reach the parking lot of my complex, and I see his sleek, black sports car parked next to my beat up, rusted Honda. Reid stops next to his car, opens the door, and stares at me. "I'll see you at work on Monday." I tilt my head and raise an eyebrow, questioning him silently. "I promise I'll be there. And this time I'm not backing out. We have a deal, after all."

Chapter Ten

MONDAY MORNINGS MEAN only one thing to me: an appointment with my therapist. I wonder if Mr. Harder warned Reid about my late arrivals on these days, and if so, what reason did he give him. Did he tell him the truth? That I am seeing a shrink? God, who knows what he might think if he knows I have weekly visits with Dr. Uria. She's been my therapist since I was a child, when I would act out and throw temper tantrums.

Of course, my mother, being the loving and doting parent she believed she was, thought I had mental issues and sought out the best help Long Port had to offer. For the first few months after my mother's death, I refused to come see her, even after multiple messages from Dr. Uria begging me to come. Surprisingly, it was Eli's mother, Jezebel, who convinced me to return. Who knew his mother, the drunken socialite, was good for something other than downing mimosas. We started off with three visits a week, then moving to two visits last year before my internship had started, and two months ago, I started once a week visits.

I'm glad Jezzie, as she likes to be called, convinced me to go back. Dr. Uria knows me better than I know myself, probably more than Elias even knows me, if that is even possible. I mean, I have been seeing her for eighteen years now, so she better know a little something about me. I look forward to our weekly sessions, and am really excited about today's visit. The nightmares are creeping back in, and she's the only one that can talk some sense into me. I've never told Eli about the dreams. I don't know why, but I just can't.

Since Dr. Uria's building is conveniently only three buildings away from the office, I park my wheezing car into my assigned parking spot on the ground floor of the parking garage, making note to take it in for a tune up or drop it off at the nearest junk yard. I really love that piece of crap. It's done well for me these past few years, but I think it's on its last leg. I sling my purse over my shoulder and exit out to the bustling sidewalk.

The air is warm this morning, reaffirming my decision to wear a playful, one shouldered floral dress, which is the opposite of my every day wear of skinny jeans, baby doll tees, and flats. I'm positive when I finally arrive to the office later this morning, everyone will go into shock at the sight of the dress and a pair of killer heels that make my legs seem a mile long. I smile to myself, basking in the pleasure of what everyone's reaction will be.

How will Reid respond to the sudden change in wardrobe? I don't know why I even care. The man irritates the hell out of me. But he opened up to me, telling me about his mother, something he hasn't told anyone apparently. I feel almost honored to know the truth. Yet at the same time, I can't get a grip on his swift mood changes. I debate whether or not I should mention Reid to Dr. Uria, but then I think, is there anything really worth mentioning? Besides the kisses. Or the fact that he lights my veins on fire, and I can't stop fantasizing about him. I immediately dismiss the idea as I open the glass door to my therapist's building.

I nod and wave at the slightly overweight, middle aged security guard sitting at the front desk. He waves in return and buzzes me through the next set of doors. I stop in front of the elevator, pressing the up button and casually wait for the elevator doors to open. Though her office is on the top floor, twenty flights up, the ride up is short. The door opens to a lavish sitting area, with pristine white walls with modern paintings hanging along them. Jesse, the male secretary, smiles eagerly at me as I move to take a seat in the lobby. He picks up the phone, letting Dr. Uria know her first patient of the day has arrived.

"The doc should be right out, sugar plum," Jesse says in a sweet voice. I laugh at his sentiment, considering last week I was "doll face".

"Thanks, Jesse," I say as I take a seat in the white plush chair closest to her office door. I lean back, close my eyes, and listen to the soft classical music playing overhead. Just sitting here brings me some measure of comfort.

I hear the door open after a few minutes and see Dr. Uria's short, petite, dark frame step out first. For a woman in her mid-fifties, she gives women my age a run for our money. Not only is she fit, beautiful, and nothing short of glamorous, but she also has one of the kindest souls I have ever known "Good morning, Liza." Her voice is light and sweet. "Let's head into my office and get started."

Dr. Uria's office isn't like a typical shrink's office, where she has you lie down on a leather couch, staring up at the ceiling while she sits just out of view, jotting things down. No, she's a more straightforward kind of person, but infinitely more welcoming. More understanding. That is her job title after all, to help and understand others. In her office, we sit on a plush off-white couch, turned so we are facing one another. Tea is set out on the ornate coffee table in front of us, along with a device to record all of our sessions. "So, what do you want to talk about today?"

"I'm having nightmares again," I say quickly. "The one with my mother."

"How do they go?"

"The same as always…" I take a deep breath. "I know I'm dreaming, but I can't snap out of it. I can barely breathe and all I see is her. She stands at the end of my bed, all bloodied and mangled, accusing me of being her undoing. That I am the cause of her death and that I should be rotting in a jail cell with my father. Which is right before she swoops down towards me and I finally break free of the dream."

"I see," she says. "Why do you think they have come back again, Liza? It's been a few years since you had them. The last time was your junior year of college. Has anything changed lately?"

"Reid." I say his name before I realize it. I bite my tongue, wishing I can take it back. It's too late; she's aware of my slipup. She sets her teacup down and then looks back to me.

Dr. Uria raises an eyebrow and eyes me curiously with her dark blue eyes. "Who is Reid?"

"Nobody," I try to deny. Dr. Uria smirks, which means she isn't buying it. So much for not mentioning Reid. I shift uncomfortably on the couch. "Reid Harder," I finally say softly.

"As in Harder's Literary Agent House?" She puts two and two together quickly.

"The one and the same," I reply. "He is Lawrence's nephew." I bring the cup to my lips and gulp a big swig of tea down before placing it on the coffee table. "He is also my new boss."

"Before we go any further, may I advise you to steer clear of him?" *It's a little too late for that,* I think to myself. "Dating your boss brings a whole lot of problems to the workplace, even more so when he is related to the man who owns the company you work for. That is a whole other issue."

I laugh loudly, unable to control myself. Have a relationship with Reid? Not going to happen. Indulge in wild fantasies with him? I would be lying if I said I am not counting that out just yet. "You don't have to worry about that, Dr. Uria. I have my list, remember... become a successful literary agent before I turn thirty, and no men. Especially not men like Reid Harder," I say quickly and laugh again.

"I'm not saying you shouldn't date, Liza. In fact, I encourage you to go out on a date. Let loose and have a little fun. Enjoy your younger years and your freedom." She pauses to refill our teacups. When she offers mine back to me, I take it with a smile plastered to my face. "I mean, do you even socialize with men outside of the workplace, or even inside the workplace? Lawrence and his nephew excluded."

"Of course I do." I really don't, and this is something she knows. "There's Eli."

"Why not go on a date with Elias?"

I laugh again, almost causing some tea to spill on my lap. "Eli? You're kidding me right, doctor? He's the brother I never had."

"Fine," she says softly. "Not out on a date, but just a night out on the town."

I shake my head and laugh. "He put you up to this, didn't he? He never stops, does he?" Leave it up to Eli to do something like this. He has my therapist on speed dial, always checking in on my progress and probably more. Sometimes I regret putting him on the list that allows him access to this sort of information, but I don't have the heart to remove him. It's comforting to know he cares so much. Besides, this topic of going out for a night comes up once every few weeks.

"Have you talked to your father?"

My body tenses, and the teacup shakes in my hand. How did this session go from my nightmares about my mother, briefly to Reid, going out, and finally making its way to my father? He is the last thing I want to talk about right now. Or ever. Just the mention of him brings back the memory of him the night he killed my mother. The crazed face he made when he confessed to killing her. And how he attacked me, leaving a jagged cut across my abdomen when I made an attempt to lock myself in their bathroom to call for help. Unconsciously, I touch my stomach and feel the remnants of his attack protruding from my skin in the form of an unattractive, unwanted scar. It's one of the main reasons I don't wear anything too tight on my torso. Anything that can reveal the outline of the damage he has done is not okay.

"You need to go see him." Dr. Uria's voice snags my attention, and I quickly remove my hand from my stomach. My breath catches, and I can feel tears beginning to sting my eyes. "Or at the very least, write him a letter. Express your feelings of anger, hurt, and the hatred you have for what he did. It's something you have to do to be able to move on."

I know she is right. But I can never face him. I will never lay eyes on him again. I never want to hear his voice, and a letter just won't simply do. I would be lying if I said I didn't hate him with every ounce of my being for everything. To be honest, if I were to tell the truth, I am happy my mother is gone. What I hate the most, why I can't face him, is the proof he left on my body of what happened. The permanent scar that forever binds me to him. I can never tell anyone this, and I never will. Not as long as I am still breathing. What kind of person does that make me, to be happy my mother is dead?

"I will soon," I lie, and she knows it. Just as I know it. Hell, if anyone else was in this room, they would know I had no intention of ever doing so.

"Let's call it a day," she says. I glance at the clock. We still have over half of our session left. "I want to leave off with how you are feeling and to take some time before heading back to work to decide what you are going to do."

"About what?" I ask nervously. I already know the answer to what is to come next, which is a big fat hell no.

"About contacting your father."

I don't know how this has happened. This is not the way my morning is supposed to start. I was supposed to go to Dr. Uria's to get some relief from my nightmares, call it a day, and go about my business. But no, I had to open my big, fat mouth and mention Reid. Thankfully, she didn't quiz me about him, and all she had to say was dating him is a bad idea. Like I didn't know that already. But that didn't stop her from mentioning letting loose and having fun most likely on Eli's behalf. The poor guy got stuck doing a whole lot of nothing with me. Instead of going out, we always stay in and watch horror movies. He says he doesn't mind, but I know him better than that.

Somehow, our conversation led to my father. Damn that woman and her psychological bull. She always catches me off guard and brings my father into the picture whenever she sees the window of opportunity. So I guess, other than not to date Reid, I really got nothing out of the session. With the money she gets every month, she better not pull this stunt next week or she is really going to have a psychotic patient.

I duck into the café and grab of cup of coffee before heading to work. I need a triple shot of espresso, and the caffeine it promises, to snap me out of this funk. I get a few extra minutes of time to myself on the ride up to my office. Almost everyone has arrived by now, and I'm thankful to have this bit of solitude before being on a floor with a bunch of people. The elevator dings, and the doors slide open, signaling the end of my personal moment. I glance over towards Reid's office, and my heart betrays me by fluttering a little when I see the blinds are fully open and he is sitting at his desk, on the phone. I catch a glimpse of one of his genuine smiles before he turns his attention to his computer. I think of Friday and our stroll through the park that almost ended in a kiss before we were snapped back into reality by the squealing little girl that sent Reid retreating back into his cold front yet again.

I enjoy the memory a moment longer before locking it away for good in the back of my mind. Like Dr. Uria said, nothing good can come from dating my boss, especially when my boss is the owner's nephew. Not that pursuing a relationship is what I'm after. That's the last thing on my to-do list. I need to clear the air with Reid, once and for all, although I've told him I don't date and I'm not even sure that's what he is after. It needs to be done. There can be no more kisses, or near kisses.

Maybe just one more. No. I shake my head. I cannot and I will not let Reid kiss me again. Not now, not ever.

Heidi greets me by my office door, asking what I want for lunch today, and I tell her to order from somewhere that delivers. I don't feel like going anywhere unless it is straight home. She nods once before returning to her desk, and I slip into my office. I boot up my computer, and as I wait for it to start and my email to load, I set my coffee on my desk, pull my cell phone out of my purse, and put it into the top drawer of my desk. My email dings, notifying me that I had new unread messages awaiting me. I hesitate before glancing at the screen, wishing — no, praying — that there wouldn't be any anonymous emails waiting for me.

After a few deep breaths, I muster up the courage to peek and sigh in relief. There are none. Just a hundred and seven new query letters waiting to be read. How the hell did this happen? I have never gotten this many letters in one night, let alone a week. My mind briefly flickers to Reid; this has to be his doing. I figure the only way to distract myself from the very short therapy session is to dive head first into the letters and try to make a dent in them before lunch. I barely make it through three before I sigh heavily and lean back. I stare up at the ceiling and try to think about anything other than my father.

Reid comes to my mind first, and I instantly push the thought away. Next thing that comes to my mind is Greece. Strange, I don't know why. I haven't been there in years, but Eli had recently mentioned the two of us going. Oh, how I would love to indulge in a vacation right now. As if on cue, a light rap dances against my glass door. I glance over and see Eli opening the door with a large bouquet of flowers in his hand.

"What are these for?" I laugh lightly as he sets them down on my desk.

"Nothing special," he says and runs a hand through his shaggy golden hair. "I just feel like I haven't seen or talked to you in ages."

"I talked to you last night." Eli sighs and turns his head away for a moment. "The shrink called you, didn't she?"

Eli's silence confirms the answer to my question. I sigh and shake my head. Eli walks around my desk, pulls me up from my chair, and wraps me in a tight hug. I am caught by surprise when tears start to prick my eyes. I can't cry here. I can't think of my father, and I can't bring him into this place. My door bangs open against the glass window, rattling as they collide into one another. Eli and I quickly pull away from each other, and I see Reid standing there. His eyes are dark, almost black, and stormy. His nostrils are flaring. I'm sure if it was cold, we could see steam come out of them like a bull. He's fuming. I quickly wipe the tears away from my face and take another step away from Eli. I glance back and forth between the two of them, both of whom are exchanging unfriendly glances. Eli seems to be assessing him, judging him from the little bit that I have told him, and whatever thoughts he has made up about him. Reid simply looks like he is out for blood, like a lion in search of his next meal. The air is rich with tension and quickly heating up.

"Uh... um..." I am momentarily at a loss for words. "Eli, meet my boss, Reid Harder. Reid, meet Eli."

For the first time, Reid glances towards me, and really looks at me. I wish he hadn't. His eyes are still dark, glaring at me, and tearing me apart. "I thought you said you didn't have a boyfriend," he all but growls at me. His words hitting me like a ton of bricks.

"I-I-I don't." I glance at Eli, who is wearing a smile plastered to his face now, from ear to ear. I can tell he is fighting to contain his laughter. Eli finally loses control and begins to chuckle. Out the corner of my eye, I see Reid tense and watch his chest rise and fall rapidly underneath his white button-up dress shirt.

"I should have believed you when you told me he was an ass." Eli directs his statement towards me but stares at Reid. I glance over at him and shake my head. I want to slap the back of his head and ask him what the hell is wrong with him. Then I glance at Reid, who is still gazing straight towards me.

His eyes waver for a moment, revealing a hint of hurt. I don't understand why for a moment, but then I get it. Because of what Eli said. What I had said to him in the first place. "I... I... was just coming by so we could get to work on some query letters." Reid finally breaks the silence that began to fill the room. "But I see you're busy right now, so we can work on that tomorrow." Before I can protest, before I can tell him that Eli is nothing more than my best friend stopping by, despite the flowers, he storms out of my office and slams the door behind him.

"Whew!" Eli laughs softly. "I see what you mean." I finally do what I wanted to do moments ago and slap him on the back of his head. Eli flinches and rubs the spot where I hit him. "Ow! What the hell was that for?'

"For being an ass."

"That's why you love me..." Eli places a kiss on the side of my forehead. A gesture he always does, and one that's comforting, not romantic in any sense.

"Leave." I point towards my door. "I have work to do."

Eli gives me a military salute. "Aye, aye, captain." I shake my head, and he laughs as he leaves my office without another word. I sigh and sink down in my chair. As if this day couldn't get any worse... my email alerts me with a new message from an unknown sender.

Chapter Eleven

From: Unknown Sender
To: LWinter@hlah.com
I see trouble brewing on the horizon. Is it a love triangle in the making? Better choose wisely. Because whoever you choose... is the one whose life is in danger. Think carefully, my dear Elizabeth. Which one are you willing to sacrifice? I'll be watching you...

IT HAS TO BE someone on this floor, someone who knows my secret, and now is threatening me. But who? And how? How do they know the truth? I've been so careful to keep my true identity hidden. And why? What the hell is in it for them? Just for plain fun? I peek out my glass windows, glad for once that they are there, and I scan the room. No one stands out. Not one single person in that lobby stands out to me. Maybe they aren't on this floor, but they have to be. They just witnessed whatever showdown was going on here. Maybe some cameras are in my office that I don't know about. I shudder at the thought and look around. I need to find out who it is, and quick. And what it is, exactly, that they want.

I try to shift my focus back to all the emails that aren't threatening, but I can't concentrate. A loud buzzing noise startles me, and I jump in my seat. I pull my cell phone out of my top drawer and see that Eli is calling. "I'm such an ass," is the first thing he says.

"Haven't I said a time or two before that all guys are asses?" I smile as I recall past conversations we've had. "I know how you can make it up to me."

"Oh really? How is that?"

I pause for a moment. I don't know why. I know it's not like he is going to say no. In fact, he'll probably start jumping up and down doing his little victory dance. "Take me out for dinner and a movie." I know it isn't a big deal, but I can't honestly remember the last time we did something like that.

"I've been waiting a really long time to hear those words." He laughs softly. "I thought you'd never ask."

"What makes you so sure I would ever even ask you?"

He laughs heartily again, the kind of laugh I know reaches his soft green eyes. "I'm a guy… we know these things. All the signs were there." He's smiling again, I can feel it, and I laugh loudly into the phone.

"You're right… you are an ass. Now seriously, I have work to do."

*   *   *

"I have nothing to wear!" I shout to Eli down the hall where he is sitting in the living room watching ESPN. I stand in my doorway with one towel wrapped around my body and one in my hair. I hear Eli pause the DVR and his footsteps leading to the hall.

He lets out a loud cat-call whistle, and I just shake my head at him. "Just wear that," he says.

"You are such a pig." I take the fuzzy pink slipper off my right foot and chuck it at him, narrowly missing him.

"You know what that means?"

"What?" I groan and roll my eyes. I turn back into my room and flop face down on my mattress. I don't like the sinister grin he had on his face. I hear a soft knock on my door, and I glance over at him. Eli is leaning against the door frame with his arms folded across his chest. A beam of sunlight breaks through my curtains and hits his face perfectly. I can see the traces of stubble along his jawline.

"It's the perfect excuse to go shopping." With just one look at Eli, you can see the man has extremely good fashion sense. It doesn't take a genius to figure that out. What people don't know is that Eli is obsessed with everything fashion, and he really does have an eye for it. Hand him a garbage bag, and he can make it seem like a thousand dollar masterpiece. He's always searching for an excuse to go shopping. "Mimi's isn't too far of a drive."

"No," I say harshly. "We are not going shopping, Elias Caraway, and we are certainly not going to Mimi's. I'll make whatever I have in my closet work."

I have the money and can afford the lavish clothing at Mimi's. I just refuse to use it. I absolutely, positively refuse to use the money in the bank account that I never touch. Unless it's a dire emergency, or my monthly charity donation that I make to the children's center in town. Other than that, absolutely not. I get by with what I get from the literary house, although to be honest, I'm not even sure I'm entitled to any money. I haven't signed an agent, but Lawrence insists that I use the money that is deposited into my bank account every two weeks. I don't like to, because I haven't earned it. But as long as it's a check from my job, I have no reservations when using it, most of the time. After all, I do have to live somehow.

"You deserve to splurge a little and go shopping." My bed dips, and I peek over my shoulder to see Eli sitting on my bed. He lies down next to me, and our noses are inches away. "You have all this money just sitting there in that ba—"

I sit up quickly and glare down at him. "No, Elias. I don't want to hear it. I'm not using that blood money, and we are not going shopping. End of story. Now, if you would, I would like to get dressed." I nod my head in the direction of my door, dismissing him from my room. Eli's face drops slightly, and he lets out an exaggerated sigh. This isn't the first time we have had this conversation, and it certainly won't be the last. Eli pushes himself off of my bed and storms out of my room.

I sit there for a few minutes on my bed, thinking about when my life all went wrong. *When Daddy Dearest killed your mother,* I say to myself. I shake my head and move towards my closet. I debate throwing the dress back on I wore to work today but decide against it. So instead, I go with the classic jeans, t-shirt, and flats. Eli will have to just get over it. I mean, I'm finally up to going out. That should be more than enough for him. Baby steps, just one step at a time for me. Although, there are still things that I will never budge on. Including shopping sprees and men— namely, Reid Harder.

I walk into the living room, where Eli has returned to watching Sports Center. He barely glances my way when I walk towards him, still obviously upset at my unnecessary harshness a few minutes ago.

Eli knows better than anyone why I do the things I do, why I have the list I have, and why I am the way I am. He pushes me all the time, and after six years, you would think he'd accept things for the way they are.

"I'm sorry," I say softly.

"No, I'm sorry." He stands up and pulls me into a hug. "It's hard, I'll admit. All the changes."

My laugh is muffled by his board shoulders. "I know. But in all fairness, it has been six years, Elias."

"I know. I just hate seeing you lose the person you once were." He pulls back but keeps his hands on my shoulders and stares into my eyes. "You used to be so vibrant, so full of life, and didn't have a care in the world. Now, you're always so worried and cautious. Constantly watching over your shoulder. Sometimes, I wonder if you forgot how to live life. You're just… just… so stuffy."

"Stuffy?" I throw my head back and groan.

"Yes, stuffy."

"Yeah, well, you would be too if your father murdered your mother," I say coldly and turn my head. Eli's face drops. He knows this conversation is over, and I can count on him not to push any further. "Now, are we going to dinner or not?"

The drive to the restaurant is silent and thick with tension. Maybe I should have indulged him in a shopping trip, not at Mimi's, but somewhere. Maybe we wouldn't have this awkward silence between us. I replay Eli's words over in my head. I almost laugh out loud thinking about how he called me stuffy. Really? Stuffy? I'm the furthest thing from stuffy. I've made decisions in my life to get me where I am today. Granted, I've been falling off the band wagon as of late, no thanks to a certain delicious creature of a man.

We pull up to the restaurant, one I have been to many times in my life, my past life. My body tenses, and I turn my attention to Eli. "We're eating at Rinaldi's?" I look back at the restaurant and shake my head. "A little warning would have been nice."

"I tried to get you to go shopping," he says with a bit of an edge to his voice. If my clothes the night at Gravity made me stand out, I am going to seem like a fish out of the sea here. "Besides, who cares what they think?"

I do. Everyone I have spent avoiding these last six years frequent here, and by the looks of it, it's a full house. Not only that, but Eli is practically famous around here, hence why I have never gone out with him until now. *Lovely, just lovely.* I really should have thought this through. When I asked Eli to dinner, I should have made it clear to take me to some mom and pop restaurant on my side of town. Coming here with him, being seen with him, is the biggest mistake of my life. I'm about to walk into the lion's den. My nerves wreak havoc on my insides, my stomach turns, and I struggle to breathe. Only one thing can make this disaster of a night worse, and that is— POP! A flashing light bulb momentarily blinds me as I step out of the car and place my hand into Eli's. It's the paparazzi, and on a Monday of all nights. Now things have taken a turn for the worse.

"Mr. Caraway!" Voices blend together as they shout for Eli. "Tell us, who is your lovely date tonight? Do we know who she is?"

Eli takes my hand and places it into the fold of his arm near his elbow. I tighten my grip to try and keep my nerves in check. My lips are dry, and my heart is pounding. "She is a dear friend of mine, and that's all you need to know."

My feet are moving quicker now as he pulls me to safety inside of the restaurant. I think I am home free when I hear something that makes me stop dead in my path. "Any news of our missing socialite Elizabeth Lewis?"

My heart stops. It's been six years, and they still haven't given up. Exhibit A of why I have made it a habit not to attend public places with him. I almost want to laugh and then throw up. The people, all of them, the ones taking the photographs and the one asking questions, they make me sick. It's in their job description to know how to find someone, even if they don't want to be found. They are obviously not that great at their jobs and should seriously think about finding new ones, since I've been right here in Long Port, right underneath their noses.

I smile at the thought momentarily. "No," I hear Eli say and glance to see the somber look on his face, "there has been no news. I don't think there ever will be."

With that, I am whisked inside by Eli, the doors closing quickly behind us. We are immediately rushed through, past the maître d standing just behind the tall wooden stand. We don't have to wait for a table and are seated along the dance floor where a big brass band is playing. We aren't in the middle of the dining floor, but we might as well be. People glance at us from the dance floor as they pass. I see everyone's heads turn, focusing on our table, as they try to gauge who I am exactly and what I am doing sitting there with Eli.

Eli has never made it a point to appear anywhere in public with a female, except to local charity events, which I refuse to go as his date. This is exactly why. I've always worried that someone will see through my façade, through my fake black hair and the simplicity of my make-up. Seriously, what was I thinking?

"Are you alright?"

I nod my head slightly. I don't know how to respond so I just stay silent.

"I really can't believe they were here tonight," he says.

I'm about to open my mouth and say something when my eye catches a flurry of red hair whip by. *Millie?* I take a deep breath and search for the brilliant strands of bright red hair. It can't be, but it is... my old best friend. I watch Millie throw her head back and laugh as the guy with his arms wrapped around her guides her across the dance floor. I hear Eli calling my name, but my focus is on the couple dancing to the band's rendition of *Zoot Suit Riot*. That's when I see the face of the man she is dancing with. My heart clenches as my eyes make contact with the man who broke my heart— Jacob.

"Shit," I hear Eli say, and I glance over and find that he is staring at the same spot. "I'm sorry, Liza. I really had no idea he was going to be here."

"Let's dance."

Chapter Twelve

ELI STARES AT ME in disbelief. I mean, I can hardly believe myself. A part of me believes Jacob recognized me, which just makes me want to go on the dance floor to prove that he means nothing to me anymore. That I have recovered from the broken heart he left me with, even if I really haven't. I take a deep calming breath and fix my gaze on Eli.

"I asked you to dance."

"Liza—"

I stand up and hold my hand out to Eli. "Don't make me ask again."

"If you're sure…" he replies hesitantly before standing up and taking my hands into his.

"I'm positive." And then I drag him to the dance floor.

The exhilaration I get from swinging around the dance floor leaves me breathless. I've always loved to dance, whether it's in a club or swing dancing. Something about it makes me feel liberated, even if dancing with Eli is nothing like dancing with Reid. I find myself easing up, as does Eli, the tension from earlier melting away. The music never stops, so we never quit dancing, forgetting the plans to have dinner and go catch a movie. The song swiftly changes to another, and it's a dance I know all too well. It's one that requires the changing of dance partners throughout the song. I stop in the middle of the dance floor and glance at Eli, who seems to have barely broken a sweat. "Let's go order something to eat."

"But this is the best dance." Before I can state my objection to staying on the dance floor, everyone starts dancing with their partners, leaving me no choice but to take hold of Eli and dance. I clutch tightly to him and scan the floor, searching for any sign of Jacob, but I can't find him.

The music indicates that it's time for a change in partners. I brace myself, prepared for whatever is to come, and release a sigh a relief when I see the plump, short, and balding man come in my direction.

I bite back the laughter that threatens to escape my mouth every time the man tries to cop a feel from behind. I graciously grab his hand and place it back where it belongs. I'm relieved and stressed at the same time when it comes time to change dance partners again. The relief I feel when Mr. Grab Ass moved on to his next victim is short lived when I come face to face with my next partner. Jacob.

He smiles and nods his head. His smile is vindictive, all too knowing, and tells me everything I need to know. He knows who I really am. *Just keep it together, Liza. It's only two minutes.* I tell myself as I place my hands into his.

Our eyes lock as we start to dance. "I'm sorry, but I don't think we've met before. I'm Jacob... Jacob Kestner." His voice is just the way I remember, smooth, rich, and deep. One that spent years saying he loved me, just one of his many lies.

I clear my throat and attempt to make my voice sound slightly different. "Liza," I say, but don't include my last name.

"Is that short for something?" He looks me in the eye and stares as he watches how I react. "Perhaps something like Elizabeth?" He twirls me around in a circle and pulls me close to him, so close that I can smell the same cologne he's always worn. I can hardly breathe, and my body is shaking. For a moment, I miss his touch and immediately throw the thought out of my head. "You know, my wife..." I wince at his mention of having a wife. "My wife, Millie—"That backstabbing wench is his wife? How could she? After knowing what he did to me? "She told me about this story, how a couple weeks ago—"

We are interrupted by another man appearing and ready to take his place. Jacob dismisses him and keeps a tight hold on my hand and waist. "As I was saying, a couple weeks ago we were at a club, Gravity. And well, she swears up and down that she saw someone who looked just like a friend she used to have. I told her she had to be mistaken. That her friend was all but gone. Poof, disappeared, and without a single trace as to where she went. I told her she was crazy, that it wasn't possible. Only now... I know she was right." He leans closer, his lips close to my ear, and my breath is ragged. "You might have fooled her that night, and everyone else here tonight, but you are not fooling me, Elizabeth."

I pull away, trying to break free from his hold, but he doesn't let go. He squeezes his hand, digging his nails into my hip, and I let out a soft cry. "Let. Me. Go," I say sharply, low enough so only he can hear it.

"No," Jacob says firmly. He pulls me closer again, too close, and my heart pounds in my chest. "You broke my heart disappearing on me like that."

"You deserved it. And you deserve much worse," I hiss. He laughs softly again. "You should be dead, right next to my mother."

A low, deep growl resonates in his throat. "Feisty… I see you haven't lost your touch. But really, is that necessary? Do you really believe that?"

"You slept with her." Tears sting the corners of my eyes. "You slept with her for four years. You pretended to love me, you even asked me to marry you, and meanwhile you were screwing her behind my back."

"It's a shame you had to find out that way. I'm sorry, Elizabeth. I really am. But I was just a boy when she seduced me. What was I supposed to do?"

"Not continue it for four damn years." I am getting angry now. He's trying to justify what he did with her, what he did to me, and what he did to us. He is putting all the blame onto her and accepting no responsibility. Just like the Jacob I once knew. "Did you know she was pregnant? And that it was your child?" Jacob tenses now and scans the room to make sure no one is close enough to hear. "That's how my father found out. He found the pregnancy tests, all five of them. My parents hadn't been together in months, so he knew… he knew she was having an affair. He just didn't know that it was you."

The truth hits him like a ton of bricks. His cool man façade quickly disappears, his eyes reflect a glimpse of sadness. I am gasping for air, fuming and angry at him. I haven't thought about that tiny detail in the last few years. The one that I was going to have a baby brother or sister. And because of him and my father, they were both taken away from me. Just like that. I've never told anyone about the baby, or about how he was sleeping with my mother. Not even Eli. I was too ashamed to admit that I hadn't been good enough for him. That he had to go to my mother, *my own mother*, just to be pleased. Whether she '*seduced*' him or not.

I break free of Jacob's hold, and this time he doesn't fight me. He stands there with a tear slipping down his face, and as pale as a ghost.

I can feel everyone staring at me and turn away as the tears start to fall down my face. I quickly shove my way off the dance floor and out one of the side doors. My eyes are so clouded with tears that I don't see the crate until after I trip and fall over it. I scrape my elbow against the cement ground and hold my hand over it, whimpering in pain. A pair of big, strong hands gently grab a hold of me. I glance up and see Reid. When did he get here?

"Here," he says gently, "let me help you up."

"Thanks, but I can manage myself." I move to stand up when a sharp pain shoots through my foot, and I collapse back down. Reid bends down, offering to help me, and I push his hands away.

"Damn it, Liza. Stop being so stubborn." I ignore him, pull my knees up to my chest, and wait for the pain to ease. Reid finally gives up trying to help me and sits down on the ground next to me, crossing his legs.

I brush my hair over my shoulder and glare at him. "What do you want?" I ask coldly.

"I want to make sure you are okay. What happened in there? Was it that guy? Elliot or whatever his name is?" He stares at me hard and waits for my response.

I start to laugh. "His name is Elias, and it wasn't him. In fact, it isn't anyone you need to concern yourself with." I take a deep breath. "Why do you even care? Why don't you go back inside the restaurant? I'm sure there are a ton of girls you'd rather be spending your time with than me." Reid laughs this time and shakes his head. "What is it that you find so humorous?"

"Are you jealous, Ms. Winter?"

"Jealous of what?" Of course I am. I'm jealous of every woman he may give the slightest bit of attention to. With all the strength I can muster, I push off the ground and wince slightly when the shot of pain courses through my foot again. "Can you just go now?"

I start to wobble away on my foot. I can't let him see the tears that are starting to roll down my face again. I only manage a few feet when he calls out to me. "Wait!"

"What the hell do you want, Reid? Like I said, there are a ton of women in there who would love the chance to talk to you... or sleep with you, if that's what you are searching for."

"I don't want any of them." He furrows his eyebrows. "I only want you."

"I hate to be a disappointment, since I'm sure you always get what you want, but that will never happen."

This time, I ignore the pain and walk away for good. I fight against every nerve in my body that wants to stop and turn around. I fight every instinct that tells me to turn around and run back to him, or wobble in my case, and let him take me right there. I barely know the man, yet I want to do things with him that I have only ever dreamed about. I continue the direction I am going and never look back.

Chapter Thirteen

HALFWAY THROUGH THE HOUR walk home, it starts to rain. By the time I get past my stubborn front door, I'm soaked to the bones. My body is shivering, and my nose is runny. The pain in my ankle intensified as I walked, and it's taking everything in me to work through the searing pain. Eli tries to call my cell phone several times, but I ignore each of his calls and send them to voice mail. I strip my clothes off, peeling layer after layer of wet clothing as I limp down my hall. I enter the small bathroom in my bedroom and turn the shower on, waiting for it to heat up. Just as the steam begins to fill the bathroom, I hear a knock on my door, and I shut the water off. I pull my fuzzy pink robe off the back of my door, wrap it tight around my body, and slip my feet into the matching fuzzy slippers.

Another knock raps across the door as I near it. The chain at the top is in place, and I decide to leave it there and open it slightly. I peek out and see Reid standing on the other side of the door. "What. Do. You. Want?" I ask sharply.

"Can I come in?"

Man, I want him to so bad. But he can't. I have a date with a nice hot shower, ice pack, and a marathon of horror movies. I can't let him come in, because I know he is either going to question me about tonight or he's going to kiss me. And I can't let either of those happen in my weak state of mind. "I'm sorry, but no." I close my door and sigh. I hear a slight thump against the door as if he lays his forehead on the door. I can hear him mumble something, but through the door, it's unintelligible.

What am I going to do?

Tonight has been nothing short of disastrous. Another sign as to why I need to stick to my list. I walk over to the window and look out just in time to see Reid's car pull out of the parking lot. I sink down on my couch and flip on the TV. I pull the fleece blanket off the back and drift off to sleep, forgetting all about the plans I had before sitting down.

The sun filters through my open window, shining brightly on my face and warming it. I wake up slowly, rubbing my eyes and groaning at the first sign of a migraine beginning. I let my eyes adjust to the light and glance over at my clock. "Oh crap!" I say out loud when I realize that it's nearly lunch time. How on earth did I sleep that long? *Great, now I am late for work.* I don't see the point in going in this late in the day, so I pull my cell phone off of the coffee table and send a quick text to Heidi to let her know that I am not coming in today.

I toss it back on the coffee table, not caring at the loud thump it makes against the solid oak wood, and close my eyes again. Finally, I get up, grab a glass of water and some ibuprofen out of the kitchen, and down them both. I return to the living room, opening up my laptop that is resting on the table in front of me, and log in to my work account. *Might as well try and do something since I'm not going in.* Over two hundred new messages flood my inbox when I log in, but the one that stands out to me is the most recent one that was sent at almost the exact same time I woke up. I hover over the message and click on it without a second thought.

From: Unknown Sender
To: LWinter@hlah.com
Dearest Elizabeth,
It seems as though you had a rough night. I would be surprised if last night wasn't a harsh one, what with your reunion with the boy who broke your heart and the near close call with the paparazzi. It's no wonder why you decided to stay home and nurse that swollen ankle of yours. Poor Eli, though, he seemed absolutely devastated when he saw you sitting out in the alley with that gorgeous boss of yours. I don't blame him for getting drunk and causing a scene last night in the bar at the restaurant. But don't forget, whomever you choose will suffer pain. Though it seems like you may have chosen already? Maybe I should go pay Reid a visit in his office today. What do you say? Think you can beat me there?

I'm off my couch in a blur. I pull the first thing on that I see in my closet, not taking the time to see if the outfit even matches. For all I know, I can be modeling stripes with plaids. I slam my front door behind me, not taking the time to lock it, and rush out to my car. My ankle protests with stabs of shooting pain, but I keep trekking forward. I open the car, place my key into the ignition, and turn. Nothing. I slam my hand on the steering wheel and scream out. I try the key again and still nothing happens. "Please, just start for me." A soft sob escapes my throat, and it seems to trigger the car to start.

Finally, the engine roars to life, and I slam the car into reverse. I pull out of the parking lot with the wheels peeling and the car making a loud screeching sound. I speed down the road, stopping only to momentarily check for oncoming cars at stop signs, and blaze through the green and yellow lights. I pull into the parking garage fifteen minutes later and park in the first spot available, not caring that my car can be towed away for not parking in my assigned spot.

I jump out of my car just as soon as I have it in park and kill the engine. The elevator seems to be taking forever, so I opt to take the stairs four flights up. The walk further pains my ankle, but I keep running up the stairs and never slow my pace. Everyone stops what they are doing when I reach the lobby of my floor, staring at me as I carelessly maneuver my way through the cubicles and desks. I open the door to Reid's office and stop dead in my tracks at the sight before me. *He really doesn't waste any time, does he?*

My breath catches, and my heart lurches as two sets of eyes turn their attention to me, both staring at me, wildly confused at my entrance. They aren't the only ones confused by what is going on here. I'm not sure what I expected to see when I barged into his office, but I certainly didn't expect to find him entangled in the arms of some nearly naked tall blonde. As soon as I enter, Reid pushes away from the girl, who lets out a yelp and stares at me. I can feel the deadly glare that the blonde is shooting my way. I spin on my heels and quickly walk out of his office, my hands clenched at my sides.

"Liza!" Reid calls out to me. I stop, aware that everyone's eyes are on me, but I don't turn around. "It's not what it looks like." His voice drops, and I am aware that he is right behind me now. "I swear… it isn't what it seems like it is." Such a classic line.

I laugh loudly, still noting that everyone is watching us and wondering what is going on. Hell, I'm not even sure myself. "Really?" I laugh again and face him again. His eyes are wide, filled with worry, and his face is pale. He seems weak, almost vulnerable, and I almost want to let it go—but I don't. "Because I'm pretty sure it's *exactly* what it looks like."

"Liza, if you wou—"

"Save it, Reid." I raise my hand. "You don't have to explain anything to me." I spin on my heels, with my head and chin held high, and walk to the only place I can get away from the burning eyes. My office. I slam the door behind me and barely manage to sit down and take a breath when Reid barges in. "Honestly, do you even know how to knock on a door?"

He shrugs his shoulders, and I can't help but feel even more aggravated. "It really isn't what you think…" He pauses for a moment. "Okay, maybe a little, but I want to explain to you what happened."

"I already told you that you don't have to explain yourself to me. You're twenty-five years old, a grown man, and if you want to have sex with some slutty blonde chick in your office, then damn it… have sex with her." Reid says nothing, and his large, million dollar smile spreads across his face. He starts to laugh loudly.

"Do you really think I would have sex in my office?" I raise an eyebrow and shrug my shoulders, as if to say I wouldn't put it past him. "Okay… so maybe I would, but I would have my doors locked…" My jaw drops at his admission. I try to regain my composure, but I'm too late. Reid's face beams with a half crooked smile, he stares into my eyes, and his voice drops. "And only if that person is you."

His words hang in the air. I am too stunned to say anything. I mean, he just said he wants to have sex with me… in his office of all places. What am I supposed to say to that? I knew he was going to be that *kind* of man, because really, what man isn't. Reid crosses the distance from the door to my desk in three long strides, leans forward, and rests his hands on top of my desk. "It really isn't what you think," he whispers. He's so close to me, and his scent overwhelms me.

"Since you are so determined, enlighten me then." I rest my elbows on the desk. We're close enough now that I can feel the warmth radiating off of his body, and I eye him curiously.

He sits down in the round leather chair in front of my desk, leans back, resting one elbow on the arm rest to prop his head up, and is quiet for a long time. I watch as his forehead creases with lines, no doubt contemplating what he wants to say and how he wants to say it, without seeming like a complete ass. He sits up, opens his mouth, then stops, and leans back into the chair. "Go to dinner with me?"

"You honestly expect me to say yes?" I straighten myself in my chair and glare at him. "You seriously have the worse timing imaginable." Reid says nothing, so I continue my rant. "You would think that working in Romance, you might know a thing or two about how and when it is appropriate to ask a woman on a date. News flash: this isn't one of those times. But even if you did, I don't think you're capable of being romantic. It's clear that isn't your thing."

"You know nothing about me." His voice is rugged and deep.

"I know enough from the pictures I have seen online. Woman after woman being displayed as nothing more than arm candy. And it's never the same woman twice." The weekend of our steamy kiss, I did what any woman would do when meeting a rich, utterly handsome man; I searched for him on the Internet. Just like I told him, every gossip blog and article showed and talked about him and his globetrotting dating life. They showed the many women of Reid Harder's life, stating that he can't settle down and just choose one woman; it isn't his forté. One reason why I try to stay clear of him. He is the kind of man that just takes what he wants, because he knows he can, and then moves on to the next person in line.

However, I still can't forget about that day in the park and what he shared about his mother. I'm sure that is something no one knows about him, the fact that he isn't as arrogant and big-headed as he portrays himself to be. Except for me. I've seen the softer side of him. I put on my best smile and stare hard into his eyes. "I've seen enough, and that's all I need to know. I'm sorry, but I have to decline your invitation to dinner, and I have to pull out of being your date to the charity event this weekend. If you remember correctly, I don't date."

"So this is what you think of me?" He stands up and gazes down at me. A flash of anger, followed by hurt, dances in his eyes before they turn into a black cold mask. "You are basing who I am by what you have seen on the Internet."

"Well, that and the make-out session I just witnessed." I slide my chair back and stand up.

"And that day in the park?"

"I've chalked it up to just being an oversight on your part. Everyone is allowed a slip up now and then. Or maybe even a ploy to suck me under your spell." If the latter, it totally worked, for a moment at least. I really don't think it is just another game to him, just another ploy to get a woman to swoon at his feet. I remember the look in his eyes when he told me about his mother and the kind of person she is. That is something you can't fake.

"What else do I have to do to prove to you that I am worth breaking whatever rule it is that you have created that doesn't give a guy a chance?"

I let out an irritated sigh. "You really haven't done anything to prove to me otherwise in the first place."

He glares at me, glances up to the ceiling, runs a hand through his dark hair, and lets out an exasperated sigh. "That's because you won't let me."

I laugh. "Are you kidding me?" I walk around my desk and towards him. "Like you have really made an effort? Let's see… first, you blackmail me into going to that godforsaken club with you, and you don't even abide by the condition I set for the interaction. Then, you show up to my apartment, kiss me, and take off after like a bat out of hell." I shudder at the memory of his soft lips against mine. What I wouldn't do to feel them again. "Then we go to lunch, where we're supposed to be talking about how you were going to help me sign an author, which if I may remind you, we still haven't started yet. So comforting to know that you are not a man of your word." Reid flinches when I say that. I really should stop while I'm ahead. "At lunch, you make fun of me because of my apartment and the car I drive, which I happen to like. You flirt with the waitress in front of me, and then you disappear for a few days—"

"I already explained to you why." His voice is low.

"Yes, you did. And while the walk was nice, I can count a couple more times where you have been a complete ass when it hasn't been necessary."

"That's your decision, then?"

I say nothing and nod my head. What is he expecting me to say? It's not like he's been the nicest guy on the block. So what if he ignites my blood on fire? Or the fact that we have some magnetic pull to one another? It doesn't excuse his jackass persona. Reid spins on his heels and heads to the door. He hesitates for a moment before turning back around and closes the distance between us. Before I can comprehend what is going on, his lips are crushing against mine, and I find myself kissing him back.

"It really wasn't what you thought." He whispers against my lips. I start to say something, and he cuts me off. "No, let me explain. Lilith, that's my secretary—" *so the skank has a name* "—she came on to me. At first, I thought I wanted it, anything to distract me from thinking about you. Which only made me think about you more, so I told her to stop. She wouldn't, and when I tried to push her off of me, her hair got tangled up in the buttons of my shirt. Th—"

I burst out laughing, a full on head thrown back, loud laugh filling the air. My stomach muscles ache at the spontaneity of it. "You seriously cannot expect me to believe that. That's like one of the most ridiculous, oldest excuses in the book." I completely forget that just a second ago our lips were locked into a passionate kiss.

Reid frowns. "I'm being serious, Liza, and I have no interest in her or any other woman that comes my way. I only want you." He's whispering again, his voice seductive and making my toes curl inside of my flats.

"Why?" I push away and turn my head. "Am I just another challenge for you to conquer? Just someone you plan on tossing aside after you get what you want?" *Way to ruin the moment with my big mouth.* But Reid makes me a little irrational at times. "Because I will tell you right now, that will never happen. We will never happen."

My heart aches as I say the words out loud, because as much as I want him, I can't go there. I want his lips to touch every surface of my body. I want to hear his low, seductive voice telling me how much he wants me. I can't let it happen. Not matter how much I want it to.

"I'll admit," he says as he comes closer to me, "I've never had to work this hard to get someone to go to dinner with me. Neither have I had someone so openly dislike me."

"I never said I didn't like you," I say quickly.

"No, but you did point out every reason why you shouldn't." I sigh. I can't disagree with that. I have been pretty cruel. "Regardless of the fact, I don't see you as just another notch on my bedpost." I raise my eyebrows. "Not that I do that. But I genuinely want to get to know you better."

"Why?"

"Because you're the first person who sees through the bullshit, the first not to be affected by whatever charm I apparently have or my money, and because… well… because when you look at me, I know you see me. You see the person I want to be, the person that I can be. *You* make me want to be a better person, and not the kind who thinks of women as an accessory."

I gasp softly. This is not what I expected to hear. I glance back at him again and find that his dark eyes have softened to a soft black, taking over his predominately glossy cold stare. "If I say yes to this, it comes with one condition."

Reid smiles. "You and your conditions."

"We can go to dinner as friends." He frowns, not afraid to show his disappointment. "We'll go to Mercury's Diner on whatever day works for you."

"How about Saturday?"

"That's the date of the charity event." Reid shrugs his shoulders. He seems to care about the event just as much as I do. While it's a good event, raising money to donate books to the local schools, I can't stand them. "If you're sure, then Saturday it is."

"It's a date," he says, finally flashing his breath taking, charming smile.

I frown and shake my head. "It's not a date. Just two friends having dinner."

"I'll take what I can get," he says before he turns and walks out of my office, closing the door behind him. As soon as the door shuts, my phone beeps, alerting that I have a new text message. I pull my phone out of my pocket and see that it's an unknown number.

Great, now whoever it is, is sending me messages. With the thought in mind, I click on the message and open it.

Next time you won't be so lucky.
Remember, Elizabeth… you can only hide for so long.

Chapter Fourteen

MERCURY'S DINER is the perfect place to go to for a 'not a date' dinner. Fifteen minutes outside of town, filled with unfamiliar faces and some pretty good burgers. I had accidentally discovered this place a few years ago, when I decided to take a drive one day and see where I would end up. The diner isn't the greatest or the nicest of places; in fact, it's quite the opposite. The booths have cracked pleather, the tables are rickety, the wallpaper is peeling, and the flooring is warped. What it lacks in style and grace, it makes up for with the welcoming, home-like atmosphere and fantastic food. I pull into the crowded parking lot and see Reid's black sports car sticking out like a sore thumb. He's early. I don't know how long he has been here, but it has to be a while considering I am twenty minutes early myself.

It's a shame, and almost an embarrassment, pulling up and parking my car next to his. But I stand by my decision. I love this beaten car of mine, even if it seems to be on its last leg. Though it isn't a date — we're just two friends having dinner — I still dress up. Well, what I consider dressing up.

The floral print, strapless summer dress I'm wearing billows around me as I step out of the car and into a light breeze passing by. My left heel gets stuck on a rock as I cross the rocky, dusty parking lot, and I know I must seem like a fool. Gee, what if Reid is watching me right now? I brave glancing up towards the diner, and I don't see his face in any of the windows. I breathe a sigh of relief. He must be sitting somewhere else, but it still doesn't mean he can't see the charade going on outside. A strong gust of wind picks up and dirt flies everywhere. I choke and cough, covering my eyes with my arm. I pick up the pace and run through the little dust storm. The door chimes as I basically fall through it, still choking and coughing from the sudden attack of wind and dirt.

That's a sure fire way to snag unwanted attention. I roll my eyes and laugh softly to myself. Everyone snaps their heads towards me, the diner utterly silent, and I am unable to move for a moment. I smooth the top of my dress and hair down, glancing around the diner. At first, I can't seem to find Reid, even though I'm almost positive that is his car outside. I keep scanning all the faces that have been staring at me since I barged in. Once I begin to move, they turn their attention back to their food and conversation.

"Liza!" I hear him before I see him. All eyes are on me again as I scan the room searching for him. There, tucked away in a small booth in the back of the diner, is Reid. I cringe. Of course, he has to go and choose the smallest table available. The one where you can only sit on the side of the table, at a small bench against the wall. I'm not sure I can sit so close to him. I take a deep breath and start walking towards the back. Reid slides out of the booth and grins as I approach him. "I figured since we're dining as friends, we'd sit next to each other. Since that's what friends do."

Uh huh, I'm sure that's exactly what you were thinking when you chose this spot. I keep the thought to myself, smile, and slide onto the bench. I move to the furthest end of the seat as possible, which doesn't make much of a difference. I am fully aware of Reid, of his scent and warmth, when he slides in next to me with a grin bigger than I have seen before. Only confirming my suspicions. He is up to something, I just have the feeling. I pick up the menu and pretend to be looking at what they have for dinner selections. Doing this is pointless though. I already know what I am ordering. I knew as soon as I suggested the place. A short, elderly woman with graying hair and a name tag that says Sally approaches our table.

"What can I get for you two love birds?" she smiles. I tense and feel Reid laughing silently next to me.

"We… uh… we're here as friends," I say quickly.

"Uh-huh, sugar, whatever you say."

"I like this woman," Reid chimes in. He chuckles again, and this time I can hear his luscious laugh. I stare at him, and he shrugs his shoulders. "I'll just take whatever my *friend* here is having."

The woman shifts her focus back to me, a notepad in one hand and a pen in the other. "I'll take the bacon cheeseburger, waffle fries, and a strawberry milkshake."

"A girl who isn't 'fraid to eat," Sally says. She turns to Reid, bends down so she's at his level, and stares him in the eyes. "That girl," she nods towards me, "is a catch. Don't let her get away."

"I know." His voice is low and serious. I tense again next to him. The woman stands back up, winks at Reid, and heads off to put in our order.

Reid grabs the glass of water off the table. His arm brushes against mine as he brings it to his lips. I watch out the corner of my eye as his tongue dances across his lips and licks off the remaining drops of water. Reid must have seen me, because I can feel his eyes on me. I straighten up and stare straight ahead. I feel him shift in his seat. He clears his throat, and I hesitate before peeking towards him. He has shifted his body so that it is angled towards me, with one arm on the back of the bench reaching behind me. I can feel the heat of his arm in my proximity. I let out a sigh.

"So what do *friends* talk about at dinner?" He's mocking me.

"Well," I hedge. I reach out, grab my glass of water, take a sip, set it back down, and turn so I can see him. "Anything, really. The weather, how their day was, what their plans are for the weekend, the newest movies. Anything…" I reiterate.

"And how was your day, Ms. Liza?" He raises an eyebrow and smirks.

"Really? You're seriously asking me that?" I let out an irritated sigh and take another sip of my water.

"You're the one who suggested it." Crap, he's right. I did. "Cut me some slack, Liza. I'm really trying here. This is all new to me."

I laugh and stare at him. Nothing on his face shows that he is joking. It's the complete opposite, and he acting as serious as he can be. "Wait a minute… you're telling me that you have never had dinner with a friend?"

"Sure I have, a million times," he says, matter-of-factly. "Just not with someone I want to be more than friends with."

I should order an ice cold beer, or three, if I want to make it through the night. "That's a good line." I laugh. "Does it work with all the women?"

"Believe or not, you are the first female I have willingly taken to dinner." He isn't finding my humor funny in the slightest bit. I bite back a smartass comment I had been preparing to say, knowing that he probably won't find it as funny as me.

"I'm sorry," I say, "It's just hard to take you seriously, given your track record and all." He shakes his head, his eyes start taking that familiar gloss stone-hard gaze. I'm pushing him too far and losing him quickly. *Knock it off, Liza.* I take a deep breath and shake my head. "I shouldn't have said that. I'm sorry… I'm not used to dating."

"I thought this isn't a date?" Reid smiles, his eyes quickly returning to his softer shade of black.

"It isn't," I answer quickly.

"It's okay. I should have expected that." He pauses for a moment. "You're right, my track record with you, or in the tabloids, isn't a good one. I'll be honest. I really did think of women as only an accessory."

"What changed?" I ask softly.

"I met you." I gaze into his eyes, searching for any trace of a lie, but I can't find anything. He doesn't falter, and I note the sincerity in his voice. "It really is hard breaking away from what I am used to doing."

"And what's that? Objectifying women by how nice they make you look when you parade them on your arm?" Reid nods slightly. I shouldn't have said it, but sometimes I can't control myself around him. "Yeah, that's a bad habit you need to break."

Reid laughs. The waitress is back with our food, and we eat in silence. Every time one of us moves to grab our drinks, our arms touch and send a jolt of energy throughout my body. Reid's finished before I am, and he sits silently, waiting for me. With his eyes on me, watching me as I chew and swallow my food, I feel nervous. I push the plate away, my burger half eaten and a pile of fries remaining. The diner is slowly beginning to clear out, and before I know it, we are the only ones left except for the staff.

Reid moves, sliding out of the booth, and I watch him walk over to the jukebox on the other side of the diner. He puts in some coins, chooses a song, and gives it a thump on the top with his wrist. The jukebox comes alive. *The Way You Look Tonight* by the one and only Frank Sinatra begins to fill the air. As he walks back, everything seems to be moving in slow motion. The way his body glides across the floor, his hand extending out to me and inviting me to join him. I hesitate only long enough to place my napkin on the table.

He pulls me close. One hand wraps around my waist, and the other grasps my hand firmly in his. We say nothing as we begin to dance around the diner, and the room fades away behind us. We somehow manage to avoid bumping into any tables and chairs as he leads us all over the diner. Our eyes are locked onto one another. Being this close, I can tell his scent is slightly different than his usual sweet, musky cologne. Instead, he smells a bit woodsy, like a forest right after a downpour of rain, mixed with a touch of aftershave. The perfect balance; he smells heavenly. I let his scent fill me, surrounding me as he holds me tightly in his arms.

The song is coming to an end, and right on cue, he dips me back. One of my feet lifts off the ground and dangles in the air. My hair flows behind me and almost grazes the ground. Reid's lips are close to mine, so close that I think he is going to kiss me. And in this moment, I hope he does. His lips are almost on mine, so close, just a little bit closer. And just like that, I'm standing back up and in the real world. The fantasy is over. The diner comes back into view, the sound of dishes being washed clatter in the background, and I can hear the staff chattering loudly.

"I-I-I, uh, I need to use the restroom," I say quickly. I pull out of his arms, turn, and rush off into the direction of the bathroom.

I splash cold water on my face and sigh. I stare at my reflection in the mirror. *What the hell, Liza?* The sound of a toilet flushing startles me. I cry out and jump away from the mirror. Our waitress, Sally, comes out of the stall with a wide grin across her face. "That was quite the dance in there," she says as she begins to wash her hands. I simply nod my head. "Whatever your reservations are about this man... toss them aside. He's just as crazy about you as you are about him. I can see it in both your eyes."

She leaves me standing alone in the bathroom, thinking on what she just said. She has no idea what she is talking about. I'm not crazy about him. As much as Reid tries to tell me, and himself, he's not really crazy about me— not in that sense. He only thinks he is, because I'm the first woman who hasn't fallen for his charm. Or at least that's what I keep telling myself. I take a deep breath and sigh loudly.

You can do this...

Reid is sitting back at our table when I emerge from the bathroom, and he quickly stands up when he sees me. Something seems off about him. I don't know what it is, but he seems to be hesitant. I put on my best pageant-like smile and walk towards him slowly. He scans the room, runs a hand through his hair, and I know that something is definitely bothering him. I can see it in his eyes. "Hey," I say softly as I approach the table.

"Hey," his voice is softer than mine. "Why don't you let me drive you home?"

I pause just for the briefest of moments. "I can't leave my car here."

"I'll have one of my men drive it home." I open my mouth to protest, but Reid stops me. "I want to show you something."

Chapter Fifteen

I CAN'T SAY no to that.

So instead, I nod my head in agreement. Reid smiles, but it doesn't quite reach his eyes. His fists clench at his side, and I can feel the nerves rolling off of him like a tidal wave. He gestures his arm towards the door, I hold my hands in front of me, and I walk towards the door first. Reid follows closely, but it's not close enough. I want his soft hand in mine again like it was when we danced. He is quick to open the door for me. I smile and head towards his car parked next to mine. Once again, he opens the door for me, hesitating for a split second before closing it behind me and jogging around the front to the driver's side.

The car starts up with a purr, so low you can barely hear it. Reid eases the car into reverse and turns toward the direction of Long Port. Soft music fills the air. Something I am all too familiar with and my heart clenches. "I didn't know you listened to Vivaldi," I say softly.

"Like I said, there are a lot about me that you don't know," he replies, staring straight out at the road. He grips the steering wheel so tightly that his knuckles are turning white.

I lean my head against the cool window. In the side view mirror, I can see my car off in the distance following us. On the open road, Reid accelerates the car way beyond the speed limit. The car handles the quick acceleration like a pro and speeds down the pavement. It doesn't take long to reach town, and he begins to bring the car down to a much more acceptable speed. He isn't saying anything, and I wish he would. Anything, just to stop the feeling that I am going to suffocate in the confines of his tiny car. *Maybe I should ask where we are going.*

For all I know, he could be taking me somewhere to kill me. I stifle back a laugh. I'm being ridiculous. Familiar buildings breeze past as

Reid navigates through the center of downtown. For a split second, I think he's changed his mind and is taking me home when I realize we are getting closer to it, but then we are past my crummy apartment complex. A few minutes down the road, we stop in front of a broken down building. Scaffoldings, cranes, and other equipment are visible in the moonlight that is quickly illuminating the darkening sky. Plastic is hanging up in all the windows and entry ways.

Reid turns the car off, gets out with his fists clenching again, and runs around to my side before I have my door open. He holds out a hand to me, and I take it into mine, noting that on the drive over here that he has developed a bad case of sweaty palms. Most women, or people in general, find this utterly disgusting. I am almost delighted by it. We walk towards the building with Reid's hand resting against my lower back as he guides me towards an entrance off the side of the building.

The room we enter isn't complete. Another thing that is obvious is its purpose. It's meant to hold books, and a lot of them. It's a library, well, in a much smaller scale than the public one on the other side of town. Still, the room is bigger than my entire department without all the walls. The built-in shelves run from the marble floor up to the ceiling that is at least thirty feet high. "What is this place?" I ask. I stand in the middle of the room, spin in a circle, in complete awe of the sheer beauty of it despite the assorted construction tools scattered around.

"I'm helping finance the new adoption center," he says quietly. My heart stops beating and drops to the pit of my stomach. Did he just say the new adoption center? "We have generous donors, a few of which donate a substantial amount every month." He eyes me curiously. He can't know that I am one of these donors, can he? Of course he can't. I deposit the monthly donations anonymously and make sure they can't be traced back to me. "While the donations are still not quite enough, I'm covering the rest of the costs. In exchange, I design the library for the children, and call it the Reid Harder Library," he adds gently.

"This is amazing." I wander over to one of the walls. I run my fingers across the delicately carved wood which is the most beautiful thing I have ever seen. "This is bigger than the one they have now, is it not?" I know that it's a silly question and that I already know the answer to it. Reid glances towards me again and raises an eyebrow.

Man, why did I have to go and say that? That's just begging for questions to be asked. Questions that I cannot and will not answer.

Reid nods his head. "It's nearly four times bigger." He smiles. This time the smile finally reaches his eyes, and he seems proud. As well he should be. "The building is divided into four sections, based on age. As much as I hate to say it, because I really think it's unfair, the truth remains that after a child reaches a certain age, the likelihood of them being adopted declines drastically. So we're implanting a program to help the older kids make the best of their circumstances. The program is designed to help them, to provide them with the materials and opportunities to make something out of their lives. To create a better and more beautiful future for them, instead of heading down a dark and narrow path. My uncle has agreed to take three teens each year in their senior year of high school and let them intern for the agency. In addition, the agency is offering five full ride scholarships to LPU to the most promising kids."

I'm rendered speechless. I don't know how to respond to the information I just learned. "This… this… this is amazing. *You…*" I stare directly at him, cross the distance between the two of us, and stop directly in front of him. "You are amazing. This center will change so many lives."

I reach up and gently brush my hand against his cheek. In this pivotal moment, all things are thrown out the window, and I can feel myself falling for him against my many inner protests. I'm taken aback by all of this. Never in a million years would I have believed someone if they told me that Reid had a hand in building this place. I slowly run my hand down his arm and clasp his hand into mine. Energy sparks between us, and I know Reid feels it too by his slight jump. I stare into his eyes, finding myself ready and waiting for a kiss that never comes. He clears his throat, and I drop his hand. The rejection stings. I turn away from him and glance around the room again, unwilling to show him the tears pricking my eyes. After a few more minutes of silence, Reid suggests he get me back home. I agree, and he drives me back to my apartment in awkward silence.

"Thank you," I say as we approach the door. "That… that was amazing. Thank you for sharing it with me."

Reid opens his mouth, but something catches his attention, and he stops. I follow the direction his eyes are staring, and I find myself just as surprised as he is. A large, obnoxious bouquet of flowers are sitting on the doormat in front of the door. "What the—?" I reach down and pluck the card that is sticking out of the flowers.

My dearest Liza,
I saw these and thought of you.
Wish you were here, but until then, I will be dreaming of you.
Love Always,
-A

I have no idea where these flowers come from, let alone who the hell A is. I glance up at Reid, who read the card over my shoulder. His eyes are dark, and his body is tense. Before I have a chance to say anything, he is turning on his heels and heading straight back to his car. I throw the card down to the ground and chase after him. He's fast, really fast, and by the time I reach the parking lot, he is already peeling out and racing down the street. I watch as he disappears around the corner and sigh heavily. The air outside suddenly turns cold, and a light brisk wind brushes against my face. I shiver and head back towards my apartment.

The flowers are still waiting for me, taunting me as I pick them up, planning to throw them away once I get inside. Opening my front door proves to be more than a struggle with the large arrangement in my arm, and the door jamb decides to be stubborn. After several minutes, I finally manage to get the door open. I walk into my apartment and am unprepared for what I see.

The vase slips from my arm, shattering everywhere, and I feel sick to my stomach. My apartment looks like a hurricane followed by a tornado struck it. My couch is flipped over on its back. The cushions are strung throughout the room carelessly. All my cabinets have been opened, and my dishes are shattered upon the kitchen floor. The few photos I have of me and Eli, as well as the store bought deco photos, have been thrown to the ground, and the glass is broken. The coffee table has been thrown up against the TV; one of the legs sticks straight through the plasma screen and out the other side. The damage goes on. I can't even imagine what my room looks like. I don't want to go and see, but apparently my feet have other plans in mind.

I run towards my room, trying not to stumble over the scattered debris that strayed in from the living room. My bedroom door is hanging off the hinges, squeaking as I push it open so I can flip on the light and glance inside. The room is a bigger mess than the living room. All the drawers are pulled out of the dresser, the contents thrown about the room. Everything from my closet has been torn off the hangers and joins the rest of the catastrophe. On the large square mirror that rests on top of my dresser, in big bold letters, the intruder leaves a note.

You can't hide forever. I plan to expose you for who you really are. Be ready.
-A

The same signature that is on the card that came with the flowers is on the mirror in bright red lipstick. If 'A' has been inside my house, why did he or she leave the flowers outside? The answer hits me like a ton of bricks. Of course, whoever it is did it so Reid would see them and get the wrong idea. And he did, he most certainly did. If it wasn't for the damn flowers, he would have come in. The flowers are what stopped him, and that's most likely what the intention was. But why? I hear a loud crash and someone yell. My heart stops, my breathing catches, and sweat beads my hairline. Whoever it is has to still be in my apartment.

I grab one of my now empty drawers, creep over to hide behind the broken door, and wait. I hear another crash that muffles a man's voice, yelling in protest. I make it behind the door just seconds before he enters the room. Without a blink of an eye, I raise the drawer up and swing. The man dodges just in time to avoid the drawer making impact with his head, catching his shoulder instead.

"Ow!" The voice is familiar. "What the hell, Liza?" Eli spins around and faces me. My hands are shaking, and I drop the drawer. He takes one look at me and scoops me into his arms. He runs his hand over the top of my hair, smoothing it down my back, and doesn't let go. "What the hell happened in here?" I shudder against his body, unsure of how to answer him. He pulls away from me but keeps a hand on each shoulder. "What is going on? What happened to your apartment?"

"I-I-I don't know," I choke out. Tears stream down my face, and my body shakes as I begin to sob hysterically. Eli's arms are around me again, and he pulls me close to the warmth of his chest.

"Let's get you out of here."

* * *

I don't know where we are going, but Eli is driving like a bat out of hell down the street. I glance over at him through my tear-soaked, puffy eyes. I can see he is on edge. He is gripping the steering wheel of his Bentley tight, and his jaw is clenched. He doesn't glance at me and remains solely focused on the road and wherever we are going. I tuck my legs up towards my chest, wrap my arms around them, and rest my chin on top of them. The vision of my apartment is burned into my mind. Someone has been inside of my house; someone has destroyed it. But who? I feel violated. My one place, my only sanctuary, is slowly slipping away from me, while the rest of my life is crumbling down around me. I always counted on my apartment to bring me solace. A reminder of how far I have come, and now that's being taken away from me. Just like everything else in my life.

The car slows down. I glance around at my surroundings and find that we are smack in the middle of town. Large buildings tower over the car, but not just any buildings. To my left is the court house, and to my right is the police station. My throat is dry, but I try to swallow, which only makes it hurt worse. "I can't go in there, Eli." My voice is hoarse.

He parks the car along the curb and quickly turns his head towards me at me. "Don't be stupid, Liza. You *have* to report this."

"No, I don't." I sigh and shift in my seat uncomfortably. "And I'm not going to."

His eyes are glossed over like he has silently been crying, and I didn't realize it until now. His forehead is creased with lines, and he frowns. "Liza." His voice is soft, but he can't hide the serious tone. "You have to."

"No. I will not go in there." *I can't.* The last time I stepped foot in there, I spent hours in the interrogation room, going over every detail I could remember the night of my mother's death. I also sat on the other side of the mirror as my father gave his confession willingly. *It's too much. It brings me too close to him, and I don't want that.* "Eli… please don't make me do this."

Eli sighs heavily. "I don't know what is going on, and I don't like it. But fine, I won't make you go in there… with one condition." I raise my eyebrow and glance over at him. "You finally let me install that new alarm system."

I know it's ridiculous. Who needs an alarm system in an apartment complex? But Eli has been hell bent on getting one since he saw the place. I have refused time and time again. But this time, I just can't. I should have done it ages ago. "Fine."

Chapter Sixteen

JUST AS I EXPECT, Reid is going to ignore me today at the office. I've seen him throughout the office, but he won't say a word to me. Not a single damn word. I have to tell him about Saturday night. Not all of it, just that I honestly don't know who sent the flowers. Which isn't technically a lie, because I don't know *exactly* who it is, in a sense, but I do know that they were purposely left there by whoever is out to get me. I try getting his secretary to patch me through to his office four times this morning, and every time it's the same response: "Mr. Harder isn't available to talk to you at the moment."

Fine. Two can play this game. If he won't talk to me about Saturday night, then that's it. I knew it was a mistake letting things go as far as they did. Dancing with him at the diner and letting him show me the center, when I should have gone straight home, was a mistake. From here on out, all interactions with him are going to be solely based on work. After all, we have a deal, and in my mind, that deal is still in effect. Whatever godforsaken desires I have about kissing him again and stripping him naked is just going to have to sit on the back burner. I cannot let my hormones control my actions anymore.

Our deal is my only saving grace. If this doesn't pan out, I'm not sure I will have a job much longer. I type out an email, detailing just that. That all our interactions are to be only for work— nothing else. No gallivanting around any small diners, and certainly not alone. Nope, not even close. If he wants to talk, we can do it in the open.

Feeling satisfied with the email, I hit send and turn my attention back to the hoard of query letters invading my inbox. After another hour of struggle, I am ready to give up. On cue, Eli rescues me. He strolls into my office, his mood better than it has been over the rest of this past weekend. He casually walks over to my desk, placing a white take-out bag and soda on top of it. The smell of Chinese food fills the air, and my stomach growls.

"Thanks for bringing me lunch." Eli grins from ear to ear. "I was af—" I don't finish my sentence, the knowing look on his face says he understands.

"Anytime, *little rabbit.*" He smiles again. "The guys just left your apartment." I nod my head. Eli had held me to my agreement and had security men come up and install a new alarm system, as well as clean it out. Since I couldn't return to my apartment yet, I had crashed at his parents' house with him instead. "Some of your stuff wasn't salvageable, so I had them bring in some new stuff, and the new alarm system is in place." If Eli has good timing, Reid has impeccable timing.

He barges into my office without knocking, as per usual. His eyes are latched on me, and we don't break eye contact as he walks towards my desk. He stops right next to the chair Eli is now sitting in and completely fails to at least acknowledge him.

"Dude," Eli says. "Have you ever heard of a little thing called common courtesy?"

"Must have missed that lesson in school." His voice is sharp, like a thousand pieces of glass piercing my skin, and his eyes remain locked onto mine. Eli pushes his chair back and stands up. Though the two men are close in height, Reid still has an inch or two on him. "Is there a problem?"

"In fact, I do have a problem," Elias says. Both of them are tense. Reid turns to his attention to Eli, his fists clenched at his side. "You're interrupting our lunch."

Reid's jaw clenches. "I didn't know you two had a lunch date."

"It's not a date," I say quickly. The two turn their attention on me. Eli seems hurt and frowns. Reid's eyes momentarily betray him and show a sign of relief; that confirmed what he was hoping. Man, these two were going to drive me insane. "And if it was... that isn't any of your business."

Eli smiles like he has won the battle. Reid flinches like I slapped him. "I came to tell you that my uncle wants you to have someone signed before the end of the month or you might as well start packing up your office." His words sting me. I try to remain poised and nod my head once. Inside, I'm screaming and want to cry. Reid coming to my office only tells me one thing— our deal is off. Before anyone says anything else, he leaves and slams my door behind him.

"I don't know what you see in him," Eli states, snapping me out of my daze.

"What are you talking about?"

"I saw the way you were staring at him. The way he was looking at you. Please tell me that you didn't—"

"Ugh." I groan. "Of course I didn't."

"Good." Eli smiles. "That guy is a jackass."

"All guys are jackasses," I remind him and smile.

"According to the book of Liza Winter." Eli laughs lightly.

"At least you are finally coming to your senses." I say coyly. The two of us both start laughing. Eli sits back down in his chair and pulls out two large takeout boxes followed by three smaller ones. I grab a set of chopsticks, grab a box, and savor every last bite.

I don't see Reid for the rest of the day, and it's probably just as well. Every time I think of him, anger sparks and rushes through my veins. I want to scream and shout at him. Tell him that he is the world's biggest asshole, but I won't, even if the opportunity presents itself. Because at the end of the day, he is nothing more than my boss, and that's all there will ever be between us. I throw myself into my work. The anger boiling inside of me must have triggered something deep down, because by the end of the day, I managed to get through four query letters. Two with the possibility of being interesting enough that I plan to make a call. It provides me with enough distraction from the walls crumbling down around me that, for once, I feel like celebrating.

I don't want to think about anything going on, what will happen when I step out into public again with Elias, or what the media will say. For once, I want to enjoy a night instead of constantly watching over my shoulder. Dr. Uria will be impressed with the progress I have made. The last time I attempted to go out with Eli, it hadn't panned out so well. So, when I call Eli up and tell him that we are hitting the club tonight, I have to bite back the laughter at his initial shock. After confirming that we have plans to go out to Gravity at nine tonight and to be ready, Eli finally stops asking for the thousandth time if I'm up to something.

Nine o'clock rolls around, and I am ready to go. I slip on a short, hot pink dress with flats, because let's face it, I'm not going to have my feet killing me while I dance the night away. I pull my hair up into a ponytail, and I wear just enough make-up that it still seems natural. I accent the dress with a chunky beaded necklace in a multitude of shades of pink. Eli looks impressive, as he always does, in dark washed jeans, a fitted black shirt, and his new haircut, which is short and styled just like the Eli I have always known. I don't object when we head outside my apartment and see he's got the limo again.

"This is a rare occasion," he whispers in my ear. "Us going out again for another fun filled night. It's only fair we do it right."

"Of course it is." I smile. "Only this time, it'll be better than our last attempt." My attitude is better than it was earlier today. It's just as surprising to me as it is to Eli. I can see the confusion written all over his face as he attempts to figure out why we are going to Gravity on a Monday night. I'm not sure what sparked the idea, either, but I just want to go with the flow. Eli stares at me, his smile not quite reaching his eyes. Nothing in his expression gives me any indication that he isn't going to go along with it. I'm glad, because whatever this is, I'm not ready to let go of it just yet.

It has to be the high from getting through those few letters.

A line from the front of the club wraps down and around the block. It'll be close to closing time before we get in. Of course, the limo pulls up directly in front of the club. Eli climbs out first, helping me out. He pulls me close to his side just as a popping noise sounds and a light flashes in my face. Of course, the paparazzi is here again. Eli holds me close as we walk right up to the door. The bouncer moves the rope aside, allowing us entrance. I can't fight the laughter that escapes past my lips at the sounds of groans growing behind us. It doesn't matter what day of the week it is. This is the hottest club in town, and everyone wants in.

Tonight feels different than the last time I was here. The last time, I was practically forced to come here, and I came in through the back. I was a nervous wreck and almost lost control with a certain guy on the dance floor. This time, however, I thrive under the strobe lights flashing, the DJ masterfully spinning the music, and the sight of bodies grinding on one another. My head turns towards the dance floor, and I stop short.

Jacob and Millie are here. Eli glances in the direction I am staring and squeezes my hand in reassurance. I smile, silently second-guessing my spur of the moment decision, and then I brush it off. Tonight belongs to me. Nothing is going to stop that.

"Let's get a drink!" I shout over the music to Eli, and he nods. Eli keeps me close as he leads me to the neon lit bar near the dance floor.

A classy bartender wearing a white button up dress shirt and short brown hair approaches us. Eli places his credit card down on the counter. The bartender smiles and takes it to open a tab. "A whiskey for me, and a rum and coke for the lady," Eli says. I smile at the fact that he remembers my favorite drink. The bartender nods and makes our drinks quickly.

We finish our drinks near the bar and take a few shots, which vary from vodka to a bit of Patron. I know I am going to regret this in the morning when I am at work, but right now, I really don't care. A warm tingling sensation creeps through my body. I'm ready. I grab Eli's hand and drag him to the dance floor.

The music is loud, the bass vibrating through my body, and I welcome it. I'd forgotten what it feels like to lose myself on the dance floor. Why did I ever deny myself this? *You know why...* I shake the thought from my head. Nothing is getting me down. I'm fully enjoying myself for the first time in six years. Song after song plays. My body is covered in sweat, and I love it. Eli mumbles something about needing a break and something to drink. I nod at him and remain on the dance floor. I lose myself to the music again. Just me, myself, and I.

That is until I feel someone press their body against me. I automatically assume it's Eli and keep grinding my body against him. Hands run over my body, caressing my breasts, down my arms, and along my abdomen. Lips brush against my ear, startling me; everything about this is out of the norm for Eli, but I keep dancing anyway. "You look absolutely delicious tonight."

I stop and face Reid.

Without hesitation, I slap him across the face. His eyes go wide, and he stares at me. "What the hell do you think you're doing? You were obviously enjoying it."

"I thought you were someone else," I practically spit at him. I turn, making a beeline for the bar, when he lightly touches my arm and stops me. "What do you want?"

His eyes soften. "Can we talk?"

"We have nothing to talk about." It comes out harsher than I want. He lowers his head, pleading with his eyes through his dark, long lashes. I sigh and search for any sign of Eli. This is not on the agenda for tonight. "Fine. You have five minutes."

Reid lifts his head, a wide grin spreads across his face. "That's all I need." He grabs my hand lightly, and I try to ignore the jolt of energy pulsating in my veins. I allow him to lead me through the crammed dance floor. We stop next to a door in the corner of the club, and I watch as he enters a code. The door opens, revealing a set of stairs. At the top of the stairs, we walk into a cozy office. A large one way mirror overlooks the entire club, and to my right is a wall lined with large flat screen TVs with different angles of the club broadcasting on them. A couple of leather chairs are placed in front of the TVs with end tables next to them

"What are we doing in here?" I say quickly and glance over my shoulder, back towards the door. "We can't be in here. We have to leave before we get caught."

Reid laughs, walks over to the fully stocked bar along the back wall, and pulls two glasses off the rack hanging from the ceiling. Without answering, he starts to make a couple of drinks. Near the bar is a large oak desk and another large leather chair. "Relax," he says, walking back to me with a glass in each hand. I take the one he offers me and sip. Rum and coke. *How does he know?* "This is my office. We won't get in trouble, and we certainly won't be interrupted." His eyes glisten with a hint of humor behind them.

"Your office?" I say. "What do you mean, your office?"

"I own this club. Well, at least half of it." No, he doesn't. I remember when the club first opened up nearly eight years ago. The only person the media talked about owing the club was some guy named Phillip Draco; nothing was mentioned about Reid being a partner. "Phillip is my cousin." I gulp and take another sip. His cousin? "I helped him get this place going." I take another drink and try to absorb this new information. He helps fund the build of a new adoption center. He helps fund a night club. And he works in the Romance department of a top literary agency. *Who the hell is this man?* To say I am not intrigued to learn more about him would be a lie. I want to know everything, despite what I keep telling myself. In another two gulps, my drink is gone.

"Want another drink?"

"No," I answer quickly, bringing a smile to his face. Another drink isn't the smartest of ideas, considering that between the shots and my drink earlier, the alcohol is taking effect. I am not thinking with a straight head. "You have five minutes… starting now." I place the empty glass on the desk. Reid closes the distance between us in a couple long strides.

He brushes a loose strand of hair behind my ear, his dark eyes gazing into mine. "Do you know the effect you have on me?" I whimper and turn my head away. He's too close. I need to get away. I take a step to move away from him and don't get very far. Reid wraps his arms around me, pulls me close, and stares me straight in the eye. This is not in the plan. This is not how tonight is supposed to go, yet I cannot stop it. His lips come crashing down onto mine. They taste of mint and alcohol. I try to fight it, which only lasts for a split second before my alcohol-induced hormones take over. I wrap my arms around his neck, pulling his lips harder against mine. His tongue dances over the top of my lips, and I part them all too willingly.

Reid groans and pulls me towards one of the leather chairs. I straddle his lap and take his lips with mine, not wasting one second. He releases my hair from its ponytail and grabs a handful. My hands run over his shoulders, stopping only to undo the buttons of his shirt. I make it halfway down before placing my hands on his rock hard chest and rubbing the contours of his muscles. His finger traces the hem of my dress, his hand slipping underneath the thin material, and he cups my cheek.

The cell phone in his pants pocket begins to vibrate against my leg, sending a thrilling sensation through my body. After a few seconds, it stops. I grind against his growing erection and moan with pleasure as he leaves a trail of kisses along my shoulder. I start to undo his belt buckle when a knock comes from the door, shattering the moment and bringing me back to reality.

"Damn it," Reid curses under his breath. That's all it takes, and I quickly jump off his lap. The shock of what I was just doing hits me like a freight train. I adjust my dress, pulling it back down to cover myself. I turn, planning to bolt for the door. "Liza?" His voice stops me; the sound of hurt and confusion surrounds me. Tears soak my eyes, and I turn to look at him.

"This is a mistake," I say. Reid flinches like I slapped him across the face again. "It will never happen again."

As I turn to walk out the door, I crash into a broad set of shoulders. "Liza?" The sound of Eli's voice instantly relieves me. "Are you okay? H-H-He didn't hurt you, did he?"

I fight back the tears and shake my head. I glance back over my shoulder at Reid, who is standing there watching the two of us. His face gives nothing away. I gaze back at Eli, who now has an arm wrapped around me for support, and I give him my best smile. "Nothing happened. I'm fine." Eli stares at me before shifting to his attention to Reid and glares coldly at him. "Really, I'm fine. I just want to go home."

His body tenses. I sense that he isn't ready to leave just yet, and now he has Reid to blame for my sudden desire to go. "I'll have the driver come get us." I hear Reid scoff behind us.

"I want to go alone."

"Liza," Eli says softly, "I do—"

"This isn't up for debate." I say in my best stern voice. I cross my arms, pull away from him, and stare straight into his eyes.

"Fine." Eli gives in all too easily. "I'll have the car pull around to the front." I relax, give him a hug, and dare to steal one last glance at Reid. His body is rigid, and his stone cold eyes have glossed back over; his walls are back up. I say nothing to him as move past Eli on the landing and make my way outside to wait for the car.

Chapter Seventeen

TONIGHT HAS BEEN one big, fat mistake. Something I seem to be making a lot of. How I ever thought going out to Gravity was a good idea is beyond me. But how was I supposed to know that Reid was a silent partner in the club? All I want now is to get home, pour myself a glass of cheap wine, and soak in the tub. It's already near midnight, which is just another reason why I shouldn't have gone out tonight. I have work in the morning. My head spins, and I feel sick. Not because of the alcohol I consumed, but because of the foolish mistakes I have been making. The first being that I thought it was a grand idea to go out, and the second was following Reid to the private office.

I sigh, lean my head back against the seat, and remember once more how Reid's lips felt against mine. The sensation of his erection pressing against me as he caressed me had filled me with desire. The sexual tension is undeniable. If we hadn't been interrupted, I'm pretty sure things would have gone a lot further. Hell, maybe I should just give in and sleep with Reid. I can finally get him out of my system and back on track.

Of course, I won't though. That would be breaking the most sacred rule on my list, which is to not have sex with a man I am not going to marry. No, the next time I give my body to someone, that person will be the one I am spending the rest of my life with. Though marriage is the furthest thing from my mind right now. I doubt I will ever even get married. The surest way to avoid any complications is to avoid all men, sex included. I've never been the kind of person to have a 'no-strings attached' relationship, or casual sex. To be honest, I have only been with one person my entire life, and it wasn't all that enjoyable.

No wonder he strayed to your mom...
No. I shake my head. I need to stop going there. I'm not going to add that to the mess that I have made these past few weeks. I may not have complete control of my life, or my dreams most times, but the one thing I can control is not thinking of *her*. The thought of my mother, her mutilated body, her death caused because I couldn't keep my *ex-fiancé* satisfied, is more than enough to put me in a downward spiral for weeks. I know because this has happened before.

Right after her death, I went crazy. Drinking and trying almost anything that came my way. I hooked up with a ton of men, always pleasing them. Nothing was ever in it for me. No one got to touch me. I felt that if could please every man I came across, whether it was a blow job or a hand job, whatever it took to get them off, that it would somehow make up for my mother's death. I was stupid and vulnerable then. And a lot of men used it to their advantage. If it wasn't for almost being raped and Jezzie coming to my rescue, I would certainly be worse off than I am now.

The limo comes to a stop, and the driver is quick to climb out to open my door before I can snap out of my head. I nod once at him and head towards my apartment. I fumble through my purse, the one that I had left in the limo when we got to the club, for my keys. I almost resort to dumping out the entire contents on the ground when I finally brush them with the tips of my fingers. I open the bag further and spot them in the porch light outside my door. Eli must have had the door fixed, because the door opens on the first try. I walk in, closing the door behind me, and pause just inside the entrance. I take a few deep breaths, letting the dark envelop me, and flick on the light switch.

A loud scream escapes my throat.

At first, I'm not sure I even made the noise. But make no mistake, it definitely came from me. I'm stunned, unable to move, let alone comprehend what is happening right now. My new couch, the soft black one that Eli bought, has been pushed aside. In its place is Jacob, who is gagged and bound to a wooden chair.

His head hangs low, and he isn't moving, with the exception of his slight, shallow breathing. The buttons on his shirt have been ripped off, exposing his solid chest that appears to be covered in cuts. I see that one of his eyes is purple and swollen. He has been hit, probably more than once. His feet are tied together against the front legs of the chair, and his hands are tied behind his back. I falter and take a step towards him until I see someone else from my past life.

"Elizabeth?" His voice is like acid. "Or should I call you Liza now?" The cold, deep voice belongs to Robert, my father's best friend. He looks exactly like I remember, only his hair has taken on a more salt and peppery hue. His jawline is tight and chiseled, his high cheek bones are still carved perfectly into his alabaster skin, and his hauntingly blue eyes still have the dark, cold, menacing stare. I'm just as afraid of him now as I was as a kid. "Do you like my present? I was going to add a bow and a bit of ribbon to the top of his head, but I thought that it might be a little bit of overkill."

My mind is crazy, and my heart is beating a mile a minute. *What is he doing here? Why is here?* So many questions race through my mind that I want to ask, but I'm distracted by the large butcher knife in his hand. One that seems almost identical to the one used to mutilate my mother's body. My knees are weak, and I hold onto the breakfast bar for support as my stomach does flips. Two things hit me at once. The first is that he is out for blood, and the second is he has to be the one that's been harassing me. But why?

"You know," he says as he takes a step towards me, "I haven't seen you since your father's trial." I stumble backwards and knock one of the stools to the ground. "Have you been to see your father? Of course you haven't. Not once in six years. Quite a shame really. Maybe he wouldn't have sent me here if you had."

My mouth gaps open. He is here because of my father. "What do you want?" My words are barely a whisper. I know he heard me because of the frightening grin that appears across his face.

"To finish what your father started six years ago."

"No!" The words come out a little shaky but louder than before. "Don't you dare touch him!"

Robert laughs loudly. "Tsk-tsk," he says shaking his head, "don't tell me you still have feelings for this bastard." Bile rises in my throat as I watch him drag the blade of the knife across Jacob's lower abdomen. I'm convinced he is dead. He doesn't move or scream out in pain as the knife cuts into him. Either that, or he's passed out and in shock from everything he has already endured tonight. And from what it seems, it has been a lot. "So, tell me... do you still love this man? The man who destroyed your family, who ripped them apart at the very seams, who took your mother away from you, and the one who took your father away from you?"

"He didn't take anything from me," I say the words clearly, confident in the truth I feel about them. "My f-f-father is the one who—" I pause, unable to breathe for a moment. "My father killed my mother, taking her away from me. Which resulted in him going to jail. As for our family being ripped at the seams, well that happened long before Jacob." I stand up on my feet, no longer needing the bar to support my weight. The anger raging inside of me is making me braver than I ought to be.

"He is to blame!" Robert shouts. "He... this man—" He grabs a handful of Jacob's hair and yanks his head up, so I can see his face. "This pathetic piece of shit was sleeping with your mother! The man you were going to marry. It's bad enough that he cheated on you for years, but it's even worse that it was with your own mother." He stops for a moment and takes a deep breath. "She... I-I-I-"

"Oh my God!" I gasp. "You were in love with her, too, weren't you?" Damn, what is it with men and my mother? Robert says nothing, which confirms my suspicions. I take a step towards him with my fists clenched at my side. "Did you ever stop to wonder why? Why she didn't marry you and married my father instead? Why she chose Jacob over you when she was no longer happy with my father?" The alcohol is definitely making me feel braver. "It's because neither of us were good enough for them. We didn't give them what they wanted. What they needed." Robert crosses the distance in two long steps. He raises his hand, and the back of it makes contact with my cheek. I stumble back, clutching my stinging cheek in my hand. Tears form in my eyes, not because I am afraid, because it actually hurt.

"I was more than good enough for her! She belonged to me first, and then your father swooped in and stole her from me. And then you couldn't keep control of this boy of yours, and that ruined my chances forever." He raises his hand, ready to strike me again when the front door opens.

It takes less than a second for the room to explode into chaos.

As soon as Reid registers the scene, he lunges for Robert. Though Reid is tall, Robert has at least three inches on his six foot plus height, and about sixty pounds more on him. But the size of Robert doesn't stop him. The two men are now rolling along the ground, exchanging blow after blow. At some point, Robert drops the knife. I kick it away from the scuffling men in order to prevent Robert from using it to inflict any harm.

"Liza!" Reid calls my name out, drawing my focus to him instead of the commotion going on. "Call the police!" Robert stops and tries to make a move for me. Reid doesn't let him get very far, and I am unable to shift my focus to anything else other than the battle. "Liza! Now! Call the police now!

Robert has Reid pinned to the ground, repeatedly connecting his elbow with the side of his face. Reid can't take much more. I can see it. He is going to black out soon, and I will be left defenseless against Robert. I grab one of the wooden stools. Without thinking any further, I raise it above my head and bring it down over Robert's head. The wood splinters on impact, flying off to various parts of the room, but it does the job. Robert is out cold and sprawls on top of Reid. Reid shifts his body, half sliding against the ground and half moving Robert's body off of him. Reid grabs a rope that I hadn't seen lying on the ground and begins to tie my father's friend up before he regains consciousness. He leaves Robert on the ground, takes three steps towards me, and presses his lips hard against my own. I don't fight back and return the kiss.

Reid breaks away first. "Next time," he says softly, "call the police."

I'm reliving the nightmare all over again.

There is blood everywhere, so much blood. Reid holds me close in his arms. I clutch him as if I am hanging on for dear life. Jacob groans. Instantly, I break out of Reid's arms and rush over to him. He is still bound to the chair, so I begin to frantically untie him. I start with his hands, freeing them from behind his back. By the time I reach the rope around his ankles, Reid is there helping me and not saying a word. We ease Jacob onto the floor, all while he groans in pain. I shudder at the sounds he is making but am grateful he is still alive. I sit down on the floor, gently placing his head on my lap, and release the gag around his mouth. "Jacob?" His name is barely a whisper on my lips. I lean over, pulling his shirt aside to examine his wounds. I cry out, pushing him out of my lap, and scramble backwards to get as far away as I can.

Reid is by my side again, pulling me into my arms, cradling me like a baby. His lips brush against the top of my forehead. "It's okay,

Liza. I'm here." The tears and sobs that follow come out uncontrollably. My body is shaking, shuddering as the tears fall, but Reid doesn't let me go. It's too much for me to handle. The sight of Jacob takes me back to the very night I held my mother in my arms, covered in blood, and screaming for someone to help her. "The police are on the way."

I barely hear him. I'm already gone and back in my parent's bedroom. As the police and ambulance arrive, I remain silent, unmoving in Reid's arms in the middle of the living room floor. The sobs have quieted down, but the tears still flow like a fountain. I glance out the corner of my eye and watch as Jacob is loaded onto a gurney and wheeled out of my house. A police officer asks if I can give a statement, and my only response is a slight shake of my head. I can't speak. I don't want to speak. Eventually I hear Reid promise the officer to have me down at the station in the next few days to give my official statement, and then we're alone.

Seconds turn into minutes as the time passes by, and I lose track of how long Reid and I sit there on the floor. Suddenly, my door slams open. I scream, and Reid jumps up off the ground, taking a defensive stance in front of me.

"What the hell happened in here?" It's Eli.

I glance up, the tears form again, and the sobs threaten to make a return. Reid moves aside, and I see Eli, who looks just as I last saw him. In a heartbeat, he takes Reid's place on the ground, holding me in his arms and rocking me back and forth. I can see Reid out of the corner of my eye, standing just a few steps away, watching us. I gaze up at Eli, who brushes a strand of hair out of my face. "I-I-it was Robert," I say softly. Eli stares at me, confused for a second. Then the realization of who Robert is crosses his face. I can tell he wants to ask more, but he holds back.

"I'm so sorry I wasn't here," he says gently. He stands up, helps me off the floor and over to a barstool. Placing more distance between Reid and I. I feel the heat of Reid's eyes on me, but I can't face him. What am I supposed to say? That sadistic, murderous people have a tendency to be a part of my life? No, I can't tell him that, even though I'm sure he has probably guessed something along those lines. But I can't look at him, either. I'm too embarrassed. God only knows what he thinks of me now.

Eli starts shuffling around the house. He brings out one of my duffle bags and starts making trips between my bedroom and the living room, placing some of my belongings inside the bag.

"What are you doing?" Reid finally speaks. My heart flutters, my body aches for his touch again, and I finally glance at him. He isn't staring at me though. His eyes are focused on Eli.

"What does it look like?" Eli's voice is harsh. "I'm packing some of her things. She can't stay here."

Reid tenses and straightens his shoulders. "She can stay with me," he says matter-of-factly.

"Is that so?" Eli laughs and shakes his head before resuming what he is doing. I watch him place my favorite pair of sweats in the bag. "That's kind of you, really, but I think that Liza would much rather stay with me."

Reid takes a step towards me, and Eli stops what he is doing. He slams the bag down against the countertop of the breakfast bar and moves between Reid and I. He's in protective mode now. I glance between the two men, unable to register what is going on, which is clearly some sort of alpha male thing here. The tension is thick in the air. Reid and Eli face one another, staring the other down and not saying a word. Reid shifts so I can see him better now, and he stares right at me. "What do you want, Liza?"

Both eyes are on me again. I take a deep breath. My stomach is in knots, and my knees begin to bounce up and down. "What do you mean?" I ask hesitantly.

"Who do you want to stay with?" Reid asks. "This bonehead…" I can't help but smile, and I see Eli's eyebrows furrow. The smile quickly disappears off of my face, and I glance back to Reid. "Or do you want to stay with me?"

"With you." The words are out of my mouth before I realize what I have just said. I hear Eli take a sharp breath and curse. I open my mouth to say something but shut it quickly. Eli is leaving, heading towards the door, and I stand up to go after him. He stops just at the door, staring at me, and his eyes are full of hatred. I stop in my tracks and frown. Eli shakes his head and then slams the door behind him.

I'm ready to cry again. I begin to fumble around with the bag, trying to place the last few things Eli had brought out of my room into it.

Reid's hands cover the top of mine, his body close to me, and I feel his shallow breath on the back of my neck.

"Here…" he whispers. "Let me do it."

I nod my head and move to the side. Reid is quick to pack my things. He disappears down the hall and reappears a moment later. He grabbed the pillow off my bed. He holds it up and smiles gently. "I thought you could use something from home to comfort you." I smile back at him and nod. With the bag packed and ready to go, Reid offers his hand to me. Instead, I smile and walk past him to the front door. I hear Reid exhale a deep breath, and his footsteps fall into place behind me.

Chapter Eighteen

REID'S HOUSE IS NOTHING like I expect it to be. Being the nephew of a man who ran the most successful agent house, the nephew of a billionaire, as well as a man who has millions himself, I honestly expect more. Another thing to add to the list of surprises. While in the dark I can't see much, I know his house sits on a lot of acreage. In the moonlight, I see nothing but trees and hills for miles. His house comes into view as we reach the end of the long, narrow, tree lined driveway. What it lacks in size, it makes up for in beauty. His home is crafted out of logs, offering a warm, welcoming feeling. Of course, his home is bigger than an average house, but isn't as big as I thought it would be. I was expecting a gigantic mansion, filled with more rooms and bathrooms than a single man needs, just to show off his wealth. Seeing his house is almost like a slap in the face. Maybe he is right? Maybe I have judged him too quickly without having all the facts. Reid pulls his car right in front of the house, jumps out of the driver's seat, and rounds the car to let me out. I place my hand in his, trying to ignore the energy pulsing under my skin, and laugh.

Reid raises an eyebrow and smiles. "What is so funny?"

"This… is not what I was expecting," I answer honestly. He smiles again and closes the car door behind me. He quickly drops my hand. In the dim light illuminating the house, I see his hand curl into a fist and release several times. He turns and heads inside. I follow him, noting the sudden change in his mood. He is tense.

Reid opens the door for me, standing off to the side, and motions me to go in first. As I step over the threshold, I suddenly wish he is carrying me. *What the hell?* Where did that come from? I shake my head and continue to walk into the house. The scent hits me intensely. The same woodsy aroma I smelled on him that night at the diner. The door closes behind me, and I hear the locks click into place. Reid starts to flip on the lights, revealing a large, open room. I glance around, immediately taken aback by the beauty of the interior. The crossbeams are intricately carved above, and across the room is a large fireplace made of stone with a large mirror hanging above it. One oversized white couch is placed in front of the fireplace, and two wooden end tables with lamps resting on top of them are placed at the ends of the couch. It isn't much. In fact, it's almost as barren as my office. Off to the right is a large open kitchen. To my left is a large set of wooden steps, and I presume that's where the rooms must be. Just like any log cabin, everything is made out of wood.

"I'll go get my blankets and some stuff out of my room and bring them downstairs."

I turn towards him and tilt my head to the side. "That isn't necessary," I tell him. *Or is it?* Reid tenses again. He seems as though he's about to say something but stops himself from saying it.

"I only have one room upstairs, besides my office." I stop my jaw from dropping and stare at a painting of a sweeping landscape on the wall next to me. "Unless you don't mind sharing…" I glance back at him and see him smiling. It's not his usual smile. It's one that doesn't quite reach his eyes, which are a hauntingly dark color. "Because in that case… we can go to bed right now."

"I can sleep downstairs then…" I say. Reid straightens his stance, stares hard at me, still smiling, and shakes his head. I'm not going to win this argument. "Fine… it probably is best if you sleep downstairs then."

Reid's smile drops, and I would do almost anything to see him smile again. Even one of the half faked smiles he does. "It probably is."

Without another word, Reid ascends the stairs and disappears out of sight. I hear him shuffling around upstairs, opening and closing things, and I move into the living room. The only difference between my office and his living room is that he actually has pictures. A few are of himself with another boy and a girl. They all look strikingly similar. Most of the photos, however, hold the same slightly older woman in them. Some of them are just shots of her, caught off guard or unaware that the photo is being taken. Others have him next to her, in several different places across the world. A photo of him and the woman in front of the Great Wall of China, in front of the Eiffel Tower, on the beaches of with white sand, and one of them at Disney World.

I walk around the living room, gazing at photo after photo. Whoever she is, she brings out a side of Reid I have never seen before. In all the photos, his eyes are light, almost a green color. A total contrast to the nearly black eyes that I have become all too familiar with. I hear Reid clear his throat behind me and quickly turn to face him. I feel my cheeks warming up, embarrassed that I have been caught staring at what is obviously private moments of his life. He drops a pillow, comforter, and a change of clothes on the couch before walking towards me. Reid stops next to me. I see out the corner of my eye that he is tense. I watch as he picks up the photo of him and the woman at Disney World. He sighs and releases a deep breath.

"My mother." That is all he says. I turn my attention towards the photo in his hands. Relief fills me as I discover the woman who covers the walls and mantle is his mother. He places the photo back on top of the mantle, and I see his hand shaking. I feel his eyes on me before I turn towards him. He is standing close, I can smell the scent of his cologne and the woodsy mixture. "I think it's best that we get some rest. You'll find the room ready upstairs for you. There's a bathroom off to the side of the room if want to take a shower or a bath."

I nod my head and turn to leave the living room, feeling like I have been dismissed. I pause on the stairs long enough to see him pull another photo off the mantle and run his finger over it. I swear I hear him let out a soft sob as he places the photo back where it belongs. In that moment, my heart breaks for him. It's clear that he loves her. I wipe the tear that slides down my face and head upstairs to the room.

* * *

I can't breathe. I can't move. I can't make a sound, frozen in place. The nightmare is back, only it's different this time. A slideshow of tonight's events and the events from six years ago blur together as one never-ending movie. I am coming home from the club and open my apartment, only to find that it's my mother tied to the chair instead of Jacob. She's already dead, though. Her throat has been slit. My father and Jacob appear, both holding knives with sinister grins on their face. They're coming towards me, both ready to attack. Just as they are about to lunge at me, I am forced awake by the sound of my phone beeping.

I jump up in the bed, sitting up and leaning over to flick on the light. The lamp casts a dim glow across the room, which is similar to the living room downstairs. Wide and open, barren of all things except for the large carved wood bed I am sitting in and the grand wooden dresser with a large mirror on it. Up here, I see no photos, no paintings, just the bed and dresser. I grab my phone off the pillow resting next to me, the screen flashing with one new message. I unlock the screen, hoping it's a response from Eli. When he refused to answer my phone calls and text messages before I fell asleep, I sent him an email. My heart stops, and my body tenses when I see that it isn't from Eli but from the unknown sender.

From: Unknown Sender
To: LWinter@hlah.com
Talk about blast from a past! How was that reunion with dear Robert and your ex-lover yesterday? Sorry it didn't go quite according to plan. It's a shame that Robert didn't get to finish what your father set out to do six years ago. That's okay though. I'll just have to finish it for him. Soon enough. In the meantime, don't be getting too cozy in that log cabin. You'll be leaving soon. Remember, Elizabeth, you can run but you can't hide.

I throw my phone across the bedroom, shattering it against the wall into a million pieces. *Great, now I don't have a phone.*

Maybe it's for the best. If I don't have a phone, I can't get any more emails. I sigh heavily and lean back against the pillow. I just start to drift back to sleep when a loud crash followed by the sound of breaking glass startles me, and I jump out of bed. I take the stairs two at a time, and I am immediately engulfed by a black cloud of smoke. I cough while flailing my arms around to try and clear the smoke. I walk into the kitchen where Reid is sweeping up shards of broken glass. The smell of burnt food hits me, and I start to laugh.

Reid looks up from the ground, and our eyes connect. "What happened in here?" I laugh again and circle around the island.

"Be careful," he says. I stop walking, narrowly missing a piece of glass near my left foot. "I, uh, well…" He rubs his temple, leaving a streak of black smudge behind. "I thought you could use some breakfast."

That's when I notice the morning light pouring through the sky lights in the kitchen. How is it possibly morning already? The room was completely pitch black upstairs. I could've sworn it was the middle of the night. "I closed the blackout curtains when I was upstairs last night. I thought you could use the uninterrupted sleep," he says as though he read my mind.

It wasn't completely uninterrupted. I think of the email on my phone, and the fact that I now need to get a new cell phone. Reid discards the remaining pieces of glass into the trash can. I walk across the kitchen and open the windows to clear the remnants of smoke. Reid follows suit and opens the French style doors in the living room that lead to a large wooden deck.

"What exactly is it that you were trying to cook?" I eye him curiously. He leans against the island, his cotton drawstring pants hang low on his waist, revealing his sexy v-cut of muscles, and I can see all the lines of his defined shirtless chest and abdomen. His hair is a slightly disheveled mess. His eyes aren't dark, but they do have bags under them like he didn't sleep last night. He looks absolutely mouthwatering. I could just take him there against the counter, savoring every taste of him.

"I'm not too sure exactly," he admits and laughs. He runs his hand through his hair and sighs. "I'm not very domesticated."

That's the understatement of the year.

I pick up a dish towel draped over the handle of the oven, walk over to Reid, and smile. "You've got a little smudge there," I say and proceed to wipe his face off. Reid takes in a sharp breath. I feel my own breath catching from being so close to him. He reaches his hand up and touches my hand. He smiles and slowly exhales.

"You do realize you are in your underwear?" His lips quirk up in a smirk. I gasp, dropping my hand quickly and taking a step back. How could I forget I was wearing only a thin tank top and my underwear? "I think I could get used to seeing you dressed like this." His voice is soft and full of desire.

"Don't get any ideas." I turn on my heels and run out of the kitchen.

I take my time showering and getting dressed, mainly because I'm too embarrassed to show my face downstairs. I'm sure it's only a matter of time before Reid comes searching for me. It's almost lunch time, and that only further embarrasses me. I take one last glimpse at my hair. I had taken the time to tame it with some mousse. I don't why I do it. My hair only cooperates that way for so long before it decides to go whichever way it wants. It's the price I pay for not taking care of it properly and dying it every time a faint sign of my blonde roots begin to make an appearance.

Reid isn't downstairs in the living room when I finally show my face. With the house having an open floor plan, I don't have to move far from the bottom of the stairs to see that the French doors are still open. A light breeze flows in and causes the sheer white drapes to dance in the wind. I take a deep breath and head towards the doors.

I bite back my surprise at the sight before me. Reid is wearing nothing but swim shorts and is lounging on a chair across the deck. The sweat on his skin glistens in the sunlight. He is devastatingly beautiful. I lean against the side of the house, watching him turn the pages of whatever book he is engrossed with. He peeks over the top of the spine, and our eyes meet. I sense hesitation as he motions for me to take a seat in the empty chair next to him.

I sit down, glancing over to see what so vigorously had his attention before I came out here, and am shocked to find what he is reading. "Bone Cold?" I ask. He is reading my favorite book by Erica Spindler. I'm not sure it's a coincidence. I'm pretty sure nothing is when it comes to him.

"I saw on the questionnaire that this is your favorite book." He doesn't look at me. Of course, being the nephew of the man who owns the company I work for, he has unlimited access to my files. After all, that is how he found where I lived the first time he showed up at my house. I wonder just how much of my file he has seen. The questionnaire is no big deal and nothing to worry about. Lawrence makes everyone fill one out, so he can 'get to know his employees better'. If Reid has snooped to find my address and has taken the time to read my questionnaire, I can't disregard the fact that perhaps he has read my entire file.

Does he know about Dr. Uria? Does he know why I see her?

The questions run through my mind a mile a minute. I feel his eyes on me, watching me, waiting for me to say something. "What do you think?" I finally say.

"You do realize this is a romance?" He tilts his head to the side and a half crooked smile appears.

"Is not," I say too quickly. Reid laughs and shakes his head in disagreement. "It's a suspense novel."

"A Romantic Suspense," he says. "You discount the growing feelings between the two main characters, the detective and the writer." My face drops. Of course it is. How could I forget? I've always been so enraptured by the suspense of the book that I pretty much ignore the other part—the romance. Maybe this is why Lawrence stuck me in Romance.

"You still never answered my question."

Reid smiles again, and a hearty laugh fills the open air around us. "And you still haven't answered mine."

"Fine… it's a Romantic Suspense." I sit back and fold my arms across my chest. "Are you happy now?"

"Very." We sit quietly side by side. Reid turns his attention back to the book, and I gaze at the view around me. It's breathtaking. Nothing but rolling hills and trees for miles, it's like we're on our own little planet out here. I spy Reid close the book and turn my head as he places it on the small round table next to his chair. "It was an alright book."

"Just alright?" I eye him, waiting for whatever might come out of his mouth next. I stare at his full lips, remembering how soft and delicate they are against mine and the way he tasted when his tongue danced with mine. Reid is smiling, like he is reading my mind again, and I quickly fix my attention on a tree straight ahead.

"I've read better, to be honest."

For some reason, this ignites a flicker of anger in me. It seems like he is mocking my favorite book. I wouldn't put it past him. He is known to mock me about other personal things. I push up out of the chair; the force I use causes it to rock on its hind legs before settling back in place. I storm across the deck and slam one of the double doors behind me.

"If he wants to make fun of me, I can be a bitch right back to him," I mutter under my breath and make my way up the stairs.

I'm being childish, I know, but I can't help it. Reid knocks on the bedroom door several times throughout the day before he finally gives up. I just want to be left alone. The reality of everything that has been happening has finally caught up with me, and surprisingly, I don't find myself crying. I am pissed. Everything I have worked so hard for is falling apart, being pulled away from me, just like everything else has.

I can't even go home right now.

I try to call Eli a couple of times on a landline I find in the bedroom, but he never answers. I call his mom, and she said that he stepped out for the day. Code for he is standing next to her, but he doesn't want to talk to me. Trust me, I know. He's done this to girls his entire life when they wouldn't leave him alone. Now I am one of those girls. I lie face down, my face buried in the pillow, and scream, letting out all my frustration on the pillow.

Earlier today, I opened the blackout curtains, hoping that maybe the sun would pull me out of this funk. Now, as the sun is setting — the most gorgeous sunset I have ever laid eyes on — I decide enough is enough. I'm not going to sulk in the room all day because some dick didn't like my favorite book as well as I did. To each their own, right?

I barely make it downstairs before Reid's lips crash against mine. A startled cry escapes from my mouth before I silence myself and find that I am kissing him back. Once again. He pushes my back against the railing of the stairs, his body forming against mine. His leg presses between mine, and I can feel his growing erection as his tongue sweeps across my lips. He tastes just as good as I remember. I run my hands through his hair, his hands clasp around my waist, and I wrap my legs around him as he lifts me up in the air. Reid breaks the kiss first, but his lips never leave. He kisses the corner of my mouth, then my chin, and a trail down the side of my neck.

I arch my back and moan with pleasure. Grabbing a fistful of his hair, I yank on his head, which sends him into a fury. Our lips meet again. He bites my lower lip gently, tugging on it, and I moan for him. He carries me toward the couch, gently easing me down, and lies on top of me. I run my hands over his back, digging my fingers into his skin and tracing his muscles. Reid's hand starts to travel underneath my shirt and begins making his way to the one place I don't want him to touch— my scar.

"Wait," I say breathlessly, "I can't do this."

Chapter Nineteen

I SHOVE REID OFF of me as quickly as I can and jump off the couch. I walk over to the fireplace, wrap my arms around myself, and stare into the glowing flames. That was too close, way too close. *I seriously cannot kiss him again.* Every time I do, I lose all inhibitions. Reid almost discovered my ugly truth, the mutilated scar on my stomach. He can't ever find out. If he does, that will only lead to questions I can't answer. That I will not answer.

This is a mistake. I should have never come here. Why couldn't I just go with Eli? Being alone and out here with Reid, in the middle of nowhere, is not good for my raging hormones. I need to get a hold of Eli as soon as I can. I don't know how much longer I can stay here without giving in to my desires, something I am not ready to do. Plus, what if Reid is completely disgusted by the scar once he discovers it? That is another thing I cannot face. I'm already disgusted by it, and I can't bear it if a man is too.

"I'm sorry," Reid whispers. "I shouldn't have done that."

I touch my lips with my hand, still swollen and moist from kissing him. I enjoy kissing him. I more than enjoy it— I love it. For a brief moment, I regret pushing him off of me. I turn back around and face him. "Don't be sorry… I kissed you back." *And I'd do it again and again.* "It's just… I can't. I can't." Tears pool in my eyes, and I sigh.

Reid closes the distance between us and pulls me into his arms. "Who broke your heart so badly that you are scared to let anyone else in?"

I release a deep breath before I allow myself to wrap my arms around him. I know I said no men, but I can't deny that I want Reid. In every way possible, including naked in bed. I barely know the man, but I know enough that, while he may piss me off most of the time, he also ignites a fire in me that I have never felt before, not even with Jacob.

Jacob... his name alone reminds me why I cannot allow myself to indulge in Reid.

"I can't tell you, Reid. Really, I can't." I feel Reid tense under my arms right before he pushes me away like I'm some disease ridden fleabag.

"This is bullshit, Liza. What more do I have to prove to you?"

"Like I've said, you haven't done much to prove otherwise." I know this is a lie and that it will hurt Reid, but I don't have any other choice. His eyes darken, and I know I'm pushing him away just like I want. "In fact, you were an ass earlier today." Not really the truth, but I'll make him think that's how he was.

"I said I was sorry." Reid glares at me.

"Oh really, when was that? Before you started to kiss me? Before you bombarded me at the bottom of the stairs as if I was yours for the taking?" In all honesty, if that is how he apologizes, I could live with that the rest of my life. "Maybe coming here was a mistake. Maybe I should leave." I brush past him with the intention to go upstairs to pack and call a cab.

"No, don't..." he calls after me. I stop and look back at him. "You're right when you say I haven't been the nicest guy around, but you really haven't given me the chance to show you who I really am."

"Reid—"

He cuts me off, "No, Liza. Let me finish. I don't know who it was that broke your heart, and quite frankly, I don't really care. What I do care about is that you have something about you that draws me to you. I can't help but to want to kiss you and make love to you." My heart stops when he refers to sleeping with me as making love. "I know I have this sort of bad boy reputation that I can't settle down and I go through women like candy. I haven't done much to prove otherwise, as you can see on the Internet. But that's not really who I am."

I take a step towards Reid and reach out to take his hand. "Reid—"

"All I am asking for is a chance," he cuts me off again. "A chance to prove to you that I am nothing like the guy who broke your heart. I want a chance to show you that it's okay to fall in love again and trust again. I want to be that guy who shows you how to love again."

His admission takes me by surprise and leaves me speechless. I wrap my hands around the back of his head and pull his lips to mine. No sexual intent is fueling the kiss, no exploring hands or lips, just two people undeniably attracted to one another kissing. And what a kiss it is.

"Don't make me regret this," I say softly against his lips.

"I won't."

I hear the truth in his voice. To hell with all my rules. In just the short time we have spent together, despite our bickering and my fighting against the building attraction, I have fallen for him. I dove in head first with no end in sight, and nothing I could have done would have prevented this from happening.

We finally manage to stop kissing, but we don't stop touching one another. We sit down on the couch. I curl up against Reid, and we stare into the fire, saying nothing at all. For the first time in a long time, I am perfectly content. Almost. I can't ignore the nagging thought in the back of my mind that I need to tell Reid the truth. I need to tell him everything. I need to be honest. Better that I do it now, get it out in the open, so he can see the kind of monster I am. And the kind of parents I am bred from.

It will be better than him finding out later. Because if he decides to walk away, I will be shattered. I wouldn't blame him, either. Who would want to be with a woman who left her ex so unsatisfied that he hooked up with her mother, which resulted in her mother being murdered by her father? *It just goes to show what kind of blood I have running in my veins. If I were him, I would run as fast as I could.*

I don't tell him, though. Sitting here, saying nothing at all, and just being held, I'm the happiest I have been in a while, and I'm not ready to let the feeling go just yet. Another reason why he should run the other way: I'm too selfish to think of what's best for him. I sigh heavily against his chest, and Reid kisses the top of my head.

At some point I fall asleep. I don't know when Reid managed to slip out from underneath me, but I wake up on the couch alone, covered in a blanket. I glance around the house and see no sign of him. My heart stops and then drops into the pit of my stomach. *He's changed his mind, and now he's gone.* Tears sting my eyes, and I throw my hands up above my head. I feel something crinkle under my hand and sit up. A small piece of paper with neat script stands out. It has to be a breakup note. I take several deep breaths before I pick it up and read it.

You seemed so peaceful, and I didn't want to disturb you.
I ran into the city to grab a few things. I will be back soon.
Until then, I will be missing every second that you aren't in my arms.
-Reid

With a sigh of relief, I lean back against the couch and smile. Okay, so I overreacted. When don't I? It's not entirely my fault that I am so cautious. I decide to get off the couch and take a nice long, hot bath as I wait for Reid to return. *I wonder what he went into the city to grab.* I walk up the stairs, my thoughts in a daze and a smile plastered on my face.

If only Dr. Uria and Eli could see me now. The thought of Eli tugs at my heart. With my phone broken, I have no way to see if he has attempted to call, text, or email me back. Maybe I'll try to call him from the landline again after my bath.

I walk into the large bathroom and to the oversized Jacuzzi tub. I crank the lever to the hottest water setting possible and wait for the tub to fill up. I stare at my reflection in the mirror and trace my fingers over my scar. I have to think of something to tell Reid. I will only be able to keep his hands off my stomach for so long. And eventually, he is going to see me naked.

What have I gotten myself into? Am I ready for this?

Yes, I am. I am ready for this. I deserve to be happy. I repeat the words that Dr. Uria has told me over and over again like a mantra. *I deserve to be happy. I deserve to be happy. I deserve to be happy.* If I truly do, why is it that I still feel so guilty? I think of my parents and Jacob.

Jacob. I need to make sure he is okay. I've long gotten over the feelings I may have once had for him, but he was nearly beaten to death in my apartment last night. I blame myself and that all this has happened because it's my fault. Reid deserves better. When I think of Reid, I wonder why he hasn't questioned me about the other night, but I'm thankful he hasn't. I don't know what I'm going to say to him.

Seeing the tub almost filled, I sigh a breath of relief. I need out of my head. I need to stop over thinking everything. I need to take things one step at a time and enjoy them. Starting with this bath. I dip my foot in the water, welcoming the feel of the hot water against my skin. I sink the rest of my body into the water, sliding down until the water covers every inch of me except for my head, and close my eyes.

The sound of a car pulling into the driveway snaps me awake. I jump up in the water and splash some out the side. The water has turned lukewarm, and my skin is wrinkly like a prune. I step onto the bathmat and grab Reid's robe from next to the shower and wrap it around me. I wrap a towel around my hair and take off down the stairs, eager to see Reid.

As I approach the front door, I notice that the vehicle in the driveway doesn't belong to Reid and stop in my tracks. I tiptoe to the door to make sure it's locked and peak out the window to the right of it. A dark, hooded figure climbs out of the front seat, wearing all black. I gasp and snap back from the window. I slide down against the door, pull my knees up to my chest, and wait.

The SUV door slams shut, and I can hear the gravel crunching under the person's feet. My heart is pounding, and my breathing is erratic. I hear whoever it is approach the front door. They knock once and then try the door handle. My heart begins to beat faster. What if they break down the door and I'm leaning up against it? I hear a loud thump against the ground on the other side of the door followed by the sounds of the person walking away.

The SUV starts back up again and slowly pulls out of the driveway. I sit there against the door, taking slow and steady breaths, waiting for what seems like forever before I push up off the ground and open the door. I crack it open, just enough to peek my head out and glance around, and notice a manila envelope with my real name written across it in black permanent marker. I grab the envelope off the ground and close the door quickly, making sure to lock it behind me.

I walk slowly towards the living room with the envelope in my hand, debating on whether or not I want to open it. After a few more breaths, I decide to see what's inside. I am not prepared for what I find. Pictures of my life, from birth until now. Most of the pictures I kept locked away in the safe at the back of my closet. How did whoever it is get their hands on them? Then I remember that my apartment was broken into. It had to have been then.

The first few pictures are of me as an infant with both of my parents. They seemed so young and happy then. A tear wells up in my eye. I haven't looked at these photos in a very long time. I had them hidden away, never to look back on them. I stare at the photo of my parents and me on my first birthday and gently touch it with my finger. The following photos are scattered from the rest of my childhood, all containing at least one of my parents in the photograph. As I scan through the photos, it's clear to see how time truly changes things. The subtle looks on my parents' faces, the fake smiles that don't entirely meet their eyes, and the obvious distance they tried to put between all of us.

My father and I share no resemblance to each other, and I'm not entirely a spitting image of my mother either. I used to question my parents about it, but they were always quick to change the topic.

Then comes the photographs of Jacob and me, from our first dance freshman year to being crowned King and Queen at the senior prom. I feel like I'm reliving another life I once had through photographs.

The last picture startles me, and I drop them all onto the floor. Though I don't have the actual photos, I never needed them. The images I have just seen have been burned on the back of my mind for six years. It's a crime scene photo. My mother's body lies under a bloodstained white cloth with police tape around the room. The photo has a caption at the top that someone added in black permanent marker. The two simple words stand out: *You're next.*

Several minutes pass by, and I haven't moved. I don't think I have breathed, either. I cannot figure out who the hell is behind all this and why or what they want. I thought it was Robert, but he can't have delivered this if he is behind bars. Which I know for certain he is.

I hear another car pull into the driveway. I run towards the door and see Reid's car approaching slowly. My heart rate goes into panic mode. I run back into the living room and gather up all the pictures as quickly as I can. I glance around the room to see where I can hide them, and I can't find a hiding place. I see the fire blazing in the fireplace and rush over to it. With a deep sigh, I toss them into the fire and watch as the only photos I have of my life become engulfed in flames.

I can hear the car pulling to a stop and rush into the kitchen, just as the last of the photos turn to ash. I need something to calm my nerves. Opening the cupboard, I see a row of liquor bottles, so I pull out a bottle of whiskey and a glass. I pour the dark brown liquid into the glass and begin to chug it before pouring myself another cup.

"Hitting the bottle a bit early, don't you think?" Reid's voice startles me. I didn't hear him come through the door. I drop the glass and watch it break into pieces on the wood floor. Reid kneels down and starts picking up the larger pieces of glass. "You know, at this rate, I may not have any dishes left in the house."

I force a light laugh and help him pick up the pieces of broken glass. "Can we go back to the city?" Reid raises an eyebrow and stares at me. He stands up, carries the glass to the garbage, and disposes of it. I know I should tell him about everything, but I can't. I need to get away from him. I have to protect him. I need to take care of this on my own.

"What's wrong, Liza?"

"Nothing, I just really miss it and all." He shakes his head as if he doesn't believe me. It's written all over the tight lines of his face. "I miss watching TV, I feel like I'm missing out on my weekly dose of reality shows." It's the furthest thing from the truth. Yes, Reid doesn't have a TV here for some odd reason, but I don't really miss watching TV. In fact, I could care less about it, but he doesn't know that.

"I'll get a TV set up here with more channels than a person needs," he says. His jaw is clenched tight as he stares at me, and my breathing hitches.

"No, I don't want to disturb the beauty and tranquility of this place. I don't want to corrupt it," I reply quickly. Reid closes the distance between us, pulls me close, and wraps his arms around me.

"Talk to me," he whispers. "What is it?"

"I just want to go home." The truth shocks me more than I expect, but it's not the apartment that I want to go back to. I suddenly feel the urge to return to my childhood home. I want to run my hand over the railing of the stairs. I want the smell of peonies from the garden to fill my nose, and I want to hear the sound of my fingers brushing against the keys of the piano.

I clench my fingers and release them slowly. The grand piano. I haven't thought about a piano in years, let alone intentionally been in the same room as one. My fingers yearn to play some Chopin, *Nocturne No. 2 in E-flat major,* to be exact. For some reason, that has always been my favorite piece to play. How did I forget about that? How could I forget about any of that? Perhaps because it reminds me of my father, the one who pushed me to learn how to play and reprimanded me whenever I missed a note.

Everything comes flooding back to me at once. The piano recitals my mother came to. The ballet recitals my father never watched. Even then, as a child, they avoided each other like the plague. I always knew they hated each other but never understood why they stayed together. Neither of my parents were the affectionate type, and only pretended to put on a display of a happy home, family, and marriage. Flashes of my childhood play in my head like a never-ending movie reel. I start to get lightheaded and collapse to the ground.

"Liza!" I hear Reid's panicked voice in the back of my mind, but I can't escape the movie playing on repeat in my head. "Liza! Come on, sweetheart, wake up!"

Chapter Twenty

THE BLACK AND WHITE piano keys taunt me as my fingers dance across them. Daring me to make a mistake, to miss one little note, and screw up the entire piece. I keep calm and let my fingers play Rachmaninov's 'Prelude in G minor Opus 23'. I play the piece without incident, fully aware of my father standing directly behind me. Once the song is complete, I feel his hand touch my shoulder, and grip it tightly.

"Again," he says sharply. "Without the sheet music."

It's not enough that he expects a ten-year-old child to master such a complicated piece, but now he wants me to play it without sheet music. I love playing. I really do, except for when my father is around. He drills me like a soldier in the army. Forcing me to play the same piece over and over again, until I feel like my fingers are going to turn raw and start to bleed. While I love playing the piano, I don't want to become the next prodigy. I don't want to become a concert pianist, like he expects me to. I play the beginning, hitting all the right keys, and it isn't until I am halfway through when I miss the first note. After that, it becomes a disaster. A tear slides down my cheek. I know what is about to come — what always comes next.

I struggle through the last half of the song, missing more notes than I play accurately. My shoulders slowly begin to hunch over. The tears are coming down my face quicker now and falling against the keys. The song is coming to an end, and I only see dread in the near future. I try to focus on the keys, trying to remember which note comes next, and all I can remember is a jumbled mess. The song ends all too soon, and I am closing the lid to the grand piano. I take a deep breath, turn on the piano bench, and stand up. I barely make it to my feet when the back of my father's hand connects with the side of my face, and I fall to the ground.

My eyes jolt open, and I take a sharp breath. My vision is blurry, and my head is pounding. I try to sit up, but I feel weak. I lie there — wherever I am lying — and feel someone brushing their hand over my hair. "Liza, darling?" It takes a minute to recognize the voice.

"Reid?" I say breathlessly and flutter my eyes. My vision is slowly clearing up, and I can see the shadow of Reid's face hovering over mine.

"Oh, thank God!" He exhales sharply. Just as my vision fully returns, I feel his soft lips press against mine, and I moan. The kiss is deep, raw, and full with love. *Love?* I am not in love with him. I can't be.

I pull back gently, breaking free of the kiss, much to my dismay. I can keep kissing him; I could kiss him all night. Reid hovers above me, his nose brushing against the tip of mine, and his eyes are soft. I try to move again, but my body is still weak. Reid sits up before he helps me shift into a sitting position. I am on the couch. I don't know how long I have been out. All I know is that Reid moved me to the couch, and the gesture comforts me.

I tentatively steal a glance at Reid and find he is staring at me with questions in his eyes. "I'm not going to ask you a million questions right now," he says softly. "But we are going to have to talk about this eventually."

I nod slightly. He is right; we are going to have to talk. He needs to know everything. He needs to know what kind of fucked up family I come from. He needs to know how screwed up I am and he needs to know that I may never be able to fully trust him enough to let my guard down and let him in. No matter how much I want to. I have a crazy stalker out there, and I don't know what they want. It's evident whoever it is really watching my every move. How else did they know where to deliver the photos?

A wave of nausea hits me, and before I can compose myself, I get sick on the floor of his living room. Reid says nothing and holds my hair back as I empty out whatever is left inside of me. My face heats up with embarrassment. Throwing up on his hardwood floor is hardly attractive. After a few minutes, my stomach finally settles down. I wipe the corners of my mouth with the sleeve of my T-shirt. Reid hesitates for a moment before he pulls me close to him. I gaze up into his soft dark eyes. His lips hover just above mine, and he moves to kiss me.

"Uh..." I pull away. "Before you do that... I need to clean up the mess I just made on your floor and brush my teeth."

Reid laughs lightly. "Go brush your teeth. I'll get the mop."

"Reid—"

"Darling." My heart jumps at the sentiment. "I've got it taken care of. Go brush your teeth. Take a bath. I'll make you some tea." I hesitate for a moment, contemplating what I should do. Reid sees right through my walls and smiles gently. "Let me take care of you."

I nod my head once and pull him close. I wrap my arms around him and squeeze him tightly, ignoring the fact that slowly but surely I can feel one of my walls crumbling down. I have never had anyone really take care of me, besides Eli, but he isn't talking to me at the moment. The thought threatens to make me sick again. How long is he going to do this? How long is he going to ignore me? "Thank you," I whisper into Reid's chest. He kisses the top of my forehead, and then I stand up to head to the stairs.

I pause a moment, gathering my bearings, and head to the wooden staircase. I take the stairs slowly, holding onto the railing for balance. My head is still pounding, and I take a deep breath. Once in the bathroom, I walk over to the tub and start the water. I scan the room for any sign of bubble bath or oils, which of course I don't find. Which really doesn't surprise me. Instead, I opt for grabbing the bottle of his body soap. Nothing like soaking in a tub full of water that smells like the man who makes your head spin. In a good way.

Once the tub is filled to the brim with water and bubbles, I peel off my clothes and step into the steaming hot water. Giving myself a moment to adjust to the temperature before sliding my body the rest of the way in, I lean my head back, resting it on the edge of the tub, and close my eyes. Not long after that I hear a slight knock on the door and open my eyes. The door opens slowly. "I've got tea," Reid says cautiously. He pauses for a moment to see if I stop him, and when I don't, he walks into the bathroom holding a white ceramic mug. Steam rises off the top off the cup, and the scent of tea fills the air.

He walks slowly towards the tub, his eyes locked on mine. I sit up carefully, making sure most of my body still remains hidden beneath the suds. He sits on the edge of the tub and holds the mug out to me. I reach out and take it from him. I bring the cup to my lips and let the warm liquid slide down my throat. I can get used to being taken care of. "Thank you," I murmur. He leans over and kisses the top of my head.

"Anytime." His eyes darken for a moment, and I can tell he's holding back something.

"Reid? What is it?" I prepare myself for the worst.

"While you were ou—" He clears his throat. "While you were napping, Office Kendrick called to let me know that they still need your statement." I let out a sigh of relief, and Reid picks up on it instantly. "What's wrong?"

"N-N-Nothing," I stutter. Reid lifts an eyebrow and gives me the 'I'm-not-buying-it' look. "It's just... I thought you might think I was crazy and had a change of heart," I admit to him.

He places a hand on each of my cheeks and stares straight into my eyes. "You are not crazy." He kisses me gently on the corner of my mouth. "And I'm not going anywhere." He kisses me on the lips. I wrap my hands around his neck, deepening the kiss and pulling him into the tub. Fully clothed.

Reid cries out, and I laugh softly against his lips. After a few minutes, Reid breaks the kiss and pulls away. My heart stops for a minute, and disappointment fills me as he shifts around in the tub. Reid turns me around, pulls me close to his chest, and I lie against him. We sit in the tub like that for a long time— Reid still fully clothed, with me cradled between his legs and in his arms. I start to drift off to sleep, feeling more safe and at ease than I ever have. Lying against his chest and listening to his heart beat under me, I feel at peace. There have been times when Eli has held me like this, usually to comfort me during the few times I have either broken down in the past or after a nightmare, but none of those times measure up to what I am feeling now.

Reid traces my arm with his fingertip, working his way down to my stomach, and I freeze. He's about to discover the darkest secret of me. The one I am most ashamed of, but I don't pull away to stop him. As he reaches the scar that runs across my stomach, I inhale a sharp breath, and he hesitates for a moment before continuing the line of the jagged scar. "Liza?" he questions softly. "What is this?"

"A scar."

"From what?" he replies, and I shake my head. I can't tell him. Not yet. "I want to see it."

"No." The word flies out of my mouth without any thought.

"But—"

"I said no." I pull out of Reid's arms and turn to glare at him. It's too much too soon. "I think you should get out. I'll be down in a moment."

Reid lowers his head and seems defeated, but he doesn't protest. He gets out of the tub, his clothes sopping wet, and walks out of the bathroom without glancing back at me. I listen as he shuffles around the room, opening and closing dresser drawers. He's changing his clothes. I wait until I hear the sound of the bedroom door close before I get out of the tub and wrap the towel around me. I pause, pressing my ear against it the door to make sure he is really gone, and then I go and change my clothes.

Reid is standing out on the deck when I come back down, fully dressed in a pair of sweatpants and a sweater. I need to be covered up. In a weak and vulnerable moment, I exposed myself to him, and I don't plan on doing it again anytime soon. He's standing next to the railing, with his hands on top of it for support, and enjoying the breathtaking view.

I stand just inside the double doors and watch him. My eyes prick with tears. This isn't fair. I can't do this to him. He deserves someone who is willing to share everything with him, and I am not that person. My heart breaks as I stand there. I know what I have to do, but it's the hardest thing I have ever done. In these few short weeks, in which most of the time he's acted like an incomprehensible ass, I managed to fall for him. It doesn't help that he is the epitome of a gentleman, so caring and giving, although he acts like a tough cookie on the outside. Inside his body, in his heart, he is beautiful. My ugly heart is no match for him.

"Reid," I say gently. He turns around and stares at me. His eyes are soft, but I can see he's got the walls up. I don't blame him. He takes a step towards me, and I just shake my head. "No." The word is barely audible. I can feel the strands of my heart pulling as I take a deep breath and prepare myself for what I am about to say. "You deserve someone better than me. Someone who can tell you everything, someone who will let you in. I thought I could, but I can't. I really wanted this to work; heaven knows I wanted this to work. But I have a horrible past that I can't burden anyone with, least of all you."

I turn to leave and start gathering my things up. "Liza." My name barely comes out a whisper. I stop and stare back at him. Reid crosses the distance in four long strides with determination in his eyes. Before I have a chance to register what is going on, he pulls me towards him and crashes his lips against mine. I don't resist. I want the kiss just as much as he does. Finally, he breaks free. "I can't lose you. I can't explain it, but you make me feel complete. Even standing in the same room as you I feel whole, like I can't breathe without you." He kisses my lips softly.

"Reid, you deserve someone who can share all of themselves with you."

"No. My heart, my body, and my soul want you, and you only. I want to feel my lips pressing against your soft, luscious mouth as much as possible. I want to be able to wrap my arms around you whenever I want. I want to be surrounded by the smell of your lavender scented hair. I want wake up every morning to the warmth of your body against mine. And I want to call you mine. If that means I only get a part of you, then I'll take it, because a part of you is better than none of you. I only hope that one day you trust me enough to show me all of you. The good and the bad."

Chapter Twenty-One

IT ONLY TAKES ME two weeks to fall for Reid, and I have fallen harder than I ever have before. Life seems normal. I'm not really sure what is going on between Reid and me, but I can't ignore it anymore. The man has more patience and heart than anyone I have ever met. Something I would have never guessed. I thought he was nothing more than a slimy sleazeball, but he keeps proving me wrong. Reid has kept his touching minimal, and hasn't touched my scar or asked about it again. The smallest of touches, however, sets my body on fire, like when he runs his fingers up and down my arm or holds me close to his chest. He ignites a flame in me that I never knew existed. I have never been so drawn, so enraptured, and so perfectly content as I am now.

Another bonus is that Reid doesn't pry. He doesn't ask any questions about my past, but I know he wants to, and I find myself telling him bits and pieces of it. Things I had long forgotten and things I know I won't regret sharing. Little simple things, like my favorite thing to eat as a kid, my love for the piano, and how I refused to wear anything except tutus for nearly a year when I was seven. Things that seem so insignificant to most people, but things I forgot I treasured. I didn't delve much into my parents, but I have shared with him that they weren't happy or the greatest parents in the world.

Everything is so simple with Reid in our little secret world, away from the troubles of the world. We are in sync; when he moves, I move. When I listen to the beating of his heart while I lie on his chest, I notice how our heartbeats are one and the same. The same rhythm, the same strong, beating heart. We have settled into a routine now. We spend most of our days hiking along the numerous trails in the vast land behind his house and having picnics. Our nights are spent curled up on the couch, with his arm wrapped around me, and the two of us reading together.

It really has been bliss.

Now, that world is about to come crashing down around us. It's time to return back to reality, and the jobs we can't keep ignoring. I don't know how Reid managed to get us this much time off, but being the nephew of the owner must come in handy sometimes. My stomach has been a wreck since Reid told me that our little vacation is coming to an end and tomorrow we head back to the office. First, it's because I am sure the rumor mill will start once we arrive. I mean, we have both been gone nearly two and a half weeks, and we are returning the same day. Yeah, I would think something is going on. Even if it isn't anyone's business.

The thing that scares me the most, that makes my stomach sicker than hell, is my computer. The idea of receiving more emails is enough to send me into hiding. I still haven't shared anything about them with Reid. It isn't his problem. This is something I have to deal with on my own, and he is already more involved than I want him to be. It's time I take a stand for myself. *The time is now.*

"Liza?" I hear Reid calling up the stairs for me. I take a deep breath and stare at the single duffle bag containing the few belongings I have here. *Time to face the music.* I pick the bag up off the bed, sling it over my arm, and head downstairs.

"I'm coming," I answer in a sing-song voice. Reid takes my bag from me when I reach the bottom of the stairs and presses his lips against the side of my head. "You really have no patience, do you?" I want to laugh because he is actually a patient man.

"I just want to be back in the city before dark and make sure you get settled in." My heart stops for a brief moment. This is it. This is the moment where I return back to my apartment, the place that has been violated twice by at least one person. At this point, I'm not even sure anymore. I really need to start searching for a new place to live.

The drive is quiet and peaceful. Reid holds my hand gently and doesn't let go during the entire trip. I watch as the trees and hills blur past us, becoming less frequent after an hour of driving and slowly starting to morph into neighborhoods. Before I know it, we are in the center of town. We are long past the turn to my apartment, and I glance over at Reid nervously. "Where are we going?"

"My place." He raises an eyebrow and glances at me as we slow down at a stoplight. I furrow my eyebrows and shake my head. I honestly wasn't expecting this. "What? Did you honestly think I would let you go back to your apartment?"

"I just assumed that I was."

"Look," he takes a deep breath, "if you aren't comfortable staying at my place, I can take you somewhere else. But I would really like it if you stayed with me so that I know you are safe."

I sit and ponder this for a moment before I squeeze his hand. "I have no place I would rather be." And I mean it. Reid smiles before he turns his attention back to the road and eases through the light. A few minutes later, we turn on a road that is very familiar.

My heart stops and drops to the pit of my stomach. My throat dries and I find myself struggling to breathe. It's the same road that leads up to the *house*, the one I grew up in and didn't have the nerve to sell after I made the drastic life change. Whether I like it or not, it's a part of me, a part of my past, and it will always be with me. That is something I can't change.

A few minutes later, we are pulling through large iron gates not very far away from my childhood home. I turn my head slightly as we drive past the gate, gaze up to the top of the hill, and see that the house is still standing there, as majestic and beautiful as it was the last time I laid eyes on it. A tear stings my eye, and I casually wipe it away, hoping that Reid doesn't notice. I turn my head back down the winding driveway when a large house appears in front of it. I hold back laughter when I see it. The house is just what I expected when we had pulled into the front of the cabin house in the woods.

Large white columns line the front of the equally white three story house. Perfectly trimmed rose bushes edge the walkway up to the grand double doors. Reid pulls to a stop in front of the house and is at my door in the blink of an eye. I smile as I place my hand into his, and he leads me towards the house.

When I reach the doors, I see the wood is carved with an incredibly intricate design. The detail in the wood is beautiful, and I stare for a moment at the twirl and swirls of the lines before Reid pushes open the door on the left hand side. We step into a grand foyer, much like the one in the house I grew up in. "So this is it," he says softly.

"It's beautiful." And it really is. I let go of his hand and walk to the center of the foyer, spinning in a slow circle. The floor is checkered with black and white tiles. A larger chandelier dangles above our heads. The ceiling has a beautiful mural gracing it, like da Vinci himself rose from the dead and painted it, and the staircase is made of dark mahogany wood.

"There's time to see the rest of the house later," he says softly. "Let's get you settled into your room."

My room? For the past two weeks, we've been sharing space. Whether we fall asleep on the couch or upstairs in bed, I've gotten used to his arms holding me tightly against his chest, and feeling his warmth invade me. Now we're going into separate rooms. The thought is absurd, and I almost say so as he leads me up the stairs. Maybe I am just overthinking things, and maybe he isn't trying to push me.

I follow him down a long hall off to the right of the top of the staircase. Photographs line the walls on both sides, much like the ones in the cabin, but here they are a bit different. Instead of just photos of his mother and him, they are family photos with his mother, a man I presume to be his father, and another male who seems to be a few years older than him but practically identical. I don't remember Reid ever mentioning he had a brother. I almost ask him about it but throw the thought aside just as quickly.

If he wanted me to know about any siblings, he would have told me. I can't start prying into his life when I have secrets of my own that I am unwilling to share. I know I am being selfish, but the thought that he is keeping something from me tugs at my heart. Reid has been nothing but completely honest with me. Now, I am beginning to wonder if I really know him all that well. Granted, he's been an open book, answering any questions that I have, but this is big. Having a brother is not something that you easily forget.

You're one to talk. I shake my head and try to escape my inner critic.

We stop in front of a simple white door. Reid glances back at me and smiles before he opens it. The door opens into a large room, just as breathtaking as the rest of the house. Huge windows across the room overlook a beautifully sculpted backyard. To my right is a large stone fireplace built into the wall with a small sitting area placed in front of it. A large four poster, canopy bed rests on top of a raised platform to my left. Thick embroidered cream colored drapes surround the bed, which are tied to the poles at the end of the bed, revealing a matching bedspread that seems like pure luxury.

"I'll let you get settled in," Reid says as he pulls me into his arms and brushes his lips against my forehead. "My room is just across the hall." I pull my head back and gaze up at him. A wicked grin spreads across his face, and he winks at me before exiting the room.

I walk across the room and throw myself on the bed. Lying there, I feel as though I am on cloud nine. The softness of the silky material brushes against my skin, and I sink deeper into the bed. I let out a deep sigh before pushing myself up and scanning the rest of the room. I see a set of double doors off to the corner of the room and decide to go investigate. I have an idea of what is behind the doors, and the thought alone excites me. I can use a nice hot bubble bath right about now.

The last thing I expect to see when I pull open the doors is a fully stocked closet with clothes in about my size. My excitement of finding the bathroom quickly diminishes and turns into rage. I don't know why I am angry over the wardrobe. Any woman would love to find a new closet full of clothes, but I am beyond pissed. I turn on my heels, storm out of the closet that is nearly the size of my room, and head straight for the room Reid said was his.

I don't knock before barging into Reid's room, and I am caught off guard when I see him shirtless. Yes, I have seen him shirtless more times than I can count over the last few weeks, but it always takes my breath away. I forget for a moment why I am in his room and take the time to admire his smooth, perfectly carved chest. My eyes finally land on the V-cut just above the top of his linen pajama bottoms. I hear Reid clear his throat and feel the heat of embarrassment rushing to my cheeks from being caught. "See something you like?"

"Y-y-yes…" I manage to say. I shake my head and glare at him. "I mean no. Stop trying to distract me. What the hell is that in my bedroom?"

He smiles and shrugs his shoulders. "I don't know what you are talking about."

"Oh no," I say, slightly irritated. I narrow my eyes on him and begin to stalk across the room like a lioness after her prey. "You know exactly what I am talking about." The smile disappears off Reid's face when he realizes I am being quite serious. "The monstrosity in my closet. What is up with all the clothes?" I stop just in front of him and cross my arms over my chest. "I don't need your charity."

"It isn't charity. I-I-I thought you would like some clothes for work."

I send a shooting glare at him. "I have clothes. If I wanted more, I would have had you stop by my apartment." Reid says nothing and drops his gaze from mine. I know I'm overreacting, but for some reason, the whole situation is getting under my skin. "Reid…" I reach out to touch his arm, and he pulls away from me.

"You're right. I'll send them back tomorrow." He turns and heads towards what I assume is his closet. My anger quickly dissipates, turning into guilt. Why did I overreact about this? It's just a bunch of clothes. I'm sure he didn't mean anything by it, other than to making me comfortable. He probably didn't think I would be feeling up to swinging by my apartment to grab more, which would be correct. Reid might have slightly gone overboard, but he meant well. Feeling defeated, I take a deep breath and follow him into the closet.

I can't find him anywhere until I see light shining from underneath a door to my right and hear water running. I knock slightly, giving warning to my entrance, before I open the door. Reid is standing at the sink with shaving cream on his chin. "You're going to shave?" I ask weakly. I take another step towards him. "I love the scruff."

Reid doesn't respond. I cast my eyes down towards the floor, afraid to look at him, but I can feel his eyes on me. "I'm sorry," I whisper. "I overreacted. It's just… you could have warned me about the clothes."

I feel his arms come around me and pull me close to him. I take a deep breath, inhaling the scent that is only Reid, and relax in his arms. "We were both wrong." He laughs deeply. "But we were both right. I should have told you about the clothes. I just wanted to surprise you."

"I hate surprises," I mumble into his chest. I can feel his laughter vibrating through me.

"I know."

I pull back and gaze up at him. I press my lips against his. He breaks free first. "Liza?" He laughs softly. "You have cream on your face."

"I don't care."

I press against him again, straining to reach his lips again, but he holds me back. "Let me get this cleaned off, and then we can make something to eat and watch a movie."

"It's a date."

Chapter Twenty-Two

THE KITCHEN IN this house would be every chef's dream. The space is enormous. My entire apartment can fit inside of it. Everything about this room screams finesse, from the spacious black granite counter tops that provide enough room that you could prepare all the food you need to serve a seven course meal on it and still have room for desert. The cherry colored oak cupboards are filled with everything you could imagine needing for cooking and snacking. The double door refrigerator secretly flush against wall holds practically every refreshment known to mankind and the widest variety of beer and wine selections. All the appliances, including the double oven, is black. The thing that wins me over the most, however, is the dishwasher. My rinky-dink, rundown apartment doesn't have one of them, and I have grown tired of washing dishes by hand.

I don't claim to be a master chef, but I like to think that I know my way around a kitchen. Which is why Reid sat at the breakfast bar nursing a dark ale beer as I whipped around, cooking up a storm. "Where do you keep the whisks?" I ask over my shoulder while adding some salt and pepper to the bowl of eggs sitting in front of me. I hear Reid laugh and stop long enough to look at him. The tip of the neck of the beer rests against his lips, and he is smirking. "What? What is so funny?"

Reid sets the beer down on top of the counter and walks towards me. He reaches up with his thumb and wipes my nose. "You had a bit of flour on your nose." I feel my cheeks blush and turn back to keep prepping the food. A long arm reaches around me and holds a whisk in front of my face.

"Thank you," I say and take it out of Reid's hand. "Now I have some eggs and pancakes to make. Let the chef work."

"You know…" Reid's voice becomes softer as he crosses the kitchen. "I could get used to this."

"To what?"

"Watching you cook in my kitchen."

"Oh yeah?" I ask. I continue beating the eggs with one hand and use my free hand to throw a handful of bell peppers into the mixing bowl. "Well, don't get used to it. I'm only cooking because I'm hungry, too."

Another loud laugh escapes Reid. The witty banter flows between us easily as I continue to cook dinner. Some people may hate the idea of breakfast foods for dinner, but nothing comforts me more than a plate full of pancakes, my signature scrambled eggs, and bacon.

Once the food is done, we eat at the breakfast bar. Reid is still sipping his beer, and I have orange juice for myself. When we clear our plates, Reid picks them up, rinses them off in the sink, and places them in the dishwasher. He finishes his beer and disposes of it in a recycling bin hiding underneath the stainless steel double sink.

We decide to head back upstairs to his room and watch a movie. As we approach his room, butterflies begin to flutter around in my stomach. I don't know why I am nervous. It's not like we haven't lay next to each other in a bed before. It still doesn't help, though. All through dinner, Reid remained shirtless, and it began to stir feelings inside of me that I forgot even existed until I met him.

Inside of his room again, I actually take a moment to really glance around his room. It's clean and elegant like the rest of the house. A fire is burning in the fireplace across the room, and I can't remember if it was burning the first time I came in here. The room is much like the room he deemed as mine, with the exception of his bed. Instead of a canopy bed, his is larger, resting on top of a raised platform, with slick black linens neatly tucked in at all the corners. Several pillows line the top of the bed against a very elegant, wooden headboard carved with a design I can't quite make out. At the end of his bed is the only thing that doesn't seem to fit in with the rest of the house, a huge, battered chest with a large padlock on it.

More secrets?

I try not to think about it. I am a total walking contradiction. Of course, he must have some things he hasn't shared with me. I don't like the thought of him keeping things hidden from me however. I mean, yes, it's only fair that he keeps things hidden from me, but Reid is seemingly perfect in my eyes. It slightly frightens me what kind of secrets he has that he feels he can't share with me. *God, I'm such a wench.*

I watch Reid grab a series of remotes of the nightstand next to his bed, hit a button, and can barely contain the squeal of surprise that escapes my lips as I witness a TV raise out from the edge of his bed. How is that even possible? I glance up at Reid, who has a slight smile on his face, but deeper down I can see the traces of uneasiness creeping in. Glad I'm not the only one who feels nervous for some reason. He motions for me to sit down on the bed as he hits another button and the wall near his bed begins to shift and reveals the biggest movie collection I have ever seen. I shift nervously on his bed in anticipation as I wait to see what he puts on. He climbs onto the bed next to me and drapes his arm across my shoulder, pulling me closer to him. It feels so right to be there with him, sitting on his bed, snuggling, and watching a movie like any normal couple. Yet I still don't know where we stand.

"Reid?" I pull away and stare at him. He gazes back at me and raises an eyebrow. "What are we?" I ask quickly. He tilts his head at me and eyes me curiously, like he doesn't understand my question. "What I mean to say is… what are we doing? Are we dating? Are we exclusive?"

"I feel sorry for any man who even thinks about touching you. You are *mine.*" It isn't the exact answer I am searching for, but if I can't understand what he means by that, then I clearly need to go back to school. I lean back against him with a smile plastered on my face and my heart beating rapidly.

As we wait for the previews to finish playing, my mind races with a thousand thoughts. What am I thinking? I can't be in a relationship, yet I want to be. But how can the two of us really be in a relationship if the both of us are hiding things from each other? I'm about to spill my life story to him when I see the menu for the DVD come on and begin to laugh. "Friday the 13th?"

"I recall you telling me that you have an unhealthy obsession with all things horror."

"That I do." *Amongst many other things, including you.* I settle in next to him, amped to be watching one of my favorite movies.

Halfway through the movie, I try to ignore the fact that Reid's hand has lowered itself to the top of my leggings, tracing circles along my waist. I press my body closer to him, kissing his neck, and smile when he moans in pleasure. Desire comes over me, and I begin to leave a trail of kisses down his neck and his still bare chest. Slowly, one kiss after another, I make my way down his chest. His grip on my waist tightens as I make my way back up his body and kiss his neck again.

"Liza…" he says, straining for control.

"Hmm?" I whisper, leaving another kiss along his chin. I flip over so I am straddling his lap and place a kiss against his lips.

"Liza…" he says again, his voice sounding more like a warning this time.

I laugh against his mouth and let out a low growl. "Just shut up and kiss me." Reid pulls me down against his body, one hand lightly gripping a handful of hair as he presses his lips against mine. I can feel his erection growing through our clothes, and I begin to grind against him. Another moan escapes from him, and he stops kissing me to look at me.

"Are you sure?" he asks softly.

I say nothing and just nod my head. I let out a yelp when he quickly flips me over onto my back and kisses along my collarbone. His fingers line the hem of my shirt. I take a deep breath as he begins to slowly lift up the bottom of my shirt. He stops once my jagged scar is revealed. I watch him, waiting to see if I can see disgust in his eyes, if he finds my mutilated body a horror. I inhale a sharp breath when he presses his lips against the biggest bulge of scar tissue protruding from my skin and lightly kisses it. "Beautiful," he whispers. Another kiss on my scar. "Every part of you is absolutely beautiful." He continues to leave kisses across my abdomen as he lifts my shirt higher until he pulls it over my head. Lying there in my bra, I feel completely vulnerable, but I don't move.

He kisses the corner of my mouth, cupping one of my breasts in his hand and massaging it. The feeling sets my body on fire, igniting a spark I thought burned out a long time ago. I press my body against him again, trying to get as close as I possibly can, and search for his lips until I find them with mine. My lips slightly part, and his tongue slips into my mouth. Our tongues begin to dance, darting around quickly. I dig my hands into his back, bringing his chest crushing down on mine, and moan out in pleasure.

Reid reaches underneath me and unclasps my bra, setting my breasts free. He breaks away from the kiss, much to my disappointment, and kisses me on my chin. A moan of pleasure escapes my throat when he takes my breast into his mouth. His tongue flicks across my nipple and he alternates the sensation with slight nips of his teeth. One hand caresses my other breast, pinching the nipple between his thumb and finger, tugging on it. His other hand slips down my leggings, rubbing against my folds over my underwear, and I struggle to keep from moving. I run my hands over his broad shoulders, feeling each cut of his muscle, and slide my hands down his backside. Slowly, I bring my hands around to the front and slip one into his pants. Reid moans as I grip his length and begin running my hand up and down. I'm taken aback by the size of him. Even with my inexperience, I know he's bigger than average, but nothing I don't think I can handle.

Touching him unleashes a caged animal, and he quickly strips my leggings off, leaving me wearing nothing but my lace underwear. "You have no idea what you do to me," he says in a heavy voice. He crushes his lips against mine, pressing his erection against the very thin material that covers me, and my body vibrates with arousal. I use my feet to slide his pajama bottoms down, and he springs free. Reid stops kissing me and traces a path down my body once more, stopping to give attention to my breasts before continuing downwards. He hooks his fingers into my underwear and pulls them down. I take a breath. No going back now, and nothing but pure excitement courses through my veins.

He gently presses his lips onto my folds and slowly slips his tongue in between. My body shudders; pure ecstasy is pulsing through my veins. His tongue darts around, pressing closer to the spot that sends my toes curling, and I scream out in pleasure. "Oh. My. God! Don't stop."

A low growl sounds from Reid as he sends me further over the edge. Just as I am about to climax, he pulls his tongue out of me, and I moan. "Are you sure you want this?" Reid stares at me. His normally dark eyes are hazy with pleasure, and I nod my head. "I promise to go easy." I bite down on my lower lip as he enters me. I wince at the discomfort, but it is quickly replaced with the feeling of ecstasy again. "Oh fuck, you're so tight," Reid says through gritted teeth. "You feel so good."

"Faster," I say breathlessly. Reid begins to pump faster, and I can feel my orgasm growing. "I'm going to come!" I scream.

"We'll go together," he says. I match Reid thrust for thrust, and we cry out together as we let our release go. He collapses on top of me, panting and breathless, and he brushes the hair out of my face and smiles. "You are so beautiful…" He kisses me. "I'm falling in love with you."

I still. I tighten my hold on Reid, not allowing him to pull up and look at me, and my mind is a cluster of thoughts. It's all too much. Going from swearing off men, to being in a relationship, to having sex. I can't deal with this emotion. But his words melt my heart, and I know I love him, too, whether I will admit it or not.

"Me, too," I whisper and kiss him again. We stay like that for a few minutes longer before he pulls out of me, and I don't want him to go. I want to lie like that forever, just him and me, in our own little world. Reid helps me up off his bed, leading me to the bathroom, and turns on the series of showerheads. I step into the waterfall cascading down on us, pull Reid against me, and kiss him. After a few minutes of kissing and touching, Reid takes me again against the marble wall of his shower. I know in that moment I will never get enough of him. No matter how hard I try.

Chapter Twenty-Three

I NEVER MADE IT back to my room last night. I never even made it back into my clothes. After our rendezvous in the shower, we had sex three more times in his bed, stopping only long enough to get a couple of hours of sleep before work this morning. Now, as I stand in the closet full of clothes, I fight to keep my eyes open. I'm exhausted, and my body is sore in a good way. I feel awakened, like I have been asleep the last six years of my life. I spot a black dress hanging on the left side of the closet, and though I haven't seen the entire collection yet, I know it's the perfect dress to wear on my first day back.

I pull the dress off the rack, finding it's plain and simple and short. I know once I put it on it will only be long enough to cover my goods. Worse, it's strapless. Definitely not office attire, but I don't care. I feel great and want to keep this feeling going. This is the perfect dress for it. I slip on the dress; the tight elastic material clings to me in all the right places and accents my body in a way that I didn't know possible. I decide to tone the dress down with a simple pair of flats and some basic jewelry. I leave my hair down and apply very minimal makeup. The dress is more than enough for me, and while I'm feeling brave, I'm not that brave. I grab a long, white pea coat on my way out.

I leave the closet and skip over to Reid's room, unable to hide my excitement to see his expression when he sees the dress I am in. Reid stumbles over himself when he walks out of his closet, his jaw drops and his eyes widen. "Please tell me you're wearing something over that?" he says in a serious voice as he struggles to straighten his tie.

"Relax," I walk towards him, "I grabbed a jacket." I point to the white coat on his bed and laugh. Reid relaxes his shoulders and relief washes over his face. I grab a hold of his tie and smile. "Here, let me help you." I straighten his tie and help him slip on his jacket. The man looks amazing in a suit, but I prefer him naked. The thought makes me giggle out loud like a school girl.

"What's so funny?" He glances at me and raises an eyebrow.

"Nothing." I kiss him quickly before turning and grabbing my jacket off the bed. "Let's go make people talk."

*   *   *

My happy mood is gone as we enter the building. The playful, brave, adventurous woman I met this morning is slowly disappearing. What was I thinking about, wearing this dress to the office? What was I thinking about, coming to work with Reid? I'm clearly out of my mind, but it's too late to go back and change my outfit now. My palms are sweaty as Reid and I head towards the elevator. I can feel everyone in the lobby eyeing us. I know they can't see the dress underneath the pea coat, but I might as well have come to work naked with how I'm feeling. I notice that no one is really paying Reid much attention, focused instead on the woman hanging from his arm as he whispers sweet nothings in her ear, and that woman is me. "What's wrong?" Reid's voice snaps me out of my haze on the elevator.

"I-I-I, uh... everyone was staring at us," I say.

"Well, let's give them something to stare at." We're alone in the elevator, so I don't know what he is thinking when he said that. He pulls me close, our bodies pressing against one another, and his mouth crashes against mine. His tongue darts into my mouth and starts the familiar dance with mine. I hear a collective gathering of gasps, whispers, and it snaps me out of the kiss. I glance around and find that we are standing in the elevator with the doors wide open on our floor. "We have nothing to be embarrassed about," Reid whispers in my ear. "We're just two people in love." With that, he kisses my temple and walks away with a grin on his face, leaving me there to face everyone on my own. I lower my head and quickly make my way through the seemingly endless cubicles and desks until I reach my office and close the door behind me.

I lean against the door and sigh. Until I remember that my office has glass windows and everyone can still see me. I grab the string above my door and close the blinds over the window before going and closing the rest of the blinds. I sink down into my chair and stare at the ceiling for several minutes before I snake out of my jacket and hang it over the back of my chair. I stare at my computer screen that is glowing in front of me. I no longer dread turning it on and staring at the hoard of query letters I once would struggle to read. No, over the couple weeks I was at the cabin, Reid helped me through that problem. What frightened me was the possibility of any anonymous emails awaiting me. I have forgotten about them momentarily, being so caught up in Reid, and now here I am. Back in the real world and back into contact with technology.

I turn on my computer, waiting for it to boot up, and tap the tip of a pen against my desk. When my email loads, I hold my breath, and slowly release it when I see that no haunting emails are waiting for me. Unless you count Viola as frightening, but I am about to remedy that problem now. I read the couple emails she sent while I was in la-la land with Reid and can't help but laugh at them. Finally after the last one, I respond with a quick email and let her know that I have decided to sign two authors, which was the truth, and am making headway on signing another.

I work through the morning, reading letter after letter, lost in thought, and jump when my office door flies open. I look over and see Reid standing there. He closes the door and leans up against it. "Would it be possible to talk you into taking a break and grabbing some lunch with me?"

"I thought you'd never ask."

As we leave the office, I realize that Heidi isn't behind her desk, just like she wasn't the last time I was in the office, and she was replaced with some blonde headed temp. I feel guilty for not knowing why Heidi is absent and wonder if she has been the entire time I was gone. I make a mental note to call her tonight and check on her to make sure she is okay.

We grab lunch at my favorite café down the street, where Reid lets me know that he was going to be staying late at the office all week to catch up from being on vacation. He lets me know that while Lawrence approved our vacation, he certainly wasn't happy that his nephew had taken so much time off as well, but that he sent his well wishes and hoped I was ready to tackle some authors. I feel guilty realizing that I kept Reid away from work, even though he assures me that he wouldn't have it any other way. After lunch, Reid walks me back to my office with promises of picking me up from the house and taking me out to dinner to celebrate our first day back at the office.

*   *   *

Being back at Reid's house alone feels weird. I didn't feel comfortable wandering around without him here. I discover that he has a workout fiend's dream gym in the basement beneath his house, that he basically has a mini movie theater on the far side of his house, as well as an indoor/outdoor pool on the backside of his house. I walk through each room, each as grand as the last, getting myself familiar with the surroundings. I don't know how long I am going to be staying here, and to be honest, I don't want to leave. I know everything is moving fast, but I really don't want to go back to my apartment. I don't want to be alone. I don't want to be without Reid. Eventually, I find myself back in his room. Curiosity wins the best of me, and I begin to snoop around. It is wrong, and I know it, but I can't help myself. I try to open the chest but the padlock is secure.

I search for a key, digging through the large mahogany desk near the fireplace, and come up empty. I move onto the nightstand near his bed. I pull out the first drawer and find nothing of importance. The bottom drawer gives a bit of a fight but I finally manage to tug it open, but inside is only two items facing downward. I pick up the first item, which is a picture frame, and turn it over. My breath hitches when I see the framed picture. In the picture is a beautiful brunette. She seems young, happy, and in love. She isn't alone, however. In the photo, Reid is standing next to her, grinning from ear to ear, holding a baby bundled in a blue blanket.

He had a family... Tears prick my eyes, and I feel my heart breaking. Yes, keeping secrets about who I really am, and who my family was, is big. I won't deny it. Reid not telling me he might possibly have a brother is big, but it's something I can live with. But not telling me that he once had a wife and a son... I'm not sure that is something I can handle.

I set the picture aside, my hands shaking, and my heart pounding. I pull out the little leather bound book. I turn it over and determine it's a photo album, and I am unsure I want to open it. I do. I open the first page, and the first photo is a close up of the brunette laughing. She looks absolutely heavenly. On the next page is an ultrasound with the name Lily Harder, and a lump forms in my throat, and I struggle to swallow it down. I shouldn't be snooping, but I can't help it. The next series of photos are of her growing belly. Reid and the male I saw in the photographs in the hall make an occasional appearance. The pictures turn to photos of the most handsome baby boy I have ever seen. Several of them have Reid holding the baby and beaming like a proud father.

The tears rush down my face. Why wouldn't he have told me about them? *The same reason you haven't told him about yourself,* my inner critic taunts me. I hear someone clear their throat, and I quickly glance up and see Reid standing in front of me, several feet away. "I-I-I…" I'm at a loss for words. "I shouldn't have been snooping."

His eyes are dark, and he is tense. He says nothing as he closes the distance between us and sits down on the bed on the other side of where I placed the framed photograph. "Lily," he says softly, staring down at the picture. My heart shatters when he says her name, as if it's a confirmation of what I have been thinking since I came across the photos. I didn't want it to be true, but the way he is acting only makes it real. "She was my sister-in-law…" *Wait, what?* "This is Ollie," he points to the baby, "my nephew. They died in a house fire." His words are weak, and I have no idea what to say. He stares at the photos for a few more seconds before placing them back into the drawer. For some reason, I feel like he isn't telling me the whole story, but I don't question him.

"I didn't know you had a brother." I finally break the silence. Reid glances at me and nods his head. His eyes are still dark, and anger is burning in them. "The guys in the photo? Are they your father and brother?" He nods again. "I-I-I'm really sorry… I shouldn't have invaded your privacy."

He reaches out and pulls me against his chest. Tears prick my eyes as I feel for his loss. "Don't worry about it. I should have told you about them," he says. He sounds distant, and I get the feeling I'm still not getting the whole story. "Now," he kisses the top of my head, "I do believe I promised you dinner."

The change of subject makes me realize that he doesn't want to talk about it or them. So I squeeze him tighter and nod my head. "Yes, I do believe you did."

Chapter Twenty-Four

THE RIDE TO THE RESTAURANT is tense. I apologize profusely to Reid a million times for poking my head around, and he reassures me that it isn't a big deal. He is still distant, and I wonder what it will take for him to open up to me. I think about telling him something about myself, if not all of it, but I still can't seem to get the words to form correctly. So I sit in the passenger seat, my head pressing against the cool window, and watch as the buildings pass us by. Mozart quietly plays in the background as we pull up in front of a restaurant. It's a newer one that just opened up in town, and I hadn't had the chance to try it out yet.

The restaurant is quaint, nothing too rich and extravagant, just perfect for a dinner date. Reid parks the car in the back parking area, rounds the car, and helps me out in typical Reid fashion. He rests his hand on my lower back, guides me around the small building, and through the entrance. Inside, the place is warm and inviting. Small, round, intimate tables are placed throughout the dining area with candle lights. The walls are painted a deep red, and a fire is burning in a grand fireplace on the farthest side of the room. Over half of the tables are filled, and the waitress leads us to a back corner table. I shed my jacket, still wearing the dress I wore to the office today, and take a seat with my back against the wall.

Reid smiles, "Have I told you how delectable you are in that dress?"

"Well, if you play your cards right, you may win the right to help me out of it tonight." I grin, seizing the moment to soak up our normal repartee. "Maybe I'll even let you have some dessert if you're a good boy." A low growl vibrates across the table, and I smile again.

The waitress comes back to fill our glasses with some wine and hands us our menus. I decide to try the chicken linguine, and Reid orders a steak with some sides. As we drink our wine, we talk about everything except for the incident in the bedroom earlier. Reid carries most of the conversation, careful to drive the topic away from my discovery. I'm sure he realizes that I know what he is doing, but I say nothing and go with the flow of conversation. The food arrives, and it's as good as it sounded. I steal a few bites of Reid's steak throughout dinner and wish I had ordered it for myself. The steak is marinated in an amazing sauce and melts right in your mouth. It is like a combination of flavors bursting in your mouth between the red wine and the seasonings. Reid takes care of the bill, and as we start to leave the restaurant, I see the last person I expected to see. On his arm is someone who looks eerily familiar, but I couldn't place her.

"Elias?" Eli stops and glances between Reid and I. He tenses but puts on his best fake smile. Since I saw him the last time in my apartment, he's cut his hair and lost some weight. Not that he needed to, but he has. His eyes look baggy, as if he hasn't slept in weeks, and just the sight of him makes my heart break.

"Oh hey, Liza," he says softly, and his eyes flicker towards Reid again. "How are you doing? Are you okay?"

"I tried to call…" My words hang in the air. "But you never answer."

"I've been busy."

"Too busy to talk to your best friend?" My voice begins to get slightly louder as the irritation builds. He glances back at the dark haired woman that came in with him, and I squint my eyes. I can't help but think how familiar she seems. She shrinks behind Eli, as if to hide from my glaring eyes. "If you didn't want to talk to me, you could've just told me, instead of ignoring me like we were in high school again."

"Can we have this conversation another time? My date and I came to have dinner." I can't believe him. He is dismissing me over some broad he is here with, someone I don't even know. *Why not?* I did the same thing with him when I chose Reid over my best friend.

"I'm sorry," I say softly, tears brimming my eyes, and I walk past him. I glance over my shoulder as I open the door and see Reid has pulled him off to the side. He is whispering, but I can see he is not happy, and I am surprised when I see Reid clap a hand on his shoulder, nod his head, and head in my direction. "What was that about?"

"Just two grown men having a chat," Reid answers.

I walk faster to the car, irritated beyond belief. My first official date with Reid since we became a couple has not gotten the start or ending I was hoping. Reid unlocks the car with the button in his hand, and I climb into the car, slamming the door behind me. Reid sits down in the car, puts the key into the ignition, but doesn't turn it. "I hate secrets, you know," I say, staring straight out the window.

"For someone who hates them so much, you seem to have quite a bit yourself." His voice is harsh. I turn my head towards him and sigh. He doesn't glance at me, starts the car, and eases out of the parking spot. *Touché, Mr. Harder, touché.*

The drive back to his house is awkward, and the tension is stronger than it was on the car ride over. I am just ready for the night to be over. Maybe I will be sleeping in my own bed tonight. How can yesterday be one of the most perfect nights in the world and today turn into a mess? The story of my life. Sure, I have no one else to blame but myself. I barely wait for Reid to park the car before I am quickly flying out of the passenger seat and making my way up to the front door. Tears streak my face as I try to punch in the code to his door. My body is shaking and I just want to crawl into bed. This is all my fault. I'm damaged goods. I'm single-handedly ruining the best thing that has ever happened to me, because I can't just spit out the damn truth.

All my fears, all my doubts, all my self-criticism is slowly breaking me down. Ruining a chance of happiness before it has even lifted off the ground. I can't do it. I can't keep stringing him along. I can't set myself up for heartbreak again. I've had my heart broken before, and I will not let it happen again. Eventually, Reid is going to get sick of my double standards. He is going to start despising the fact that I expect him to share every part of himself with me and only give him a part of me. Although he claims that he'd rather have only a part of me than none at all, I can't really expect him to hold onto that. One day, he's going to wake up, and realize he doesn't want that anymore, that he doesn't want me anymore, and I will be left shattered in a million pieces again.

I hear Reid call out to me as I push open the door and rush to the stairs. I make my way down the hall leading to my room, where I left my duffle bag yesterday when we arrived. I never unpacked, so it'll be easy to grab and leave.

"What are you doing?" I hear Reid say behind me. I stop, glance back at him, and see him standing in the doorway.

"I can't do this." I take a deep breath and snag the bag off the bed. "I thought I could, but I can't. So I'm going home."

"I'm not going to let you run away when things start to get tough. It may have worked in the past, but it's not going to work now." I try to push past him, and he stops me. "I won't let you Liza; it's time to stop running." He pulls me against his chest, and I sag against him. "I'm not letting you go so easily. Do you not get it? I... love... you. All of you. The good, and the frustrating. Just because things have been tense today doesn't mean anything. Some days, things are going to be hard. Some days, we're going to fight. We're going to scream and shout. We're going to disagree, whether it's about what color of sheets we want or how to wash laundry. That's what couples do. That's what people who are in love do. They call each other on their bullshit, they fight, and then they have the most amazing make up sex."

I laugh against his chest. "But I'm lying to you. I can't even open up to you. One day you're going to get sick of my secrets and leave."

"You have secrets. So do I. Everyone does, but that's the way of life." He kisses my forehead. "I will never leave you unless you tell me to. You hold that power. You have my heart in your hands."

"You're perfect," I whisper and tighten my arms around him. "Absolutely perfect."

"Not perfect... just right." I can't disagree with him. I know he's wrong, but I'll let him think he is right for now. One day, he will get sick of me, and he will leave. I just have to prepare myself for that day. "What do you say to a bath?"

I never, ever want to leave Reid's bathroom or bathtub. With the jets, the bubbles, and the never-ending candles providing the only light in the room, I am in heaven. Of course, the only way I will stay is if Reid agrees to never leave. I snuggle against him in the crook of his legs, and he holds me tight. Classical music plays softly over the speakers in the bathroom. When the music first came on, I searched around the bathroom for any sign of them and found none. I quickly gave up the search when Reid joined me. I close my eyes and rest my head against his chest, listening to his heart beating steadily beneath me.

We stay in the bathtub until our skin becomes like prunes, wrinkly and old looking. Reid holds out the towel for me as I step out of the tub and dries me off. He wraps the towel around me, and I can't help staring at his naked torso as he repeats the process on himself. He really is a sight to behold. Neither of dress as we head back into his bedroom. He shows me how to work the controls that bring up the TV and how to access his collection of movies. I stick with the horror theme from the other night and go with *Halloween*. Halfway through the movie, Reid lets me know that I don't have to go into the office tomorrow if I don't want to. He already cleared it with his uncle. I don't know if I should be happy or angry that he assumed I wouldn't be up for work tomorrow, but I'm glad he thought of me. The idea of missing more work kills me, but after the day I had, I really can use another day off. So I tell him that I will stay home and just relax for the day.

Something Reid said earlier stuck with me. It is time for me to stop running from my past, and I know exactly how to do it. Tomorrow, I will adventure up to the house I have avoided like the plague for the last six years. I will face my inner demons. I will overcome all the pain and suffering I have locked away. It is time to move on, and I want to with Reid. The only way I can do that is returning to the place that haunts my nightmares, and then tell Reid the truth about everything. And I mean *everything*.

Sometime, after another night of lovemaking, I finally manage to fall into a fitful sleep. For the first time in weeks, I have another nightmare, but it's not the one with my mother blaming me for her death. Rather it's one of the house, the one I grew up in. I am wandering around, searching for a way out, but I am trapped, and the walls are caving in on me. I wake up in a panic, gasping for air, and sweat pouring off of me. The sun is just beginning to rise and filter in through the large windows next to the bed. I peek over at Reid, who is still peacefully sleeping, and brush a strand of his hair out of his face. I pull the covers aside and slip out of the bed. I walk into the bathroom, turn the shower on, slip out of my clothes, and step under the spray.

The hot water beats down on my body as I sit on the floor of the shower. Tears fall down my face, as if a dam has busted open. The nightmare was doing strange things to me, and I can't make any sense of it. I was watching a montage of walking down the familiar hallways as they closed in on me. I don't know if it was the sight of the blood that smeared the walls, or the echoing sound of banging on the doors, is what has me terrified of my plan for the day.

Two strong arms scoop me up off the floor and out of the shower. I can barely make Reid out in the stream of tears steadily falling down my face as he sets me down and wraps a towel around me. "Liza? What's wrong?"

After a few calming breaths, I begin to feel more in control of my emotions and glance up at Reid. His eyebrows are creased, his eyes full of worry, and he is staring at me tenderly. I fight to bring a faint smile to my lips and know I failed when he frowns slightly. "Just another nightmare," my voice comes out softly.

"Want to talk about it?" I shake my head. "Do you have them often?"

"No." Not for a long time at least. "Just occasionally." He pulls me close to him. I can feel his chest rising as he takes a deep breath and releases it slowly. "What are you doing out of bed?"

"I woke up and found your side of the bed empty. I thought you snuck away and left me while I was asleep."

I laugh softly, gaze up at him, and press a kiss against his chin. "You would know it if I was leaving. As you see, I can be quite dramatic when it comes to you."

"I hope you never leave."

His confession tightens around my heart. I will never leave, but nothing is stopping him from walking away one day. Today, I will make sure that doesn't happen. "The same goes for you… unfortunately, you do have to leave me." He glances down at me and raises an eyebrow. "You can't afford to miss any more work, whether your uncle owns the company or not."

Both of us laugh, and this morning's episode is quickly behind us. I get dressed and wait for Reid to get ready for work. I don't wait long before Reid pulls his laptop out of his bag and writes down the password in case I want to access my email account for work and do some work while at the house. After he makes sure I know and have everything I need, he's pulling me into a deep kiss and whispering how I will be invading every thought he has today. I head back into the house when I see his car disappear down the street and go into the kitchen to make something to eat. After breakfast, I head upstairs, pull his laptop onto the top of his bed, and turn it on. I enter the password and wait for it to quickly load and log into my email.

No emails from my stalker. I slowly let a breath of relief out, which is quickly replaced by fear. The silence has gone on long enough. I don't know if this means whoever it is has given up or if it means they are waiting for something. What that is, I don't have any idea. Ignoring the wave of uneasiness, I scan through the emails I do have, randomly choose one, and open it. The author sounds promising; her story sounds like it will be amazing. I read the three required chapters that are in the email and quickly respond with a request for the rest of her manuscript.

I'm finding it easier to filter through the hoard of emails bombarding my inbox. By noon, I have requested full manuscripts from four more authors. I decide to take a break and eat some lunch. I bring the laptop downstairs to the kitchen with me and set it on the breakfast bar while *Panic Station* by Muse blares through the tiny speakers. I dance throughout the kitchen as I search for the ingredients I need to make the meanest grilled cheese sandwich mankind has ever known. With all the ingredients in hand, I start cooking. The music switches over to Justin Timberlake's *Sexy Back*. I laugh softly to myself at Reid's eclectic taste in music, which is very much like my own. Halfway through the song, it cuts off, and I assume it's because the battery has died and keep singing the lyrics out loud, still dancing.

I hear a laugh behind me, one I know intimately, and I freeze. The heat rushes to my face, and I slowly turn around and come face to face with Reid. "If you promise to be doing that every day at lunch time… I promise to be home every day at lunch time." He smiles and pulls me against him.

"Ha ha, very funny. I'll have you know that I am not going to be one of those women who stays at home with bare feet and a million children running around." I snuggle against his chest.

"I didn't think you were. But the idea is appealing." I push away from him and see the humor dancing in his eyes.

"Lunch?" I ask. I wasn't expecting him home for lunch, but I am glad he came. Reid nods his head, and I turn back to make him a sandwich. He laughs softly to himself, and I pause to look at him. "What's so funny?"

"N-n-nothing." His face flushes red at being caught. He sits down on one of the bar stools and watches me. "Don't let me keep you distracted."

With that, I finish making our lunch. I set his plate down in front of him and take a seat next to him. Reid tells me about his uneventful morning at work and how it isn't the same knowing he can't come bother me at my office. I remind him that it's work, not a playground, and that we can't be horsing around. Of course, he doesn't see it that way. He doesn't stay for very long, because he has to get back in time for a meeting, but doesn't leave without pulling me into the most sensational kiss I've ever experienced.

I watch as Reid pulls out of the driveway and sag against the door frame, missing him already. He's going to be late again at the office. Once his car is no longer in sight, I close the door and head back into the kitchen. I stop at the computer and see that it hasn't died, but rather he paused the song. I push play and begin to dance around as the song begins to fill the room again. I look through the pantry and refrigerator in search of what to prepare for dinner tonight. I settle on making some lemon pepper salmon with a nice fresh salad and a glass of wine. With dinner decided and Reid on his way back to work, I am left with nothing to do but get back on the computer and do some more work.

My luck has run out from this morning. None of the emails I read sound appealing, none are eye catching, and none give me the sense that I have to request more from the author or I will regret it. After a couple more hours, I decide to take a break, prep what I need to for dinner, and grab a plate full of cookies and a glass of milk before getting back on the computer. After about an hour of reading absolute nonsense, like an author who wrote a book about a girl who can't decide between three men she claims to love and which one to marry.

Sure, the book might sell, readers love these kind of things. They love a woman torn between X amount of men. I just don't want my name tied to a story like this. To something I don't believe in. No way. Call me critical, call me whatever you please, but I stand by my beliefs and my decisions. I check the box next to the email and send it to the trash. Just as I do so, my inbox beeps with a new message. My heart drops when I see that it's from an unknown user. I hesitate before finally clicking it open.

From: Unknown Sender
To: LWinter@hlah.com
It seems as though the two love birds have finally come back to reality. I do hope, darling, that you make a move soon and tell lover boy the truth before I do. Or before something happens to him. Let's not forget your dear, sweet friend Elias. Rumor has it that you guys had quite the showdown at a quaint little restaurant downtown. However, it seems as though you have made your choice. Watch your back and that lovesick puppy of yours. You never know when I'm coming for either one of you.

I delete the email, more determined than ever to get to the bottom of this. First things first, I have a trip to make, the one I have put off all day, and then I'll tell Reid everything— including this anonymous stalker of mine. Then, I will track whoever it is threatening me and the ones I love deeply and put an end to all this bull, and to them. With a new found strength, I close the laptop and head upstairs. I pull on the first pair of jeans, T-shirt, and flats I find. I pull my slightly wet hair back in a ponytail. I make my way through the house and exit through the front door, slamming it behind me.

This all ends today.

I am no longer going to hide. I am no longer going to be ashamed of who my parents are, what my mother did, or what my father did. Their actions are no longer going to define me. I am my own person, and today is the first time I start to own up to that. Today I am taking a stand. Today I begin to live life the way I want to and not the way my fears want me to. My fears will no longer control my actions. With determination, I leave the driveway and head up the street towards the house I have always feared.

Chapter Twenty-Five

THE SKY IS BURSTING with shades of pink as the sun sets. The temperature is quickly dropping, and I wrap my arms tightly around myself. As I reach the end of the driveway, I see the house coming into view. The grand, crisp white structure towers over me as I reach the end of the circular driveway. It's a picturesque sight, a home that people can only dream of, a place where they dream of raising a family in, a place where memories are made. The house is a house of dreams, but to me it's a house of horror.

Nothing good has ever come from this place. This house is the very place that haunts me deep in the night. A constant reminder of what little I had that was stripped away from me. My mind is telling my body to move, to step away from the beautiful marble fountain that sits in front of the house. To take one step at a time until I reach the elegant double doors, but my body refuses to listen. I am frozen in place, trapped in the memories of what this house means to me. I can barely breathe, my heart is pounding in my chest, and my knees are shaking. For a split second, I wish Eli was here with me, but I quickly dismiss the thought. Immediately, my mind goes to Reid, but I still haven't told him about this part of my past— yet. Maybe it's better this way. Maybe it's better to face my demons alone.

With a deep breath, I slowly move to the front door. I pull out the key, insert it into the lock, and turn it without a struggle. I step through the door, and it's like I've been transported back into time. My vision tunnels, my heart races, and all I can see is blood. Tears stream down my face as I try to regain some control of my emotions, but it's no use. No matter how many times I blink my eyes, shake my head, or how many breaths I take, all I can see is red. I close my eyes, slowly inhaling through my nose and exhaling out of my mouth.

"Fear doesn't control you. Own your fears. Take control. Face your demons." I repeat the words that my therapist has told me on more than one occasion. I say them over and over again until I can feel the power behind them begin to strengthen, and I finally open my eyes and see the blood is gone.

Everything seems to be just as it had all my life. Everything has been restored to all its former glory. The blood has been cleaned up, and the broken furniture has been replaced with exact replicas, just as I had ordered. The marble floor glistens under the sun filtering through the windows in the vaulted ceilings above, the sun's rays bouncing off the chandelier and dancing along the walls, and the stairs have been restored to the way they looked before the murder. Time has a way of changing things. However, it's as if time hasn't touched this room at all.

The scent of fresh roses pulls me back into the vicious cycle of nightmares as I begin to climb up the stairs. The memory of the bloodshed begins to taunt me, and I can see it again. Finding my mother battered and dead hits me full force, as well as my father making a move to attack me next. My hand subconsciously moves to the jagged scar along my abdomen, and I gently rub it. As I reach the top of the landing, I swear I can hear the soft sounds of a piano playing from the third floor. I pause, glancing down the hallway where my parents' room resides, but I don't dare linger towards it. Being in their room is more than I can handle today. Maybe one day I can step foot into their room, but that day isn't today. So instead, I begin to climb the next set of stairs and make my way to the music room.

The climb is excruciating, and I don't remember there being as many stairs when I was younger. As I reach the top of the stairs, the music becomes louder, dancing towards me, and calling for me to come and play. I get lost in the moment, my focus on nothing but the sound of the beautiful music coming my way. I yearn to play again. The hole in my heart is missing the very core of its being. Beethoven's *Moonlight Sonata* calls for me, taking me back to the time I spent weeks trying to perfect it until I could play it without sheet music— when I was only eight years old.

I walk towards the room apprehensively, and doubt begins to fill my mind, questioning if I am ready to face the music, literally. I press the door open slowly, and a low gasp escapes my lips. My mind must really be playing tricks on me. It's bad enough that I am hearing music playing in my head, but now I am actually seeing someone sitting at the piano playing. I can see a familiar shade of strawberry blonde hair cascading down the person's back. I don't have to see her face to know who it is.

"Heidi?" Her name comes out a whisper. When the piano stops playing, she turns her head towards me and confirms that it is indeed her. Her blue eyes stare daggers into me. If looks could kill, I would probably be dead right now. "What are you doing here?" *How do you know about this place?*

"I was wondering when you would finally make your way home, *Elizabeth.*" My name slides off her tongue like acid. *How does she know my name?* Heidi laughs, a laugh that sounds like it belongs to an evil villain in a movie, and it sends chills down my spine. She crosses the distance between us, and I smell something familiar and try to wrap my head around the scent. It's my perfume, the one I use to wear as a teenager. The scent sends me spiraling back into my past, and flashes of memories dance in front of me like a movie. The recitals my mother never came to… my carefree days with Jacob, Millie, Eli, and the rest of my friends… finally settling on the night of my mother's death.

"Hello…" Heidi interrupts the montage. "I am here to make you suffer the way I have had to suffer for the last twenty-four years of my life."

I stare at the woman who is supposed to be my assistant, my eyes wide, and feeling utterly confused. "What are you talking about?"

"As if you didn't know."

"Heidi… whatever it is, I honestly have no idea what you are talking about." She brings her hand up and slaps me across the face. The hit stings, causing tears to form in the corner of my eyes, and all I can do is stand there frozen in place.

"It's because of you… and that whore of a mother you had… you two are the reason my father neglected me and never wanted anything to do with me." I'm speechless, unable to comprehend what she is trying to get at. "It's time you pay. You have spent all these years pretending that your past is nothing but a distant memory. You gave everything up, and for what? To hide like a scared little kitten? I'm going to make sure you never see the light of day again. You don't deserve happiness.

You don't deserve Elias or Reid... they will pay for what you have done!" she screams at me, and I flinch. I move to take a step back, but she reaches for me, grabbing a handful of hair at the back of my head, and slams my head into her knee.

The sight of blood pulls me back to the night of my mother's death. I crumple to the floor, hyperventilating, and barely hearing anything Heidi says as I stare at the blood falling from my nose. "My father," she strikes me on the back of the head with a sharp object, "was in love with your mother." Another blow hits my head, and I can feel the warmth of the blood trickling down my neck. A glint of sliver flashes in the sunlight pouring into the vast open room, and I barely glance in time to see that she has a knife. "He spent years pining for her while she was busy screwing around with that boyfriend of yours."

That's when I realize who she really is. "Your father is Robert?" The same man who broke into my apartment a few weeks ago.

She laughs and strikes me again. "Have you paid attention to anything I have said?"

I push off the ground. I have to get out of here and call for help. I feel the heel of her shoe dig into my back as she pushes me back down onto the floor. A sharp pain hits my side, and I cry out. She stabs me with the knife. Blood pools around me as I begin to lose consciousness. The last thing I see before I black out is the memory of my mother's contorted body. "Reid..." I say softly before the blackness engulfs me.

* * *

I jolt awake to being splashed in the face with cold water. It takes a few minutes for my vision to clear, and when it does, I find myself in another part of the house, the one room I was avoiding— my parents' room. My side stings from where I was stabbed. I instinctively reach down and find a bandage wrapped around me. The room is dark, with a lamp on the nightstand next to my parents' bed providing the only light in the room. The light is dim, and I can only see about a foot around me. I hear footsteps moving around but can't see where they are coming from. "I took care of your wounds for you, so you don't have to worry." Heidi's voice sounds throughout the darkness. "I have plans, and they don't include getting rid of you so soon."

The footsteps grow closer, and I fight against the restraints that have me pinned to some sort of chair. I squint my eyes, trying to see through the pitch black in front of me, and find which way Heidi is coming from. I sense her presence behind me before I hear her. "I think it's time our company joins us, don't you?"

Before I can respond, the overhead bedroom light flickers on and blinds me for a moment. After blinking my eyes a few times, my vision comes back. I cry out as tears form in my eyes. Across the room are the two people I care for the most— bound, gagged, and seemingly unconscious.

"Let them go," I say harshly. Heidi laughs and walks around me. She finally comes into view, with a large knife in hand. She walks slowly towards Eli and Reid, who are both shirtless. I start to fight against the chair and doing everything in my power to break free. It's useless, the rope she is using is tied tightly. "No!" I scream as she glances back at me, holding up the knife, waving it back and forth with a sinister grin plastered to her face.

"Let's see…" She places the knife against Reid's stomach and starts to press in. I hold my breath and wait for some sort of reaction from him, but he doesn't stir. "Right about here" — the knife digs into his skin — "is where your scar starts… is it not?" I close my eyes so I don't witness her cutting him.

I hear something drop against the floor and force my eyes open. Blood is trickling down Reid's stomach from his open wound. I glance back to Heidi, who is standing back with her arms across her chest and admiring her work. On the floor, near Reid's foot, is the knife that she just used to cut him open. The tears stream down my face, and all I can do is blame myself.

"Before we continue," she winks to me, "I want these two to be awake. They need to hear what I have to say."

Heidi turns her attention to Eli. While walking the few feet between the two of them, she sweeps up her long hair into a bun on the top of her head. I watch as she walks past Eli and into the master bathroom. I listen as the faucet turns on and the sound of water echoes out into the room. My mind starts to reel at how she possibly subdued them, much less get them up here, but I'm not able to give it much more thought. My focus shifts as I watch her exit out of the bathroom with a bucket I presume is filled with water. I hold my breath and turn my head as she dumps the contents of the bucket over Eli's head. I hear the sounds of Eli coughing and glance towards him. His eyes are wide and disorientated. He fights against the cloth that is gagging him in attempt to say something. "Oh look, pretty boy wants to say something." Heidi chuckles and pulls the gag out of his mouth.

"Liza! Wh—"

"Nuh-uh-uh," Heidi interrupts. "It seems that you too have forgotten who she really is. If you are to speak, you will call her Elizabeth."

"Fuck you!" Eli shouts. Heidi smirks, reaches behind his chair, and pulls out a bat. She raises the bat and brings it smashing down against his knee.

"Stop!" I scream. "It's me that you want! Leave them alone!"

Heidi hits Eli again and I wince as if I can feel his pain. She pulls the gag back over his mouth with ease while he is grimacing in pain. "Keep your mouth shut." She peeks over towards me. "Speak out of line and you will only make it worse for them." She starts to walk towards me. Behind her I hear Reid groan and see that he is starting to wake up. "Yay!" Heidi cries out and claps her hands in excitement. "Now, we can really get the party started."

Chapter Twenty-Six

I WATCH IN HORROR as Heidi stitches the wound she created on Reid's stomach. Every time he grimaces or cries out in pain my heart breaks just a bit more. This isn't fair. It's all my fault, and I really don't understand the full extent of it all. All I know is that Robert is Heidi's father, who was in love with my mother, who cast him aside because she was screwing around with Jacob. Sure, I am connected to all of them, but none of what has happened is my fault. No, the blame is on them. More importantly, it's on my mother, but she's gone now. Isn't that enough?

After Heidi's done stitching Reid up, she wraps a white ace wrap around him, just like she did with me. Blood is covering her hands and smudged onto her clothes, but she doesn't seem to notice. She stands up from her kneeling position and turns to glances at me. Her eyes are crazed with terror and she looks wicked.

"Now," she says as she licks her lips and walks towards me. She stops, leans close to me, and stares straight into my eyes. "I'll let you have the honor of telling everyone why we are here."

My eyes flicker over to Reid, who is still clearly in pain, and he is staring at me with confusion written on his face. When I can't take it anymore, I turn my attention to Eli, who seems less confused. Heidi told him to call me Elizabeth, but I know he is still confused as to why. "I still haven't got the slightest idea. Sure, you have a vendetta against me for whatever reason, but them—" I glance over to the two men "—they have nothing to do with this. Just let them go." I begin to cry.

Heidi raises her hand and slaps me across the face. "You are not the victim here! I am!" she shouts. "Now, you can start by telling Reid everything. You can tell him the truth about who you really are and whose house we are in."

I can barely see the man I love through my tear soaked eyes. I squeeze my eyes closed tightly and open them when I feel the tears sliding down my cheeks. I didn't want to tell him this way, but I have to go along with Heidi until I can figure a way to get all of us out of this situation. "T-t-this is my house," I say weakly.

"I'm sorry... what was that?" Heidi laughs. "Speak louder so we can all hear."

"I said that this is my house." My voice is still weak but significantly louder. "I mean, the house I grew up in. I haven't stepped foot in this house for six years, until today."

"Why is that?" Heidi interjects. This is the part I am going to have the hardest time telling. I'm afraid once Reid learns the truth, he will see me as a product of two seriously messed up people. People who are nothing but monsters, and decide he wants nothing more to do with me. Add in the fact that he is being held captive and just had his stomach split open because of me. It's over between us before we really got started. Heidi hits me again, and the force of her strike splits open my lip. I stick my tongue out and taste metal. The taste of blood. I can't look at Reid. The way he is staring at me, with hopelessness in his eyes, is killing me piece by piece. I glance at Eli, sympathy clearly shining, and he knows I haven't told Reid. That I haven't told anyone. He nods his head slightly, encouraging me to spill the secrets I have been hiding.

"My father murdered my mother. Right here in this room." The look in Reid's eyes isn't what I was expecting. I was expecting disgust, or perhaps shock, but neither of those make an appearance. Instead, sorrow fills his eyes. He is staring at me softly, slightly nodding his head, as if he has known all along. Oh my, what if he has known all along. "My real name is Elizabeth Lewis..." I take a deep breath. "My father is Jared Lewis." I don't have to explain who he is because my father was a big time defense attorney.

"The prodigal child has returned!" Heidi exclaims. I'm not entirely sure what she means by that, but I'm not sure I know what or who she is anymore. "This is where I come in." Heidi walks a few paces until she is standing in the middle of all three of us. "You see, *Elizabeth*, over there," she is speaking to Reid, "Her mother was a whore. She didn't know how to keep her legs closed, no matter who it was. First, she was with my father. She got knocked up, and when he asked her to marry him, she went running into the arms of Mr. Big Shot. Her mother kept a relationship with my father. She kept telling him she made a mistake and promised that she would get a divorce and that they could raise their family together."

Wait…what? "It's not possible that my mother was pregnant with another child. I'm an only child."

"Don't you get it?" Heidi says in a low voice. She stalks towards me with a smile on her face. "Jared wasn't your father… Robert was. My father is your father… which makes us sisters. Crazy, isn't it?"

No, no, no. She can't be telling the truth. It's all some sick twisted ploy of hers. No way in hell is Robert my father. I close my eyes and shake my head. She's lying. She has to be. "Believe what you want." I open my eyes and stare at Heidi. "But we are sisters."

"I could never be related to someone as twisted as you are."

"Which brings me to my next point. The reason we are here." She glares at me, and I'm sure hatred is filling her every bone. "After your mother married Jared, my father was heartbroken and distraught, and began a relationship with my mother. When she discovered she was pregnant with me, he left her high and dry. Yeah, he sent money every month, but he wasn't there. He was too busy crawling into bed with your mother and watching you grow from a distance. When your mother grew tired of him and cast him to the side, he came crawling back, begging for forgiveness, but it was too late by then. He tried to explain that love made him stupid, that he regretted not being there. But I know if it wasn't for your mother trading him in for a much younger boy toy, your boyfriend, he would have never come back at all."

"You still aren't making any sense."

"I'm not? Let's see if you can make sense with this." She picks up the baseball ball lying next to Eli's chair and smashes it against his other knee. "Tell me, am I making sense now?" She hits his knee again.

"Stop!" I scream. "What do you want?"

"I want you to suffer. For what your mother did and for what my father did."

"You can't blame me for their actions," I whisper. My body is wrecked with sobs. I can hear Eli groaning in pain. The sound of the baseball bat making contact with his knee is playing like a broken record over and over again.

"Your mother isn't alive, which I have Jared to thank for that. Since he didn't finish the job with you, it's my duty to do so."

"But your fat—"

"He is paying for what he has done. Why do you think he was in your apartment all those weeks ago? Because I coerced him into it."

I think back to the night that Robert was in my apartment. That night has replayed in my mind a thousand times, trying to make sense as to why he was there that night with Jacob. Why after all these years, he was doing something about it. The pieces are starting to fall into place. The emails, how the person knew my every move. It was all Heidi. She knew my every step, her desk was outside my office, and it was easy for her. But I still can't figure out where Eli and Reid play into this.

"Fine. Do what you want with me, but just let them go," I plead.

"No, they are staying. It's part of your suffering. I am going to kill both of them, painfully and slowly, and thrive off the torture it brings you. Then, once I am finished with them, I will do the same for you. None of this is going to be short and quick. We're going to be here for a long time. Now, why don't you get comfortable for a little bit. I have to go check on a few things, and then the fun times will resume."

Heidi turns and walks out of the room, closing the door behind her, and I hear the sounds of locks clicking in place. She's locked us in here, leaving just the three of us alone. I glance around the room, a heavy weight bearing down on my shoulders, and I can't stand to look at Eli or Reid. Eli is still softly groaning in pain and I feel helpless. Nothing in this room has been touched. The room remains unchanged and just like it always has. The four poster bed sits just to the right of me, a large fireplace sits empty across the room, and a night stand by the bed. That's it. Neither of my parents made this room personalized. They left the personalization to their offices. Rooms I only caught a glance of once or twice in my life.

Finally, I muster the courage to glance at the both of them. At first glance, Eli seems unharmed except for the low groans emanating from his body across the room. His upper body remains untouched. Reid has only experienced the one wound as far as I am aware of. My eyes drift to the bandage around his stomach. Traces of red seep out through the patched up wound, making the wrap turn to a slightly pinkish color around the cut. I'm sure he is in pain, but he isn't showing it in any way. I watch as both of them move their heads back and forth, trying to wiggle the gags out of their mouths. I pull against the chair again and barely manage to budge the rope. After a few minutes, I give up and sag against the chair. I cast my eyes down to the floor, tears brimming in my eyes, and let out a soft sob. "I'm so sorry. You two shouldn't be here. This is all my fault."

"No," Eli's rough voice surprises me and I jump, "That woman is sadistic." I glance over at him and I start to cry. "Don't cry, *little rabbit.*" Another sob escapes my mouth. "None of this is your fault. She has got her panties twisted up in a terrible bunch, or perhaps a stick was shoved up so far up her ass that she couldn't remove it."

"This isn't the time to make jokes," I say as I laugh softly. In the time of trouble, I can count on Eli to make me smile. "I'm sorry, Eli, for whatever I did wrong. I have missed you so much."

Eli lets out a long sigh, "You didn't do anything wrong. I just let my ego get the best of me. I missed you, too."

"If you two are done playing make up, I think it's best we try and figure a way out of here." Reid's voice cuts into the conversation. I turn my attention to him and find him smiling. A smile at a time like this. What is wrong with these guys? "I mean, don't get me wrong. I'm glad you guys are making up. I'm tired of Liza hurting over this, but now is not the time."

A low groan comes from Eli, and I see the regret in his eyes. "Pretty boy is right. We need to figure a way out."

I try not to laugh as the two of them, mainly Reid because Eli can hardly move, fight against their restraints. I know the situation we are in is quite serious, and that Heidi can come back at any moment, but watching two big men fight against a chair and some rope is quite humorous. Eli gives up first and I can't say I blame him. He's probably got two busted knee caps and that cannot feel good. I try again to fight against the ropes, but my body is aching from the movement.

My head is pounding and where I was stabbed feels like it is on fire. I pulled a couple of stitches out trying to wiggle my wrists from the ropes. Tears sting my eyes, and I bite my lip to avoid crying out in pain. *This is useless. We can't get out of these ropes.* These ropes are as snug as they can get.

I give up before Reid, who is still twisting and turning his body every which way he can. The determination on his face says he's not going to stop. I glance around the room, searching for anything that might help us if we can figure out how to get to it. A glint of sliver flashes in the light, and I remember the knife. I glance over to Reid, and then to the floor where the bloody knife she used to slice him open is still laying. "Reid… the knife." He looks down at the knife and then back up to me, nodding his head. "See if you can kick it over here to me. If you can, I can try to get the chair to tip over and use it to cut myself free."

"Let me do it since it's right next to me." He starts moving back and forth, building momentum to knock his chair over.

"No, I can do it if you can get it to me," I say quickly. He stares at me and raises an eyebrow.

"Now is not the time for heroics, Liza."

"Shut your mouth, Reid." He smiles, and I shake my head. "I'm just saying that my hands are smaller than yours, and I can maneuver the knife better than you can." He nods his head, accepting what I am telling him. I inhale a deep breath and hold it while I watch him slide his foot towards the knife. It's just out of his reach, and he curses. "Calm down," I say softly. "See if you can slide your chair over a tiny bit."

For a moment, he stares at me like I am crazy before he decides to go for it. Inch by inch, he makes his way closer to the knife, the carpet making it tougher than it should be. After several long minutes, Reid finally gets himself into a position where he can reach the knife better and get a good kick behind it. He brings his foot back as far as he can and swiftly kicks the knife.

Time slows down as I watch the knife fly up into the air. No one makes a sound, and all I can hear is the sound of our deep breathing. The knife begins to make its descent to the floor, and I watch in anticipation as it gets closer and closer. My heart drops when it stops just short of me. It will be hard to reach, but I figure if I can get my chair on the floor, I might be able to wiggle it towards it. I rock the chair back and forth until I get enough momentum to tip it on its side. When I land, the chair makes a loud thud against the floor, and

I cry out in pain, quickly quieting myself and listening for any signs of Heidi coming back to the room.

I lie there for a minute, waiting for the shooting pain to subside in my side, and try to figure out how I am going to reach it. I wonder if I slip my foot out of my flat if I might be able to slip it out of the rope and use it to push me across the floor. Without another thought, I slip my foot out of the shoe and begin trying to pull it free. Unlike Reid, who didn't have his feet bound for whatever reason, mine were just a few inches above my ankles. The rope tugs against my skin, creating a friction like burn against it. After what seems like forever, I can feel the rope begin to slightly loosen, unlike the one that has my hands tied behind my back.

A few more pulls and my foot springs free. Eli and Reid let out a cheer of excitement and I glare at them for being so loud while stifling back my own excitement. I push my foot into the carpet and use it as leverage to push me forward. It's working, but slowly. After a few minutes I am right next to the knife, but my hands are behind my back. I use my free foot to slowly turn around while still on the side.

"You're almost there," Reid says. "See if you can get the chair to move backwards. The knife is just within your grasp."

I do as Reid says, and in seconds, I feel the butt of the knife graze against my fingertips. One more soft push off the ground and I'm able to wrap my hands around it. My heart leaps with joy. I'm so close. I move my hands to the best of my ability and get the blade of the knife under a piece of the rope. The position of my hand is awkward and uncomfortable. The rope is rubbing at my skin, and I can feel it cutting it open and stinging. Slowly, I move the rope back and forth, little by little. Just as I cut through the last strand of rope, I hear the locks on the door clicking. I am frozen in place with fear just as the door swings open and Heidi steps through.

Chapter Twenty-Seven

"WHAT THE HELL do you think you are doing?" Heidi's voice vibrates across the room from the door. I lie there, unmoving. I don't want her to know that I am free. I watch as she walks across the room and wait. Once she is close enough, I pull my hands from behind my back and stand up. The chair is still tied around my foot, and I kick at it until I break free. Heidi's slow saunter turns into a dead run just as my foot pulls free, and I barely manage to block her incoming blow. She grabs a handful of my hair and yanks on it. I scream out in pain. My arms flail around, trying to reach her and break free. My hand makes contact with her face and she releases my hair.

Now that I am in control again, I stand there waiting for her, slowly breathing in and out. "It's over, Heidi."

She throws her head back and laughs. "Not yet. Those two—" she jerks her thumb over her shoulder towards Eli and Reid "are still tied up. So that leaves you and me." She lunges for me. Clenching my fist, I throw all my strength into the swing. I miss, hitting her shoulder instead. She tackles me to the floor as if my punch didn't have any effect on her. As she tries to pin me, I struggle harder. I bend my leg, kneeing her in the back. Her grip slips. I seize the moment, bucking her off of me. She lands on top of the chair. A piercing scream fills the room.

"Liza!" Eli yells. "Use the knife."

I glance at the knife just as Heidi recovers, and when she dives for me, I plunge it into her side. She falls to the ground, screaming and thrashing her body around. I push the knife a little further into her torso before pulling it out. I search the room for something heavy enough to render her unconscious and snatch the lamp off the night stand. I stand above her, and for the first time, Heidi seems terrified. I close my eyes and bring the lamp down against her head. She instantly becomes quiet. I collapse against the ground, pull my knees up to my chest, close my eyes, and rock back and forth.

The vision of my mother comes back. The one where she is blaming me for her death. I'm stuck in the montage of blood and her dead corpse trying to get to me. "Liza!" I can faintly hear my name being shouted, but I am stuck in this nightmare. "Liza… baby… you have to help us out of these ropes." I finally register Reid's voice and snap back to reality.

I glance over and see Heidi's unconscious body next to me, and the knife protruding out of her side. I close my eyes, wrap my hand around the hilt of the knife, and shudder as I pull it out of her body. I don't open my eyes until I am sure I have crawled past her far enough so that I don't have to see her. My hands shake as I cut through the rope behind Reid's chair that bounds his hands. My heart is pounding and my breathing is ragged. I don't realize that Reid is free until I feel his strong arms wrap around me and pull me close. I open my eyes and gaze up at him. He crushes his lips down on mine. "It's going to be okay. We made it," he whispers between kisses.

"Ahem," I hear Eli clear his voice, "Did you forget I was still here?" Reid lifts one finger at a time off the knife, prying it from my hand, places a kiss on my forehead, and goes to free Eli. Once the ropes have been cut free, Eli doesn't move. He can't move.

Reid returns to my side, pulls my face into his hands, and gives me a kiss. "I've got to go call for help."

"There's a landline in the office two doors down." He tilts his head and stares at me questionably. "I never disconnected anything in the house." He raises his eyebrow, and I smile slightly. "Don't ask."

Reid leaves the room, I glance at Heidi for a moment and push myself off the floor. I round the chair and stop in front of Eli. "I am so sorry," I say gently. "For this and everything else."

"Don't apologize. We're okay because of you." He shifts in his chair and lets out a deep groan.

Eli and I remain quiet while Reid is gone. We don't say anything else about what has happened today, or the past few weeks. We don't have to. I know I have him back, and I will never let him go. He's my best friend, my rock, and means the world to me. Although I have Reid in my life now, no one will ever take his place. Reid and Eli will just have to figure out between the two of them whatever problem they have with one another. They both have a place in my heart, whether they like it or not, and will have to figure out how to work that out amongst themselves as well.

"Reid isn't as bad as I thought." Eli breaks the silence first. I smile and nod my head in agreement. "Do you love him?"

"I do. With all my heart."

"He loves you, you know," he says softly. "I mean, he like *really* loves you."

"I know." I smile.

"And you're okay with that?" Eli shifts again uncomfortably in his seat.

"Try not to move around so much. And yes, I am. Okay with him loving me, I mean."

"What does that mean is going to happen to us?" Eli casts his eyes down to the floor and grips the arm of the chair tightly.

"Nothing. Absolutely nothing." I stand up, place my hand under his chin, and turn his face so he is facing me. "He's the love of my life, and you're my best friend. I have room for the both of you."

"I love you, too, you know."

I drop my hand from his chin and turn away. "I know." That's all I can manage to say. Until now, I might have never admitted it. But I have known the only reason Eli has stuck around is because he loved me in more than the way of friendship. And while he has never attempted to do anything about it, I always knew. Which might explain why he refused to talk to me when I chose Reid over him.

I love Eli, but not in the way he loves me. He's family. He is everything that has held me together over the past six years of my life. He's like my brother. Always watching out for me, even when I didn't want him to. He is someone I never want to lose. "You have to move on, Eli," I say regretfully. "I know this is cliché, but there are millions of other women out there who will be lucky to have your love. It just isn't me. I love you, but you have to find someone who can reciprocate the same level of feelings."

"Love sucks. I'm never falling in love again." I laugh and jump when someone wraps their arms around me from behind. I instantly know who it is and pull his arms tighter.

"Ah man, love isn't all that bad." Reid says. Eli shakes his head, and I laugh softly.

"Says the man who won."

The room falls quiet after that. I hate feeling like crap, but I had to be honest with Eli. It's time for him to move on, in the sense of finding someone new to love, but not leaving me completely. I know it won't be easy, and that I will have to spend time with him away from Reid for a while. Eventually, he'll get over it and move on. He has to. That's the only way we can still be friends. If he can't, then I will have to say goodbye to him, even if I don't want to.

The police arrive faster than expected, along with a few ambulances. Reid talks to some officers, giving them the rundown of his side of the story and how he ended up here. From what I gather, he was drugged and doesn't know much of anything else. I stand off to the side and cry softly as I watch the paramedics lift Eli out of the chair and onto a stretcher while he screams in pain. It's just as I suspected. Both of his knees are completely shattered, and he is going to need surgery to replace them. Reid rejoins me as they begin to wheel Eli out of the room and sticks by my side as I tell them my story. Starting at the beginning, I tell them about the emails and packages I have received. I tell them about the mystery person who showed up at the cabin, and what happened today when I arrived. I can feel Reid tense next to me as I replay every detail from the beginning. I glance up at him, and he mouths, "We'll talk about this later." I know he isn't happy with me for keeping this a secret, but I know he isn't going anywhere.

I clutch onto Reid as Heidi begins to stir back to consciousness, and as soon as she is awake, they place her on a stretcher and handcuff her to the bed. They read the Miranda rights to her, and I bury my head into Reid's chest as she shouts obscenities as they wheel her out of the room. One by one, the police officers trickle out of the room, leaving us alone with the police captain. He leaves his card with Reid and gives him instructions to call if we remember anything else that is important. The captain tells us that Heidi said she hired a homeless man to help her get the men upstairs and that it was all a game they were playing. The thought makes me cringe. Nothing about tonight has been a game.

Once he leaves, the two of us are alone. Reid squeezes me tightly and presses a kiss against my temple. "Let's get out of here." I nod my head in agreement. He holds me close as we exit the room and he leads me down the stairs out the front door. As we walk down the driveway, I gaze back towards the house one last time with a new resolve settling in. First thing tomorrow morning, I am calling a realtor and putting the house on the market. Of course, after the police finish their investigation and the house is cleaned out. With the plan set in stone, I am ready to let go of the past and start working on my future with the man beside me.

Chapter Twenty-Eight

Six weeks later

I WALK THROUGH the halls of the hospital, following the path I have followed every day for the past six weeks. In one arm, I am carrying a bouquet of flowers, against Eli's request. He'll get over it, just like he's gotten over the last five bouquets I have brought him. Every person deserves to have fresh roses next to their hospital bed, whether they are male or female. The scent of chemicals mixed with the roses fills the air. It reminds me of hand sanitizer. Fresh, clean, and germ free. The walls are blinding, the white walls clashing with the white flooring, and it sends my senses into overload. I enter Eli's room and find that he is sitting up in bed and talking — more like flirting — with a cute, petite nurse. I clear my throat, and the two stare at me; their faces flush and turn a shade of pink, embarrassed at being caught. The nurse says something low so that only Eli can hear, and he smiles. As she walks past me, I nod and smile, and she returns the favor.

"Well, she is certainly cute." I place the vase of flowers on the table next to his bed and sit down in the boring white chair next to him. "This room is seriously depressing," I say, scanning the room.

"Try being stuck in here for the past six weeks." Eli shuffles around the bed and tucks a pillow behind his back. "One more week of therapy and I can break free of this place."

"What shall we do first?"

Eli laughs, "All I want to do is sleep in my oversized, over-fluffed bed and not to be disturbed for a couple days. This bed is seriously the most uncomfortable thing I have ever slept on."

I laugh and we fall into our familiar pattern of joking, teasing, and just talking. Neither of us have once mentioned the incident with Heidi since it happened, but I have to bring it up. Eli needs to know what is going on. "So... they finally set the hearing." Eli stares at me and frowns. "Her attorney is going to try to get an insanity plea."

"Well, the bitch is crazy."

"True." I laugh and shake my head. Crazy she most certainly is. I had to change the number for my office shortly after her arrest. Heidi decided she had the balls to call and harass me several times the first week. It got to be too much.

I lean back in the chair, take in the silence passing between the two of us, and reflect on the changes over the past few weeks. The first change was I packed up my apartment and officially moved in with Reid. The next change was I decided to stay in the Romance department and signed my first author. Reid's uncle tried to give me a promotion as an apology for what Heidi did. He felt as though he is to blame, because he offered her the internship. I refused, of course, because I didn't want the promotion to come from the terror of what we endured. No, I want to earn it fair and square.

Another surprise, no more harassing emails from Viola. Not one single email. Lawrence finally got his head out of his ass and filed for divorce when he found out that she was sleeping with someone in the Sci-Fi department. He vows that he is not going to marry again and that it will be a while before he dates. We'll see how long he really lasts. Now that he is single, he will be going through women more than he changes his underwear. The thought is frightening and sickening.

Eli has come to terms that he and I will never happen, unless our relationship remains solely focused on the friendship aspect of things. Things between him and Reid are still a little tense, but I can see that they are both trying. Eli has promised to come to our place — still getting used to that — for dinner once he is out of here. After a daylong surgery, both of Eli's knees were replaced, and he's well on the road to recovery.

Things with Reid and I are far better than great. After we got checked out at the hospital that night, our wounds properly attended to, we went home and had a long talk. I told Reid everything he needed to know about my life, starting with my childhood. I shouldn't have been surprised when he told me he knew my true identity and who my parents were, but to hear him confirm it was shocking. What he didn't know were the small, intimate details. It took a while to hash the story out, considering there were years I had to tell, and I had to stop every so often because I couldn't stop crying.

Things were rocky a couple of weeks ago, when I asked Robert for a DNA test, and what I hoped was a lie was actually the truth. Heidi did one thing right, something neither of my parents did, and that was telling me the truth. After talking about it with Reid, things from my childhood started to make sense. Like why my parents couldn't stand each other, why my father was as hard on me as he was, and why they avoided me, and each other, like a plague. I am the child they never wanted. Though I already knew that.

The biggest step I took, with Dr. Uria and Reid's encouragement, was that I went to the prison. I sat down, with Reid by my side, and told my father to his face everything I have ever wanted to say. Jared said nothing, and when I was finished, he stood up and just walked away. Since then, I haven't been plagued with nightmares. The police finally finished up with their investigation, and my childhood home was no longer a crime scene. It's up on the market now, and I am counting down the days until it is nothing more than a distant memory. A piece of my past.

"Hey, so Reid came and talked to me the other day," Eli says, cutting into my thoughts. I stare at him and wait for him to elaborate. Reid never mentioned anything about coming to see him. I am going to have to talk to him when I get home. "I guess congratulations are in order."

"Hmm, what?"

"The two of you are getting hitched, aren't you?" Eli asks. His voice is soft, but carries a tone of hurt underneath it.

"Oh yeah," I whisper. That's the biggest change in my life. I'm getting married. Reid asked me last night. He left work early yesterday, and when I got home, all the lights were off inside. A trail of rose petals and candles greeted me at the front door and led me out to the balcony, where he had a four string quartet softly playing and a candlelight dinner waiting for me. Before I could say anything, he kneeled down on one knee, gave me some long speech that I can barely remember because I was so focused on the man himself, and then he asked me to marry him.

"Can I see the ring?" I nod and pull the ring out of the front of my pants pocket where I placed it before coming into the hospital. I slip it onto my finger and hold my hand out for Eli to see. "At least he knows how to pick a diamond out. That thing is a rock!" I smile at Eli and lean down to give him a hug.

A soft knock raps across the door, and I turn my head to see Reid standing in the doorway. "You ready to go, sweetheart?" I nod to him and squeeze Eli one more time. "I hear you're getting out of this hell hole next week. Let me know when you're up for that round of golf you promised."

I glance between the two men who hold my heart and smile. "You got it," Eli says. I smile at Reid as I walk towards him. He winks at me and holds his hand out to me.

"See you later, Eli." I wave over my shoulder.

"See you later, *little rabbit.*"

After we reach the car in the parking lot, I peek over at Reid and smile. "Rumor has it that you came to see Eli the other day… what gives?"

Reid moves his hands off the steering wheel and shifts in his seat so he is facing me. "The truth?" I nod my head. "I came to ask him if it was okay if I asked for your hand in marriage."

Tears brim my eyes. I lean over the center console and pull him into a kiss. "You…" Another kiss, "Are…" kiss… "Perfect."

Reid chuckles and plants a soft kiss on my lips. "I know."

He starts the car, puts it in reverse, and slowly backs out of the parking space. We reach the house in no time, and I head inside to start dinner. I glance through the pantry and refrigerator and decide to make spaghetti. Reid pulls open his bag and pulls out his laptop. As I start prepping dinner, I glance over at Reid and smile as he clicks away on the keyboard. Just as I get the sauce going, Reid's phone starts to ring, and he steps out onto the patio to answer it. At first, it used to bug the hell out of me when he stepped out of the room, but now I have grown accustomed to it. Especially since I know that if I was to walk outside, I wouldn't be forced back inside. I can listen in if I want to, but the moment I leave the office, I like to leave work behind.

Everything between us has settled into a bit of a routine now. Reid returns to the kitchen just as I'm dishing up the plates and pulling the garlic bread out of the oven. We eat dinner, talk, and then make our way upstairs. We share a shower before crawling into bed and watching horror movies. I'm no longer ashamed when he sees or touches my scar, especially now that he has one similar to mine. Although, I still haven't been able to see it without the guilty feeling that it's my fault. I try to avoid looking at it as much as I can. Not because I find it unattractive, but the weight of guilt is overbearing. Eventually I will overcome that, but in the meantime, I will keep loving the man next to me in bed.

Sometime during the movie, I drift off to sleep, something I am no longer afraid of. None of my nightmares haunt me any longer, as they are now a thing of the past. I jump awake when I hear the doorbell ringing in the middle of the night. I glance at the clock glowing in the dark on the night stand and see that it is a quarter past two in the morning. I have no idea who would be ringing the doorbell at this time of night. The bell rings again, and I glance over at Reid, who is sound asleep. The poor guy has been working hard over the last few weeks. When the doorbell rings again and Reid doesn't make any indication that he is getting up, I quietly slip out of bed, pull on my robe, and head down stairs.

I can see the shadow of a tall man standing in front of the door as I approach it. I flick on the porch light. Slowly, I tiptoe to the door and peek outside to see a man I don't recognize. I should go back and wake up Reid, but the man seems harmless enough, so I open the door. "Can I help you?" I ask softly.

The man jumps and turns to stare at me. My face meets a set of broad shoulders and I glance up into a pair of brown eyes. He removes the battered hat off the top of his head and reveals a headful of dark blond hair. "Oh sorry," he says deeply, "I think I have the wrong house. Is this Reid Harder's house?"

"It is."

"And who are you?" The man tilts his head to the side and raises an eyebrow.

"I don't see how th—" The man barrels past me and leaves me standing by the front door in complete disbelief.

"Reid!" he bellows out.

"Excuse me, but I think you should wait outside until I get him."

The man laughs and spins on his heels to look at me. "Nonsense. Just go tell him Marco Rodriguez is here to see him." My feet stay planted to the floor, unwilling to move, and I'm not sure what to do. "It's okay... I mean no harm. Now, hurry along and go wake him."

Chapter Twenty-Nine

"REID!" I NUDGE HIM on the arm. Reid stirs in the bed and doesn't respond. I shake his arm a bit harder, and he slightly opens his arms.

"Liza?" His voice is groggy. "What are you doing? Get back into bed."

"I wish I could, but some guy downstairs is eager to see you. He came barging in the front door and insisted on me telling you that Marco Rodriguez is here."

Instantly, Reid jumps out of bed. He is wide awake now. "Why didn't you tell me that in the first place?" He rushes past me in nothing but his plaid pajama pants.

"I just did," I whisper. *What the hell?* I make my way downstairs to find out what is going on and who exactly this man is that came barging into my house in the middle of the night. When I reach the foyer, I discover that it is empty. I can hear voices coming from the kitchen and follow them into there.

Reid is standing across from the stranger, who is sitting on a bar stool and sipping on a beer. The two of them are in a deep conversation when I walk into the room, and I clear my throat. They stop talking, turn their attention on me, and for the first time, I get a clear look at the man. He's handsome in a rugged, manly kind of way. His features are soft and kind, and his eyes seem to have a trace of green mixed into them. He's taller than Reid and has a bigger build. I have no doubt in my mind if these two were to start knocking fists around this very second that he would overpower Reid in a heartbeat. My eyes flicker over to the knives along the back of the counter near the stove. If I am quick, I can make it over there before he can stop me. I laugh silently at being so absurd. It's obvious they aren't going to fight, and in fact, I can see they are good friends.

"Marco," Reid says, "I would like to introduce you to my fiancé, Liza." Reid walks towards me and wraps an arm around my waist.

"Fiancé?" The man seems slightly confused for a moment before a beautiful smile crosses over his face. "Hell, congratulations, man." He walks over towards us and pats Reid on the shoulder. "Sorry about earlier; I didn't mean to scare you."

"It's okay." Reid squeezes me tightly. Marco heads back over to the stool and sits back down. As Reid begins to lead me to a stool across the bar from his friend, I lean in and whisper to him. "Is everything alright?"

"We're about to find out," he whispers back. I take a seat across from the man and watch as he takes a sip of his beer. Reid stands behind me, his body pressing against mine, and his chin resting on top of my head.

"Wow, I seriously can't believe what I am seeing here." The man laughs and takes another sip of the beer before placing it down on the countertop. "Reid Harder is finally settling down."

"Cut to the chase, Marco. Why are you here? At two in the morning?" I can feel Reid slightly tense behind me. I debate asking him if I should leave the two of them to some privacy, but curiosity wins, and I stay planted firmly in my seat.

"It isn't good." Marco sighs. "I lost him." The hand Reid is using to rub my arm stops and digs into my skin. I don't know if he realizes he is squeezing me or not, so I just bite my lip and say nothing to him. "I fucking lost him, man."

Reid releases my arm and rounds the breakfast bar. I've seen this look in his eyes before, the one filled with anger, and one I haven't seen in a long time. It's more intense than I have ever seen it, like a storm is dancing in his pupils, and I start to wonder if grabbing a knife just might be necessary. Reid stops just in front of the man, his face inches away from him, and his breathing is shallow. I squirm in my seat, worry and fear begin to fill me as I wait to see what might happen next. After a few seconds, Reid takes a deep breath and a few steps back, allowing some room between the two of them.

"Where? Tell me what happened," Reid says. His voice is hoarse. He glances at me, and I see a glimpse of fear flash in his eyes. *What in the world is going on?* Who did this Marco man lose and why was he following him for Reid in the first place?

"We were in Russia, man," Marco says. "I had been following him in and out of bars and clubs for four days straight, never stopping to get any rest. I think he was on drugs at the rate he was going. He was plowing through drinks and women as if it didn't faze him. He was chatting up some escort in a bar, and I figured I would be okay if I used the bathroom. I was gone for less than five minutes, and when I came back out, he was gone. Poof! He vanished into thin air."

"What were you thinking?" Reid shouts. He begins to pace across the kitchen, and all I can do is sit and try to figure out what the hell is going on.

"I wasn't, man," Marco admits. "He must have finally caught on that I had been following him the past few weeks and disappeared the first chance he got."

Reid stops pacing, quickly looks at me, before turning his attention back to Marco. "Do you have any idea where he is? Or where he is going?"

"I have reason to believe he hopped back on a flight to the States using an alias. I'm still trying to figure out where he came in at and where he is going."

"Shit! Shit! Shit!" Reid says loudly. "This isn't any fucking good."

"You think I don't realize that?"

I can't take being silent anymore and finally muster up the courage to speak. "What the hell is going on?" Reid stops walking around the room and stares at me. "Is anyone willing to clue me in on what is going on?"

"You haven't told her yet?" Marco asks Reid, who shakes his head. "Shit, man. You need to tell her. I'm going to leave you two alone and grab some shuteye. One of the guest rooms, okay?" Reid nods his head and Marco leaves the kitchen.

He glances at me before stomping towards the refrigerator. He yanks open the door, pulls out a beer, and slams the door closed. Reid pops off the top of the beer and takes a big gulp of it before walking towards me and placing it down on the breakfast bar. "We need to talk."

"I would say so." I laugh softly, trying to make light of the situation. On the outside, I seem calm and collected. Like nothing that's been said in the past few minutes is doing anything to me. On the inside, my head is spinning with confusion and a hundred and one questions I want to ask.

"Marco is a friend of mine," he pauses and takes a sip of his beer, "He's ex-Special Ops. The best there is and he's been keeping an eye on someone for me." *Who?* I say nothing and wait as Reid takes another gulp of his beer. "The person he has been watching is my brother. He's been watching him, because he is a dangerous man caught up in some dangerous business. Business that my moth—" The landline begins to ring and interrupts Reid for a moment. Neither of us move to answer it. "Look, he's dangerous. That's all you need to know for now. Okay? Let's go back to bed, and I will tell you everything tomorrow, but for now, let's just leave it at that."

I want to protest. I want to demand that he tells me everything I need and want to know right then and there. Instead, I get up off my chair and wrap my arms around Reid. He presses a kiss against my forehead and holds me close to him. "Sounds like a plan to me," I finally say.

Reid stands up, walks towards the sink where the hidden recycling bin is, and pounds down the rest of his drink before tossing it in with the rest. The glass bottle clinks against the rest of the bottles and echoes throughout the kitchen. Reid takes my hand and begins to lead me out of the kitchen when the phone starts to ring again. "Maybe you should answer that."

Reid shakes his head, "Nah, let the answering machine get it. I mean, who calls phone lines anymore these days anyways? Whoever it is clearly hasn't heard of a cell phone before."

I laugh, and he pulls me into his side. As I flip off the light, the answering machine clicks on with the standard greeting. When the robotic voice stops talking and beeps, a haunting voice plays out through the speaker. "Silly brother."

Reid stops and tenses next to me. We are frozen in place as we listen to the rest of the message. "You really didn't think you could get rid of me forever, did you? What a shame. You clearly don't know me as well you think you do. You don't think I didn't notice the man you've had following me? What a joke he is! He stuck out like a sore thumb. Here's a little advice for you, baby brother. Don't play in the big leagues if you can't keep up. In the meantime, while you are awaiting my arrival, don't let that pretty woman of yours out of your sight. You never know what is going to happen to her if you do. Oh! Before I go, I should tell you that our mother says hello and that she can't wait to have both of her boys under the same roof again. I'll be coming for you when you least expect it, and when I do… you will have hell to pay."

MORE GREAT READS FROM BOOKTROPE

Four Rubbings **by Jennifer L. Hotes** (Young Adult Thriller) Fourteen-year old Jose, haunted by the death of her mother, leads her best friends to an ancient cemetary to rub graves on Halloween night. Convinced she will come away with proof of her mother's spirit at last, her journey and that of her friends takes a very different turn.

Mocha, Moonlight and Murder **by MaryAnn Kempher** (Romantic Suspense) Scott and Katherine face jealousy, misunderstandings, lust, and rivals, not to mention attempted murder—and all before their first real date.

Tea and Primroses **by Tess Thompson** (Romantic Suspense) Money, love, power and loss – a mother shares the truth about them all with her daughter, but is it too late to help her shape her life differently?

The Puppeteer **by Tamsen Schultz** (Romantic Suspense) A CIA agent and an ex-SEAL-turned-detective uncover a global web of manipulation that will force them to risk not just their fledgling relationship, but their very lives.

Unbridled Hearts Collection **by Heather Huffman** (Romantic Suspense Collection) The "Unbridled Hearts Collection" bundles together three works of romance and suspense, spanning the globe from the South Seas to the jungles of Ecuador in a sparkling yet socially relevant collection.

Discover more books and learn about our new approach to publishing at www.booktrope.com

CPSIA information can be obtained
at www.ICGtesting.com
Printed in the USA
FFOW02n0817010514
5174FF

9 781620 153673